Arrogant HEIR

USA TODAY BESTSELLING AUTHOR
MICHELLE HEARD

Cover Designer: Sybil Wilson, PopKitty Design

Cover Model: Chase Mattson

Photographer Credit: Michelle Lancaster

TABLE OF CONTENTS

Dedication

Taken too soon by unspeakable violence.

Never forgotten.

To the victims of gender-based violence.

Songlist

Go to ***Spotify – Arrogant Heir***

Synopsis

Mila West.
The feisty girl with ironclad determination.

Beneath all the quick comebacks lies a broken heart.
Nothing sucks like unrequited love. Especially when it's for
one of your best friends.

Jase Reyes.
Beautiful. Arrogant. Untouchable.

He's the playboy every girl hopes to catch. The future CEO
of a billion-dollar empire. People worship the ground he
walks on.

Jase and Mila fell in love,
but they fought each other at every turn.
Jase fell down,
and broke his crown;
And Mila?
Mila's life shattered to pieces.

Arrogant Heir

THE HEIRS
Book 2

College/New Adult series of interconnected STANDALONES.

"Expectations and assumptions are the mothers of all fuck ups." — **Mila West.**

Family Tree

JASE REYES

↓   ↓

Julian Reyes   Jamie Truman
Father   *Mother*

Godmother: Della Truman

Godfather: Falcon Reyes

Best Friends: Hunter Chargill, Kao Reed & Noah West

MILA WEST

↓   ↓

Logan West   Mia Daniels
Father   *Mother*

Godmother: Miss Sebastian

Godfather: Rhett Daniels

Best friends: Fallon Reyes, Jade Daniels & Hana Cutler

Jase and Mila fell in love,
but they fought each other at every turn.
Jase fell down,
and broke his crown;
And Mila?
Mila's life shattered to pieces.

Chapter 1

MILA

Mila 15; Jase 19

My eyes keep darting to the clock on the wall. The last couple of minutes feel like forever as I wait for the bell to ring.

I asked Jase to come pick me up after school so we can talk. It's taken me months to gather the courage to tell Jase I'm in love with him. At first, I thought it would be enough to dream about him, but my feelings kept growing until all I could think about was Jase.

Dreams are no longer enough. I want the real thing with him, and I'm hoping he'll feel the same way.

Staring out the window at the pouring rain, my thoughts are consumed with all things Jase. I keep reassuring myself I'm doing the right thing.

Jase always hugs you longer than the other girls in our group.

You're the only one he kisses on the forehead.

You're the only one he's always teasing.

It has to mean something, right?

The shrill sound of the bell yanks me out of my thoughts, and I rush to grab my bag. I'm the first one up and out of the classroom.

"Mila," Jade calls from behind me. "Wait for me."

Reluctantly, I stop and wait for my cousin to catch up with me.

"Fallon ran to the office quickly. Let's wait inside for her."

"You can go ahead. I have other plans."

Jade, Fallon, and Hana have been my best friends since forever. I didn't tell them I'm planning on declaring my love for Jase. I'm scared they'd try to talk me out of it.

We've all grown up as a tight-knit group of friends, and with Jase being Fallon's cousin, it might complicate things even more.

"Oh?" Jade frowns at me. "What plans? You didn't mention this before."

I shrug and begin to walk backward. "It's nothing. I'll catch you later."

Before Jade can ask more questions, I dart down the hallway and burst through the doors. Using my bag to cover my head from the rain, I quickly make my way to the parking area while my gaze darts from car to car, looking for Jase's.

When I don't see his vehicle anywhere, I take cover under a tree. He's probably just late because of the rain.

I hear screeching laughter, and when I see Jade, Fallon, and Hana run toward Fallon's car, I duck behind the tree so they won't see me.

As soon as they drive away, I step forward to have a clear view of the entrance for when Jase pulls in.

The minutes slowly begin to tick away, and with each one, a disappointing feeling sinks heavier into my stomach.

After waiting for thirty minutes, my disappointment begins to change into anger.

How could Jase forget?

Not caring I'll get wetter than I already am, I begin to walk. Jase lives in the same neighborhood as me, and I decide to stop by his house before going home.

I'm determined to talk with him because I can't keep weaving dreams around him if nothing will come from them.

To make my crappy day worse, the rain comes down harder, and by the time I reach Jase's house, I not only look like a drowned cat, but I'm also freezing my butt off.

I walk around the mansion to the chalet Jase moved into when he turned eighteen. He had to beg his parents to let him move out of the main house, but like with everything else in his life, he got what he wanted.

When I step onto the porch, I set my bag aside, and first, try to squeeze the water from my hair.

Maybe I should first go home and get changed.

"No," I whisper. If I go home now, I'll chicken out completely. I lift my hand to the door, and I'm just about to knock when I hear a girl giggle from inside.

A frown rumples my forehead as dread begins to spin a web around my heart. Not wanting to make a fool of myself, I inch closer to the window and peek inside. When I see Jase sitting on his couch with a girl straddling him, my heart cracks right down the middle. He grins at her in a

13

way he's never looked at me before, and then he wraps a hand around the back of her neck and pulls her down into a heated kiss, and it splinters my dreams to shards.

Stupid, Mila!

I grab my bag and run away from the truth I never wanted to see.

Jase just thinks of me as a friend.

Two more girls come dashing around the side of the house, and I freeze. They're laughing as they try to avoid getting wet, and I recognize them from school. They were in Jase's senior class.

Before I can search for a place to hide in the perfectly landscaped garden, the door to Jase's chalet opens. My broken heart begins to thunder in my chest, and my insides tighten with nerves.

"Mila?"

Unable to form a smile on my face, I refrain from turning around and just call out. "You're busy. I'll catch you later."

I dart around the girls who don't even seem to notice me. They only have eyes for Jase.

Like me… and every other girl on this planet.

I don't make it far before a hand clamps around my arm, and I'm pulled to a stop.

Crap, this day isn't turning out like I hoped it would.

"Hey, you're soaking wet," Jase says as he comes to stand in front of me.

"Yeah." I point up. "Rain." I lower my eyes to the cobblestone path. "I don't want to keep you from your friends."

I begin to move around Jase, but he doesn't let go of my arm, and tilting his head, he frowns at me. "Why did you come over?"

Seriously?

My fragile heart doesn't have the strength to deal with the wave of disappointment Jase's words cause.

"I asked you to pick me up after school, remember?" I ask because I want him to at least remember he said he'd pick me up.

Understanding flashes over his way too handsome features. "Shit, I'm sorry, Mila. I was on my way to your school when Angela came over."

Angela. So that's the name of the girl who gets to kiss Jase.

The thought is a sting to my bruised ego.

"No worries," I mumble as I pull my arm free. I walk as fast as I can.

"Wait, I'll take you home," Jase calls after me.

15

"I love walking in the rain. Go back to your friends," I shout, quickening my pace even more.

When I finally get to the road, I break out into a run.

I try to get away from my broken heart and lost dreams. I try to outrun the intimate image of Jase and Angela.

Mostly, I try to get away from the wave of hurt because I should've known better. Jase has always been surrounded by girls. Older girls. More experienced girls.

Why did I ever think he'd be interested in me?

Chapter 2

MILA

Mila 18; Jase 22

Finishing my assignment, I make sure to save the document before I close my laptop.

"Damn, that took forever," I groan as I stretch my arms above my head. My stomach growls, and it reminds me I haven't eaten anything today.

Climbing off the bed, I slip on my shoes and walk out of my room, hoping one of my friends wants to eat dinner with me.

I've been attending Trinity Academy for a month now, sharing a suite with my best friends, so there's usually someone I can hang out with.

Walking into the living room, I grin when I see Jade and Hunter snuggling. The movie that's playing on the TV is totally forgotten.

"You guys are so cute," I say. Every time I see them together, I'm thankful they worked past their problems. I was really worried about them. "I'm starving. Have you eaten?"

Jade lifts her head long enough to nod. "Yeah, we had dinner an hour ago."

Leaving the two lovebirds, I check Fallon and Hana's rooms, but not finding them, I decide to see if they're at the restaurant. If not, I can always grab something to go.

I leave the suite and take the elevator down. The doors ping open on the ground floor, and I freeze in my tracks when I come face to face with Jase and Jessica lip-locked.

Ugh, does it have to be Jessica? I can't stand the girl or any of her friends.

Jase manages to pull free from Jessica's octopus hold on him, and his eyes widen when he sees me staring at them. The doors begin to slide shut, and I don't bother stopping them.

Well, that sight made me lose my appetite.

Soon after I started at Trinity, Jase asked me to be his date for the welcome ball. Even though everything in me wanted to scream yes and do a happy dance, I had to say no for the sake of our friendship. I've loved Jase Reyes for three years, and every day it gets more challenging being around him.

18

He keeps flirting with me, and it confuses the hell out of me. I know he doesn't mean anything by it because every weekend he's out partying. Jase is a playboy, and no matter how much I love him, I won't give him the chance to break my heart.

I let out a sigh and press the button for the top floor, but the doors slide open again, and Jase steps into the confined space.

"What, no Jessica?" I grumble, crossing my arms over my chest.

He doesn't answer my snide comment about Jessica and instead comes to stand right next to me. Our arms press against each other, and I scoot a step to the right, but Jase just moves closer to me again.

Nothing will ever come of my feelings for Jase, and I won't risk the friendship we have for a quick fling. I love Jase too much to lose him.

Shooting him a glare, I ask, "Ever heard of personal space?"

Slowly he turns to me with his trademark sexy grin plastered on his face. It only makes my glare darken.

Jase leans his head closer to mine and whispers, "You love having me in your personal space."

The low timbre of his voice sends goosebumps rushing over my skin. My heart flutters, and my insides quiver. Everything about Jase makes me weak in the knees. From his thick brown hair to his golden-brown eyes. Let's not forget his toned body and sun-brown skin. The guy is my wildest fantasy incarnate, which doesn't help shit in my struggle to keep him at a distance.

It's a reaction I've grown accustomed to whenever I'm near Jase. I'd love nothing more than to grab hold of his shirt and to yank him down so I can kiss that grin from his way too sexy face. But my determination to keep things platonic between us once again triumphs over my attraction for him.

I bring up a hand between us and shove him back. The doors open, and I dart out of the elevator, snapping. "In your dreams, Jase."

He catches up to me and throws his arm around my shoulders. "Babe, I've told you before, you don't want to know what I do to you in my dreams."

The first time Jase said those words to me, I was too stunned to react. I shrug his arm away as I walk into the suite, growling, "Don't touch me with your Jessica infested paws."

Jade and Hunter glance between us, then Jade asks, "Weren't you going to eat?"

I roll my eyes in Jase's direction. "I lost my appetite." Walking to my room, I slam the door shut behind me, but it just swings open again as Jase follows me inside. "I haven't had dinner. Let's go."

Turning around, I cross my arms over my chest and glare at him. "I'm not hungry."

Ignoring me, Jase stalks to me, and, wrapping an arm around my waist, he pulls me out of my room.

"Dude, I said no," I protest even though my deceitful heart is doing a happy dance that Jase is giving me attention.

Pathetic, I know.

Jase continues to ignore me and pulls my left arm free so he can take hold of my hand. To the wide-eyed expressions Jade and Hunter are giving us, Jase says, "I'm going to feed grumpy. Catch you later."

"Grumpy my butt," I scoff as we leave the suite.

When we stop in front of the elevator, Jase again leans into me. "Careful, babe. You'll have me thinking you're jealous because you saw Jessica kissing me."

"Ugh." I roll my eyes so hard, I'm surprised they don't fall right out of their sockets. "There's a difference between being traumatized from you and Jessica sucking face and actually giving two shits."

Jase grins at me as the doors slide open, and he pulls me inside. "Yeah, keep lying to yourself, Mila. It's fun watching you squirm."

I pull my hand free from Jase's and shake my head. "You're delusional. Stop seeing things that aren't there."

Jase moves quickly, and placing his hands on my hips, he pushes me back until I'm pinned against the panel. He lowers his head, and feeling his breath on my face makes the spit in my mouth dry right up. My heart skips a beat before it sets off at a crazy pace, and my stomach knots up with anticipation.

Jase shifts his hands up to my jaw, and when our gazes lock, I forget to breathe. Those golden-brown eyes have always been my greatest weakness. They have a way of hypnotizing me.

Jase's voice is low and husky when he whispers, "So you don't want to kiss me right now?"

Somehow I manage to shake my head.

Vaguely I hear the doors open, and then Fallon says, "Whoa! Let's take the stairs, Hana."

Hearing my friend's voice yanks me out of the lovesick spell Jase put me under, and I pull free from him. Darting out of the elevator, I rush out of the dorm and hurry around the side of the building. Breaking out into a run, I make a mad dash in the direction of the lecture buildings.

I only stop when I'm sure Jase is nowhere in sight. Leaning against a wall, I catch my breath while I try to rein in my emotions, which almost got the better of me.

You know better than to be alone with Jase! That was too close. No matter how much you want to be with him, you can't give in. Jase will soon find someone new to flirt with, and you'll be able to just be his friend. Just hold out.

But damn, the past month of flirting is starting to really get to me. A girl can only say no so many times before she gives in.

I can't give in. Not now. Not ever.

I sink down to the ground and take a couple of deep breaths. I'll wait ten minutes before I go back to the suite.

Forcing myself to remember Jessica and Jase's kiss helps solidify my belief that Jase is just a player. No good will ever come from a quick fling between us.

JASE

I let out a chuckle as Mila runs away from me, and it earns me a slap upside the head from my cousin, Fallon.

"Stop teasing my friend," she chastises me.

"It's too much fun." I quickly get out of the elevator and shoot the girls a grin before I head out of the dorm to see if I can catch up with Mila.

When there's no sign of her, I walk to the restaurant, figuring that's where she'll be.

My grin widens when I think of how her breaths sped up as I leaned into her. Mila might be feisty and fight me at every turn, but her body's reaction to me speaks louder than words. And damn, it's so much fun getting her all riled up.

'Just don't push it too far, or you'll risk your friendship with her.' my conscience whispers.

Moving in the same circle, we've always been around each other. I used to see Mila as nothing more than a friend until she moved into the dorm a month ago. Little things about her started grabbing my attention.

At first, I flirted with her just because she shot me down when I asked her to be my plus one to the welcome ball held at Trinity every year. But seeing how riled up she got, my flirting intensified, and now I'm fucking addicted to the push and pull between us.

I know Mila wholeheartedly believes I'm a player, and it doesn't help that she keeps catching me in compromising positions like the one earlier when Jessica laid a kiss on me. One minute, Jessica was declaring her undying love, and the next, her lips were locked with mine. I had nothing to do with the situation, and come to think of it, I was practically assaulted.

I never used to mind girls coming onto me, and I guess I created that monster by not saying no. But then I got slapped upside the head with the realization that little Mila isn't so little anymore.

I shrug the thought away because Mila's just a friend. One I obviously love teasing, but a friend nonetheless.

Walking into the restaurant, I feel everyone's eyes lock on me.

"Hey, Jase," Jessica says, and it's only then I see her sitting at a table with her group of friends. She makes a point of glancing over at the empty table reserved for my friends and me, then says, "Don't eat alone. Sit with us."

"I'm just here to grab an order," I say, trying my best to hide my disappointment because Mila's not here like I thought. Knowing she has to eat, I walk to the nearest waiter and get her a chicken salad and pizza. Either one should be okay with her.

"I can keep you company while you wait?" Jessica pipes up behind me.

Shaking my head, I pull my phone from my pocket. "I have emails to check. Thanks, though."

I've been preparing for my future position as CEO with my grandfather, and he's taught me the importance of not burning bridges. You never know when you might need someone, so it's best to always be polite. It sucks, though, because it puts me in a catch twenty-two with the girls. You give them an inch, and they want the whole damn body.

I never used to mind, but lately, it's all starting to become exhausting. I also have to consider my future position as chairman of CRC Holdings, and a playboy image won't be tolerated by the shareholders.

Suppose it's time to start growing up.

I clear my damn spam folder, so I'll look busy, and I let out a sigh of relief when the order is finally ready. Taking the food from the server, I keep my eyes on my phone, so I don't accidentally encourage a student to approach me as I walk out of the restaurant.

When I'm outside, I tuck the device back in my pocket and glancing around, my eyes focus on someone coming from the lecture halls' direction. A grin begins to spread over my face, and I jog until I reach Mila. When I wrap my arm around her shoulders, she lets out a shriek, and slapping me against the chest, she quickly moves to the side.

When she sees it's me, she darts forward and punches me against the shoulder. "Dumbass! You'll give me a freaking heart attack. Don't ever sneak up on me again."

"Bet I made your heart skip a beat," I tease her. I shove the food against her chest, and she has no choice but to take hold of the bag and box. "I got your dinner. Go eat." Not waiting for her response, I begin to walk toward the dorm.

"You got me dinner?" she asks behind me, sounding dumbstruck.

"You have to eat, right?" I ask as I shove my hands in my pockets.

"Yeah, but you didn't have to get me food," she says as she catches up to me. I can feel her eyes on my face but keep mine trained on the building ahead of us.

"I know," I say.

"Oh… well… thanks, I suppose," she stammers, and it makes a smile form around my lips.

"You can always thank me another way," I say as I tap my pointer finger against my cheek.

"Ugh," she lets out on a huff and begins to walk faster while mumbling, "Should've known there was a catch."

"You bet your pretty little ass, I'm a catch," I call after her.

Chapter 3

MILA

Fallon, Jade, and I have just attended our last lecture for the day, and we're walking back to the dorm when two juniors, Nate Sparks and Justin Green, approach us.

"Ladies," Nate says, a grin playing around his lips. "I'm having a party next Friday and was hoping you'd come?"

I glance at Fallon, knowing she'll decide for all of us.

She looks at Jade and me before she answers, "Sure, we can show our faces. Where will it be?"

"At Studio 9. I've booked the club." Looking happy that we'll be attending, he begins to turn away. "Catch you later."

I'm just about to continue walking when Justin touches my arm to get my attention. "Hey, Mila. Can we talk?"

I've never actually spoken to the guy and have no idea why he would want to talk to me. My eyes dart to Jade, who's downright scowling at Justin.

Raising an eyebrow at him, I say, "What about?"

29

He shoots a glance at Jade and Fallon, and realizing they aren't leaving my side, he sighs. "Seeing as you're all going to Nate's party, I was hoping you'd go with me?"

Huh?

His question takes me totally by surprise because we've hardly interacted with each other.

What happened to first getting to know a girl before asking her out on a date?

"Ahh…" I hesitate, not wanting to hurt his feelings, but then answer, "We're going in a group, so I'll see you there."

He looks taken aback by my answer but then shrugs. "Sure. Save a dance for me?"

"Yeah," I agree, figuring one dance won't hurt.

"Great, see you around."

I watch him walk away then turn my frown to Jade and Fallon. "Well, that was a surprise."

"Yeah," Fallon agrees.

Jade's still scowling at Justin's back, then she grumbles, "I saw him checking you out the other night."

"For real?" I ask as we begin to walk again. "I'm not interested, though. He's not my type."

An arm falls around my shoulders, and as my head snaps up, I get an instant overdose of Jase.

His sexy as hell grin. His woodsy aftershave that smells heavenly. His muscled body pressing against my side.

Sigh, total ovary-exploding worthy.

"That's 'cause I'm your type, right?" Jase teases, his eyes slowly drifting over my face.

Giving him an irritated scowl, I shrug his arm from my shoulders. "That would be a solid hell no."

I'm such a liar.

"Ouch." He places his hand over his heart, pretending to look wounded. "You're so damn cold." And then his attention turns to all of us. "I'm hungry. Wanna grab an early dinner with me?"

"Sure," Fallon answers, and we change direction toward the restaurant.

Jade and I fall back behind Fallon and Jase, and my cousin hooks her arm through mine. "So... Justin Green?"

"That's never happening," I say, shaking my head.

"Don't you think it's weird he suddenly asked you out?"

I shrug, not caring. "Let's change the subject. Things look good between you and Hunter."

Jade knows I don't open up easily, and not pushing, she smiles like a lovesick teenager. "Yeah, I still get moments where it's surreal."

"I'm glad you realized he's the one for you," I mention.

"Yeah, me too." Then Jade wags her eyebrows at me and whispers, "How about you and Jase?"

Giving my cousin a disgruntled look, I shake my head. "That's another solid hell no." Just then, Jessica and her group of friends approach Jase, and I pull a face when she hugs him. "Jase will never be a one-girl kinda guy."

Jade lets out a disappointed sigh. "Yeah, I had high hopes, but with that dream up in smoke…" she grins at me, "we should find you, someone."

I pull my arm free from hers and shake my head hard. "No." When she gives me a pleading look, I adamantly state, "No, Jade. I don't want to date."

She takes a deep breath, then concedes, "Fine. But the second you're ready to climb into the dating pool, you better tell me. There are a couple of hot fish in the sea."

"I've never liked fishing," I joke as we walk into the restaurant.

I wait for everyone to pick a seat, and leaving a couple of chairs empty between Jase and me, I sit down and grab a menu.

"What's everyone having?" Jade asks.

"The shrimp linguini alfredo," Fallon answers, not even looking at the selection on the menu.

"I need some meat," I murmur, and then I see exactly what I want. "I'll have the filet mignon with shoestring potatoes."

"You should've said something," Jase says.

"Huh?" Setting down my menu, I give him a confused look.

"Babe, I have all the meat you'll ever need."

"God help me," I groan. Slumping back in my chair, I glance at the restaurant's décor to avoid looking at Jase. "You're so freaking full of yourself. Doesn't it get tiring carrying that big head of yours around all day?"

Jase begins to chuckle. "You have no idea. I can hardly walk." I try not to laugh, but the second my lips twitch, Jase lets out a bark of laughter. Then he says, "It won't be so funny when I die of blue balls."

Covering my eyes with my hand, I do my best to school my face into a scowl as I mutter, "I'm never going to win with you."

JASE

A waiter takes our orders, and then I lean back in the chair and stare at Mila until she glances at me. "What did Justin Green want?"

She just shrugs. "Nothing."

A courier carrying flowers catches my eye. He asks one of the servers something, and then he's pointed in our direction. A frown starts to form on my forehead as he walks toward us.

"I have flowers for a Mila West?" the guy asks.

Mila's head snaps in his direction, and surprise flashes over her face. "That's me."

"Could you sign here?"

My frown darkens as he places the bouquet down on the table. The thing is nothing short of half a damn garden.

"Who would send me flowers?" Mila asks as she searches for the card. Finding it, my gaze narrows on her as she reads the message.

She grimaces, and looking rueful, she says, "They're from Justin." Her shoulders slump, and she glances around the restaurant. Spotting Justin where he's seated with his friends, she rises from her chair, muttering, "Now I feel bad for saying no. Ugh. I should, at least, thank him."

My face sets into a scowl as I watch Mila walk to his table. There's a possessive twinge in my chest when she smiles at him.

Fallon sneezes, and it yanks my attention away from Mila. Getting up, I grab hold of the arrangement and set it down on the open table next to ours.

"Thanks," Fallon says, then she grumbles, "Why did I have to be allergic to flowers? It sucks not being able to receive any."

My eyes find Mila as she walks back to us. She sits down and gives Fallon an apologetic smile. "Sorry, my friend. Now your sinuses will be acting up again."

Fallon waves it away. "I'll take something for it when we're done eating."

My gaze is still locked on Mila. "So, you and Justin?"

She shakes her head and places her napkin over her lap. "There's no Justin and me."

A server brings our food, and while we eat, my eyes keep finding their way to Mila.

Drop it, Jase. You're just overprotective because she's your friend.

Obviously, Mila's going to date, and with her fucking beauty, I'm actually surprised one of the guys on campus hasn't swooped in to claim her.

The thought makes me freeze, and the glare on my face darkens.

"What's wrong?" Fallon asks.

I continue cutting a piece of my steak. "Nothing."

"Yeah, right," Jade says. "It looks like you're about to kill someone."

"I said it's nothing," I snap. I drop my cutlery and take a deep breath before I give the girls a remorseful smile. "Sorry, I didn't mean to snap."

Fallon reaches over to me and gives my arm a squeeze. "Let's enjoy the meal."

My eyes meet Fallon's, and hers clearly say we'll talk later. Thinking of a quick lie to get me out of the hot seat, I say, "I'm just worried about working with my father this summer."

"I'll be there to help. We'll be fine," Fallon says, a look of encouragement on her face.

I force a playful smile around my lips. "Yeah? Any way I can bribe you into doing my work?"

Fallon glares at me. "Nope." But then her expression softens. "You won't be alone. You'll have Hana, Hunter, and myself there."

I let out a heavy breath before I glance at Mila. I catch her staring at me with concern tightening her features.

Giving her a grin, I focus on my dinner so the girls will drop the subject.

Why did Mila getting flowers piss me off so much?

Ignoring the question, I shove it deep down.

My eyes drift to her face again, and I watch as she nibbles on a shoestring potato. I take in her long silky black hair, and her sharp green eyes and full lips.

Those damn cheekbones of hers make her look fucking sexy.

My eyes glide down her neck, her skin snowy white. It's in total contrast with her dark hair, and it makes her look more feminine.

I'd be blind and castrated not to notice she's fucking gorgeous.

And every day, I'm becoming more aware of her beauty.

Fine, so you're attracted to Mila. So what? It's not like anything will ever come of it. Stick to flirting with her because that's as far as you can take things without fucking up your friendship.

My thoughts turn to the past month, and I remember how teasing the ever-loving shit out of Mila was only for fun.

And for fun, it will remain, Jase.

Needing a drink, I get the attention of a waiter and quickly place an order.

My eyes drift back to Mila, and I watch as she cuts a piece from her steak. Her hands are small and probably half the size of mine.

Something stirs in my chest again, and my eyes narrow at the foreign emotion.

I wonder what would've happened if she weren't my friend.

The sudden thought packs one hell of a punch.

Yeah, I know what would've happened. Without thinking twice about it, I'd pursue her.

"Jase," Mila snaps, and my eyes fly up to her face. "Why are you staring at me like that?"

I clear my throat and shift uncomfortably in my chair. "I'm not staring at you."

"Could've fooled me," she mumbles. Her eyes linger on my face for a couple of seconds. "It really looked like you wanted to kill me. Are you that worried about working at CRC?"

Taking the out she's unknowingly given me, I nod. "Yeah, it's a lot of pressure to know I'll be taking over as the CEO of CRC Holdings. I don't know how my dad handles it."

"You'll be fine." Mila's mouth curves into a soft smile, one I haven't seen in a while. "I believe in you."

My heart starts to beat faster, and a cold sweat breaks out over my body. Shifting my chair back, I climb to my feet. "Shit, I think I'm coming down with something. I'll see you at the suite."

Fallon abandons her meal and jumps out of her chair. "The flu? I'll walk back with you and get you some meds."

"Don't worry. I'm just going to sleep it off."

I stalk out of the restaurant, my heart hammering against my ribs, and placing my hand over my chest, I suck in a deep breath of air.

What the fuck is going on with me?

It's probably just a cold.

I will my heartbeat back to normal and shove all thoughts of Mila to the farthest corner of my mind. I'm sure I'll be fine tomorrow. I just need a good night's rest.

Chapter 4

MILA

Worried about Jase, I knock on his door.

"Yeah?"

Pushing the door open, I peek inside. "How are you feeling?"

His eyes snap from his laptop to me. "Better. Thanks."

I take in his features, looking for any signs that he's not feeling well. "You sure? You didn't look too hot earlier."

A grin spreads over his face. "Babe, I always look hot."

I roll my eyes. "Yep, you're definitely fine."

I begin to pull the door shut, then Jase calls out, "Glad you're finally admitting it."

Shaking my head, I walk to my own room. I grab my pajamas, which basically consist of sweatpants and a t-shirt, and go shower.

When I'm done washing and drying off, I lather my body with my lily scented lotion. Searching for my panties, I let out a huff when I realize I didn't bring any. I quickly wrap a towel around me and dart back into my room. Seeing Jase lying on my bed, I come to a sudden stop.

His eyebrows pop up, and his gaze sweeps over my body.

Gripping the towel tighter, I snap, "Dude, come on. What happened to personal space?"

He shakes his head and plasters an innocent look over his face. "I'm nowhere near your personal space." Then he climbs off the bed and saunters closer to me. His eyes drop to the towel. "By the way, I love your PJ's."

"Ha-ha." I go to my walk-in closet and grab a pair of cotton panties. Turning around, I come face to face with Jase, who followed me inside. Even though my heart skips a beat and there's a flutter in my stomach, I force a scowl to my face. "Do you mind?"

His grin turns seductive as he slowly shakes his head. "Not at all."

I know myself, and I'm reaching the point of no return at the speed of light. If Jase were to try anything, I wouldn't be able to stop him, and I'd give in.

I can't keep doing this with him, though. It hurts when he dangles the damn carrot in front of my face, and I know I can never have it.

The scowl on my face is replaced with a serious look as I say, "This has to stop, Jase."

He tilts his head. "What?"

"This thing you're doing," I say, and when he takes a step closer to me, I begin to feel panicky. I can't let him find out how I feel about him. I'd just die of embarrassment.

Jase comes to stand way too close to me, and I'm wrapped in a cloud of his woodsy scent.

I groan inwardly as my resolve slips some more.

Lifting a hand, Jase brushes my hair off my shoulder. He leans down, and when I feel his breath on my cheek, my eyes drift shut.

Oh, God. I have zero resistance right now.

"Thing?" he whispers so low, it almost sounds like a growl.

My stomach buzzes like a beehive that's been disturbed, and my heart beats so fast I'm afraid my chest won't be able to contain the wild organ.

Pulling back, Jase tilts his head, and he locks his eyes on mine. After a couple of torturous seconds, he says, "You know I'm only joking with you, right?"

Yeah, sadly, I do know.

I nod, trying very hard to ignore the sting in my heart.

42

There's a weird look on his face as he smiles at me. "It's just 'cause you're one of my favorite people."

Knowing he won't take it wrong, I grab the chance to speak the truth without bearing the consequences of it. "Yeah, I love you, too."

I love you so so so much.

I keep the smile on my face as I watch him leave, and then my shoulders slump.

Nothing sucks like unrequited love.

To Jase, it's nothing more than innocent flirting, but for me, it's torture.

Letting out a sigh, I walk back to the bathroom so I can get dressed.

You need to get over Jase, Mila. Nothing will ever come of it.

JASE

My heart is practically pounding in my chest as I shut my bedroom door behind me.

Fuck, why did I do that?

I was a split-second away from grabbing hold of Mila and kissing her.

Confused, I lean back against the door, sucking in deep breaths of air.

I admit I've felt an attraction toward her, but tonight? Seeing her only in that towel?

Fuck, she looked sexy and… totally fuckable.

The thought makes me choke on a random drop of spit, and coughing, I rush to my bedside table to get some water. I swallow half the bottle down before I come up for air.

What the fuck was that?

Feeling claustrophobic, I practically jog out of my room.

"Where are you going?" Kao asks as I rush past the kitchen where he and Noah are busy scarfing down burgers.

"For a walk," I call back.

I can't get out of the suite fast enough, and not wanting to be stuck in the elevator, I take the stairs down. When I burst through the main doors of the dorm, I stop to get some air in.

Holy shit, do I have a thing for Mila?

Noooo.

But…

Fuck.

Panic begins to bleed into my chest.

You just need to get laid, Jase. There's nothing between you and Mila. She's hot, and you saw her half-naked. It's only normal for your cock to take notice.

I let out a frustrated groan and glancing around me, my eyes land on Jessica as she comes out of the opposite dorm.

She spots me, and crossing the road, there's a broad smile on her face. "Hey, Jase." Her voice is low and inviting.

"Hey." Mine sounds like it's breaking all over again. I clear my throat.

"You want some company?" she asks, and I can hear the double-meaning. I should stay away from the girl seeing as Fallon, Hana, Mila, and Jade don't get along with her and her friends.

But instead, I ask, "What did you have in mind?"

She points to the dorm across the road. "I just redecorated my suite. Wanna come and see?"

No.

"Sure."

I shove my hands in my pockets and follow an ecstatic Jessica to her suite.

Everything in me wants to run back to my own suite, but I push through and walking into Jessica's private space, it just feels… wrong.

"Soooo," she turns to stare at my face, "what do you think?"

I don't even take in the decor. "It looks good."

Gripping hold of my arm, she pulls me toward her bedroom. "This is my favorite room."

The feeling that this is all wrong keeps growing in my chest until my breaths begin to speed up.

Jessica must read my reaction wrong because the next second, her mouth is plastered against mine.

Instead of pulling away, I force my hands to her face and kiss her back. I take a deep breath of her scent, and the sweet smell instantly clears my head. Yanking away from her, I feel the first ripples of regret.

Nothing like the soft scent always wrapped around Mila.

"This is a mistake," I grumble, and I leave her standing in her bedroom. I let myself out of the suite, feeling like a zombie as I walk back to my own building.

Now I'm even more confused.

Frustrated and confounded, I walk into my suite, and come to a standstill when I see Mila lying on the couch with the other girls. They're watching Smallville.

Fallon spots me first. "Where were you?"

"I just went for a walk." I move closer to the couch Mila's on, and I can't stop myself from saying, "Make space for me."

Mila sits up, but keeping her back to me, she leans her left shoulder against the couch. Then she warns me, "You better not mess with my Clark Kent time."

I force my eyes to the television and manage to watch a couple of seconds before my gaze drifts to Mila's back. She looks uncomfortable, and not even thinking twice, I reach for her. Pulling her down, I let her head rest on my thigh.

Her startled gaze flits to me before it snaps back to the TV screen.

Yeah, babe, me too. I have no fucking idea what I'm doing.

All I know is Jessica's scent and touch irritated the fuck out of me, where Mila's… everything about her has become fucking exhilarating.

And like an idiot, I sit and watch four damn episodes of Smallville while torturing myself with the unexplained emotions swirling in my fucking chest.

47

I've come to the conclusion I just feel protective of Mila because the fucker, Justin Green, is showing interest in her.

It's taken me two days to realize this, but at least I don't feel so fucking confused anymore.

Man, it's great being back to my old self. For a moment there, I thought I was losing my mind.

I'm grinning at every student passing me by. Nate and Justin fucking Green come toward me, and my good mood sours a little.

"Hey, I was looking for you," Nate says, a broad smile plastered over his face. The guy's not that bad, but his best friend irritates the fuck out of me.

"I'm having a party at Studio 9 next Friday and was hoping you'd come. Fallon and the girls already said they would pop in."

Like I have much of a choice now. If the girls are going to the club, then it means Hunter, Kao, Noah, and I will definitely be there. We never let them go to that club alone because who knows when a seedy fucker will try his luck with one of them.

"Sure, I'll make an appearance," I grumble, not too happy about the fact.

"Thanks." Nate looks like I've just made his year.

I glance at Justin, and when I see his attention is elsewhere, I follow his line of sight, and then a dark scowl shadows my features.

"Are you interested in Mila?" I ask outright.

Justin looks caught red-handed as his eyes dart to me. "Ah… yeah."

I take a step closer to him, not caring that I'm starting to draw the attention of the students around us. "Don't fuck with her. She's off-limits."

"Who's off-limits?" Fallon suddenly asks behind me.

I glance over my shoulder, and seeing Hana, Jade, and Mila with Fallon, I hesitate, but then I push through and answer, "Mila's off-limits."

Just like I expected, a frown settles on Mila's face. "Who are you to decide that?"

"Seriously?" I let out a bark of laughter. "Do you really need me to answer that?"

She crosses her arms over her chest and daringly lifts her chin. "Yes."

Slowly, I saunter closer to Mila until I'm right in front of her. Looking down at her, I tilt my head, a grin tugging at the corner of my mouth. "I'd thought it was self-explanatory, babe."

"Let's pretend my IQ just dropped. Explain it to me," she fucking sasses me.

I lean down slightly, and the space between us shrinks. "As the leader of this group, it's my duty to make sure no one fucks with any of my girls."

'You're lying,' my conscience whispers. 'It's because you can't stand seeing another dick anywhere near Mila.'

Mila's eyes narrow on me, and her voice drops to a hiss, "I'm not one of *your* girls."

My eyebrow darts up, and the grin widens on my face. "Keep lying to yourself, babe. We both know that's not the truth."

Mila's breaths begin to speed up, and for a moment, there's a flash of panic on her face before she darkens her glare. "You better stop this crap, Jase. People are going to start thinking you're in love with me."

Whoa... hold up a second.

Say what?

Mila sees the shock on my face, and her sexy as fuck mouth lifts into a smile. "Careful, Jase. Your playboy image is in danger of going up in smoke."

She pushes past me, and I turn to watch her walk away, still dumbstruck she actually called me out in front of everyone.

"Who's the one dreaming now?" I manage to call after her.

Mila stops and gives me a seductive look, and then she throws my words from the other day back at me, "Oh, babe, you don't want to know what I do to you in my dreams." She glances me up and down, then grumbles, "I'll give you a hint... it involves me throat punching you."

I let out a chuckle as I watch her walk toward the lecture halls.

The sass of that girl will drive me absolutely wild.

I suck in a deep breath of air, and then noticing Nate and Justin are still standing by me, I snap, "Like I said. My girls are off-limits."

I stalk away, feeling like I'm on a high from the altercation with Mila.

Yeah, I'm definitely getting addicted to the push and pull between us.

But the real question is, does Mila feel it too?

Chapter 5

MILA

What the hell was that?

The past two days, Jase gave me a break, and things were actually good between us. Then wham, we're back to him giving me crap.

Ugh, for a moment back there, I was worried my secret was out.

My heart is pounding a mile a minute, but I'm proud of how I reacted. I stuck to my guns and gave Jase a taste of his own medicine.

I attend two lectures before lunch, and the moment I meet up with Fallon and Jade in the restaurant, Fallon gives me a confused look. "I can't figure out whether you and Jase are flirting or fighting."

I shrug and mutter, "He's flirting, and I'm fighting."

Fallon glances from me to Jade, then asks, "But he's just teasing you, right?"

Jade leans her forearms on the table and wags her eyebrows at Fallon. "You can always ask Jase if he likes Mila and put us all out of our misery."

I give my friends a look of warning. "Don't ask him anything. Besides, even if he did like me as more than a friend, nothing will come of it. I'm not willing to risk our friendship for a fling."

My friends stare at each other before they both settle their gazes on me.

"Do you like Jase?" Fallon asks, and her eyes sharpen on me.

Knowing she's undeniably loyal to Jase, I give her a non-committal shrug. "Can we change the subject?"

There's a flash of disappointment on Fallon's face. "Not that my opinion counts, but I think you and Jase would make a perfect couple."

I give her a pleading look to let it go, and lucky for me, a waiter comes to take our orders.

Everyone is starting to notice something is going on between Jase and me. The only problem is that Jase is just joking. And Me? I'm hopelessly in love with him.

I let out a sigh, and then I jerk when a hand settles on my shoulder. Glancing up, I give Justin a questioning look.

"Hey, sorry to interrupt your lunch." He sits down in the empty seat next to me, earning frowns from Fallon and Jade. "Will you have dinner with me tonight? I'd like to get to know you better."

For a split-second, I consider accepting his offer. Maybe then my friends will back down, and Jase will get the message.

But I'm not the kind of person who uses people, so I shake my head. "Sorry, Justin. I really appreciate the offer, but I'm not interested in dating right now."

He hesitates for a moment, a confused expression on his face.

"You're in my seat," Jase suddenly barks from behind me.

Justin gets up, and giving me a rueful smile, he says, "Maybe another time."

Jase slumps down in the chair Justin vacated, and giving me a pissed-off look, he growls, "I'd seriously fucking appreciate it if your boyfriend didn't sit at our table."

My jaw drops, and I stare at Jase while searching for the right come back.

Hunter takes the seat next to Jase, and leaning forward, says, "Calm down, Jase."

54

Jase's head snaps to Hunter. "I'll fucking calm down when people start respecting boundaries."

"Boundaries?" I hiss, my temper shooting through me like a missile.

Where were the boundaries when I repeatedly pointed out he was in my personal space? And all the times he's flirted with me, giving me the impression he was about to kiss me?

And now he's losing his shit with me? I haven't done anything wrong to deserve him talking to me like that, and it's the last straw.

"You're one to talk!" Getting up, I throw my napkin on the table, and I glare at Jase as my breaths race over my lips. When Jase finally looks up at me, I say, "Lately, you're a real shitty friend, Jase."

I stalk away while another crack is added to my bruised heart. I can't take much more. He's pushing me to the point of breaking, and for the first time, I regret coming to Trinity.

I'm so damn angry I can't stop the tears from falling as I rush out of the restaurant.

I... I just can't do this anymore.

I can't keep loving Jase while he treats me like one of his hoes.

JASE

My anger gets the better of me, and before Hunter can stop me, I dart up and run after Mila.

I catch up to her outside the restaurant, and grabbing hold of her arm, I yank her back. She stumbles and crashes into me. Her head snaps up, and the second I see the tears on her cheeks, my anger diminishes a little, and I start to feel like shit.

Wrapping my arms around her, I hug her, and pressing my face into her neck, I whisper, "I'm sorry, Mila."

Mila shoves at me, pulling herself free. She begins to walk away, then stops and swinging back to me, her voice is hoarse as she says, "I can't do this with you, Jase. You treat me like crap, and I didn't do anything to deserve it. I've been nothing but a friend to you." She begins to walk again, then stops and cries out, "Why?"

Why?

It's the first time the question gets stuck in my chest.

Because I'm attracted to you?

Because I hate seeing Justin near you?

Because you've always been my Mila, and I never had to share you before?

I ignore all the why's and take the easy way out, "I'm sorry, Mila."

Anger tightens her features, and she stalks back to me. Shoving a finger at my chest, she snaps, "I don't want an apology. I want to know why you're such an asshole to me, Jase. You owe me an explanation."

I know I do, but I don't even understand it myself. Where do I begin to explain it to Mila?

Shaking my head, I say, "I'm a dumbass. There's no reason."

Her face is shadowed with a sad look, and she stares at me for a moment before she whispers, "It feels like I don't know you anymore."

This time when she walks away, I let her.

I suck in a breath of air, but it does nothing to ease the turbulent feeling in my chest. My pride keeps me from admitting out loud that I'm attracted to her.

What if Mila doesn't feel the same? I'll end up making an ass of myself.

My eyes stay on her until another thought rattles through me.

You're losing Mila. You're fucking losing her friendship.

I break out into a run, and not caring who sees, I dart in front of Mila. "Wait. Let's talk about this."

Giving me an exasperated look, she asks, "Talk about what exactly, Jase?"

The students are starting to gather nearby, watching the fight between Mila and me. "Not here. Let's go up to the suite." Taking her hand, I don't give her much of a choice as I pull her into the dorm.

Our anger simmers in silence as we take the elevator to the top floor, and once we walk inside the suite, I follow Mila into her room. She crosses her arms over her chest as she turns to face me. A heavy sigh escapes her as she raises an expectant eyebrow at me. "You wanted to talk. Let's talk."

Her anger is etched into every inch of her face, and I can feel it coming off her in waves. I know I have to defuse the situation, but I don't know how.

Again, I take the easy way out. "I'm sorry I snapped at you. Justin just aggravates the fuck out of me."

Her gaze narrows on me. "Is that all you have to say?"

No. I have so much more I want to say. If only I had the guts.

Again my pride wins out, and not willing to admit I'm attracted to her, I nod.

Mila shakes her head, a frustrated expression tightening her features even more. "So you have nothing to say about the way you've been treating me? All those times you made crude comments about giving me a piece, about the handjob so you don't die of blue balls... and the damn kiss the night we played that game? You have nothing to say about any of that?"

Her whole body is tense, and hearing her call me out for my actions the past month, makes regret ripple through me. I never meant to hurt her by flirting with her. I thought she was enjoying the banter. It has me admitting, "I thought you were okay with it all."

A frown settles hard between her eyes. "That's so freaking arrogant of you, Jase. How does me repeatedly telling you to stop give you the impression I enjoy being treated like one of your lays?"

My self-control begins to slip, and throwing my arms wide, I snap, "Fine, I won't fucking flirt anymore. God, if I knew you were so sensitive, I wouldn't have started in the first place."

Seething, Mila stares at me for a long moment, and then a look of loss darkens her green irises. She closes her eyes and sucks in a deep breath of air. When her gaze settles on me again, her voice cracks over the words as she says, "I should've known better."

"What does that mean?" My voice is sharp while I feel a flutter of panic in my chest. The expression on Mila's face looks like she's done with us.

She lets out an empty sounding chuckle. "You've always been a player. It just hurts so much because you don't treat Fallon, Hana, or Jade that way. You just keep chipping away at me, and I don't understand why."

Mila shakes her head, and it looks like she's come to a conclusion. As she turns around and heads to the walk-in closet, she says, "I can't do this anymore. I'll move back home for the time being. Then you don't have to be around my sensitive ass."

Something snaps in my chest, and I lose the last of my control. Darting forward, I grab hold of her shoulder, and I force her to turn around. "Fine, you want the fucking truth?" I growl. I lean in closer and shout, "I'm fucking attracted to you. I know it will fuck up our friendship, but seeing as that ship sailed, I might as well fucking admit it."

Mila's lips part with surprise, and her eyes widen. She stares at me until I can't take it anymore, then she whispers, "What did you just say?"

The rage I felt gives way to the realization of what I just admitted, and I close my eyes against the truth.

Fuck.

Chapter 6

MILA

It feels like someone dropped a nuclear missile on my heart.

I'm torn between the anger pulsing through me and the love I feel for Jase.

Why did I fall in love with the one guy that's so far out of my damn reach, he might as well be in a different solar system.

And it hurts. So damn much.

For the last month, he's been pushing me relentlessly with all the flirting and innuendos hidden in his words. Jase was the one who asked me to the welcome ball. He's the one who danced the opening dance with me. He's been dropping hints of us being together… and it's all just too much.

I can't handle the teasing when it's the one thing I want with my whole heart. Not able to take it anymore, I know I'm a coward when I turn away from Jase and stalk to my closet. "I can't do this anymore. I'll move back home for the time being. Then you don't have to be around my sensitive ass."

Suddenly Jase grabs hold of me and spins me around. "Fine, you want the fucking truth?" he growls, leaning in so close, I can feel his breath burst over my face as he shouts, "I'm fucking attracted to you. I know it will fuck up our friendship, but seeing as that ship sailed, I might as well fucking admit it."

What?

All I can do is stare at him as the shock of his words hits me like a tidal wave.

Jase is attracted to me?

His words revive my broken heart, where it lies in a bloody mess at my feet, and sends it rocketing back into my chest.

Not able to believe what Jase just admitted, I whisper, "What did you just say?"

The same shock I feel ripples over his features, and then his eyes drift shut. I hold my breath when it looks like regret furrows his brow.

Don't give me hope, only to rip it away again.

Jase can't be that cruel.

When he opens his eyes, his golden-brown irises look like liquid gold. His gaze darts away from me, only to flick right back. Confusion mars his attractive features, and it makes my heart sink again.

"I… I don't know what I feel," Jase stammers, which is so unlike Jase. He's always sure of himself. If anything, he's overconfident when it comes to everything in his life. To see him unsure – makes me feel anxious.

I take a step backward, needing to put some space between us. It feels like I'm being thrown from one emotion to the next. Futile hope keeps warring with the disheartening despair that nothing will ever come of my love for him.

I begin to shake my head. "You don't get to do that to me, Jase. I can't handle you being hot and cold with me. You're torturing me." I take another step back, trying to retreat from the final crack that rips my heart in two. I shut my eyes tightly, not wanting to see his reaction as I let the words tear their way out of me, "I've loved you since I was fifteen. You were supposed to pick me up after school so I could tell you, but you forgot. Seeing you with another girl that day made me realize how stupid I was." I lower my head and opening my eyes, I stare at the floor. "Just when I think I can move on, you shove your way right back into my heart. How am I supposed to get over you when you keep dangling the damn carrot in front of my face?"

I gasp for air, filled with a weird combination of regret and relief for finally getting the secret off my chest.

I feel Jase move closer to me, and as I raise my eyes, his hands take hold of my face, and then his mouth crashes against mine.

At first, the shock of feeling Jase's lips on mine stuns the hell out of me, and I stand frozen.

When his mouth moves against mine, and he takes the final step between us, fusing our bodies together, my traitorous heart and body betray me in the worst way.

JASE

My emotions are out of control, and it feels like someone took a bat, smashing everything I've ever known about Mila and me to pieces.

Hearing her admit she loves me fills me with a desperation to find out whether I feel the same. And it drives me forward. I frame her face with my hands and slam my mouth down on hers.

And nothing is what I thought.

My carefully planned life spirals into a world of chaos. Instead of finding the answer I wanted, I'm left with more questions.

My lips move against hers, and the moment her body melts into mine, I'm fucking lost.

My tongue drives into the heat of her mouth, and the desire that's been hidden in every flirty comment flares into a fucking inferno.

Only one certainty remains – kissing Mila calms the storm that's been raging. And in its place, a wildfire begins to reap destruction through me.

I'm filled with a desire I've never felt before.

It's like the gates of hell have been thrust open, and there's no stopping the unadulterated need the flames breathe to life between us.

What the fuck is happening?

I shouldn't cross the line with Mila, but I have zero self-restraint left. The kiss grows more seductive, and I begin to devour her mouth, my body demanding more. The uncontrollable desire makes my heart thunder in my chest.

Fuck, tasting her sends my blood roaring through my veins.

My hands drop to her hips, and I pull her as close to me as I can while my tongue wars with hers for control.

Wanting… no, needing to feel more of her, my hands slip down to her ass, and I grip her tightly.

Mila gasps into my mouth, and it drives me fucking wild.

She fucking wants this as much as I do.

Heat flares through my body, and it makes my hands greedily explore her curves.

Fuck, I want Mila naked. I want to quench this ever-fucking thirst for her.

MILA

I'm swept up in the release I feel. I'm finally getting to kiss Jase and to express my emotions, until his hands brush up my body and his touch grows more frantic.

My mind clears up, and knowing I have to put a stop to this, I pull free and take a couple of steps backward.

Our breaths rush over our swollen lips as our eyes meet.

And then the shock of what just happened rocks me to my core, and I lift my hands, covering my mouth as I gasp for air.

Oh, God. How am I going to salvage our friendship now?

My eyes drift over Jase, and it doesn't help that he looks like sex incarnate. The heat in his gaze sets his eyes on fire, and it makes my resolve fade to nothing but a distant echo.

But then he takes a step backward, and realization ripples over his face. "Fuck." A flash of panic tightens his features. "I… I didn't mean for that to happen."

I close my eyes against the sharp pain in my chest as Jase brutally rips my heart out.

He must see the pain on my face because he moves forward and places his hand on my shoulder. "I need some time, Mila. I don't know where to begin to understand what just happened."

Jase makes it sound like I blindsided him, and it freaking devastates me. Pulling away from him, I say, "Then take the time you need, but don't you dare blame me for this. I didn't force you to kiss me."

He holds a hand up. "I didn't mean for it to come across like that. I'm just confused right now. We both need to process what happened."

No shit. I told you I love you, and you kissed me.

Seeing how rattled Jase is, and knowing I need some time alone, as well, I nod. "Go think about it and let me know where we stand once you've figured everything out."

Jase hesitates for a moment, then says, "Can we keep this between us?"

Ha, like I'm going to tell everyone about the most devastating moment of my life.

Having my love rejected by Jase is the worst thing that could've happened. He didn't even bother saying anything about the fact that I laid my heart at his feet.

"Sure," I mutter.

Watching Jase walk out of my room is so damn hard, and it makes a lump form in my throat. When the door shuts behind him, everything that just happened rips the ground from under my feet, and I sink to the floor.

I can't keep the sob back and quickly cover my mouth.

I just told Jase I love him and... nothing. It's like he didn't even hear my confession – words I've never said to another man before.

Why? Why do I even love him? He's done nothing to deserve it.

I cry for my teenage dream shattering to pieces once again. I mourn our friendship because deep in my heart, I know there's no way we'll ever come back from this fight.

Chapter 7

JASE

Holy fucking shit!

Not wanting any of my friends to see me in such a state, I grab my car keys and dart out of the door. My body is still buzzing with left-over adrenaline, and I take the stairs down to the ground floor.

When I run out of the dorm, I hear Hunter call, "Jase, let's talk."

I only pause long enough to yell, "Later." When I reach my car, I notice my hands are trembling as I yank the door open.

I keep the thoughts from flooding my mind as I start the engine, and flooring the gas, the tires spin. I'm not even out of the gates when my phone starts to ring. I dig the device out of my pocket and switch it off before throwing it on the backseat.

I don't know how I manage to drive without causing an accident, but I finally pull up to my grandfather's house.

Switching off the car, my body sinks back against the seat, and I close my eyes.

And then the torture begins. I remember what it felt like to kiss Mila. The devastation I saw on her face knocks the air from my lungs.

God, what have I done?

I've ruined our fucking friendship.

There's a tap against the window, and my eyes fly open. My grandfather opens the door and gives me a questioning look. "Why are you sitting in the car?"

I get out and slam the door shut behind me, and then I lie, "I have a headache."

His sharp gaze searches over my face, then he mutters, "If you say so. Let's go inside."

It's impossible to lie to my grandfather, and I should've known better. I wait until we walk into the living room before I admit, "I'm just dealing with something... ah... unexpected."

He gestures for me to take a seat behind the chessboard. It's been our thing since I turned thirteen.

"I take it you need some advice?" he asks as he makes his first move.

I stare at the chess pieces and move a pawn. "Yes, Sir."

We continue to play in silence while I try to figure out where to start. "There's a girl."

Granddad lets out a chuckle. "Isn't there always?"

The corner of my mouth twitches, and I shake my head. "She's different."

"Oh?" He takes one of my pawns. "How so?"

My eyes dart around the luxurious room before they settle on him. "She said she loves me."

One of his eyebrows rises slightly. "I can't tell you how many times women have told me they love me. Be careful, Jase. I'm not saying it's the case, but the girl might love your last name and wealth more."

"Mila West," I blurt her name out.

My grandfather's attention leaves the game, and his eyes settle hard on me. "Her father is a partner, Jase."

"I know."

He leans back in the chair, his gaze never leaving my face, and it has me admitting, "I don't know how I feel about her. We've been such good friends, and today it all went to hell."

My grandfather gets up and goes to pour us both a tumbler of whiskey. He hands me one and sits down again before he asks, "Mind if I tell you a story?"

I lean back against my chair and pay attention because every story he's ever told me was a lesson.

"While I was married to your grandmother, I fell in love with an amazing woman."

My lips twitch because I know this tale. It's about how he met my step-grandmother.

"God, she gave me hell," he breathes with a tender smile he only gets when he talks about Stephanie. "She fought me at every turn. Even after I divorced Clare, Stephanie still wouldn't have me."

"Sorry to interrupt," I say, leaning my forearms on my knees, "but what does this have to do with Mila and me."

"Stephanie is the heart of CRC Holdings, Jase. If things had gone wrong between us, it would've been a huge risk to the company. She knows every trade secret."

For him to admit something like that is huge. Warren Reyes is the most powerful man in America, and he took the risk to be with his personal assistant. Stephanie is still with the company, now serving as my father's PA.

My grandfather raises an eyebrow at me as he takes a sip of his drink. "Now that I have your attention." He sets the tumbler down on a table. "Is Mila West worth the risk of losing her family's shares and probably the other members of Indie Ink's, as well?"

74

I blink slowly as his question rattles between all the others in my head. "I don't know. I don't even know if this thing between us is worth risking our friendship for… or what's left of it."

"And you don't know how you feel about the girl?"

I shake my head. "Of course, I love her like a friend. She's been a huge part of my life."

"But?"

"But… How do you know when you really love someone?"

Without missing a breath, Granddad answers, "You're willing to risk everything for them. Remember what I taught you about being careful not to burn bridges?"

I nod, my drink forgotten in my hand.

"The West's are one hell of a bridge to burn, son."

"I know, Sir."

He sits forward in the chair. "But if you're unable to return Miss West's love, and she holds it against you, I'm willing to make the sacrifice of losing their business for you."

I glance up at the ceiling as his words sink in. He doesn't say the words I love you a lot, but damn, he shows it every chance he gets.

I search through my chaotic emotions, then admit, "I don't want to lose her, though. What do I do if I can't be more than friends?"

"Then you be the best goddamn friend she's ever had. You respect the love she's given you. Just because she cares for you doesn't mean your friendship is over, son."

I nod, drinking in his advice like a man dying of thirst.

"It took nineteen years before I could be with Stephanie. Not once did I make her feel like she was less. Just respect Miss West for the amazing woman she is. You wouldn't be sitting across from me if that was not the case."

My attention returns to the chessboard as I nod. "You're right. Thank you for the advice, Sir. I'll do my best to salvage the friendship."

He scoots forward and rubs his hands together. "Good, good. With that settled, I can now enjoy beating you again."

As I continue to move pieces across the board, I try to sift through the emotions inside me, knowing I have to come to a conclusion soon, so I can save what's left of my friendship with Mila.

MILA

After crying my eyes out, I went to shower, and now I'm keeping myself busy with my school work.

There's a knock on my door, and thinking it's Jade, I call out, "Come in."

I finish typing the sentence I'm busy with before I glance up, and my eyes connect with Jase's.

All the emotions I've managed to force down bubble back to the surface, and I suck in a deep breath.

He shuts the door but doesn't come any closer. There's a serious look on his face, which is rare, and I know it means nothing good.

"I managed to clear my head enough to realize one thing," he begins.

It feels like we're having a meeting. There's no warmth of friendship.

Then he continues, "Your friendship means a lot to me but…"

My mom once told me whatever precedes a but is meaningless, and I scramble to steel myself for what's to come.

"I don't know if I'm willing to risk it to find out if there can be more between us."

Not the sentence I expected.

I was expecting something along the lines that our friendship was unsalvageable. I let out the breath I'm holding. "So you would rather just remain friends," I say to make sure I'm on the same page as Jase.

"Yes." Then there's a flash of indecisiveness on his face, and he adds, "I need to make sure what I feel for you isn't just friendship, Mila. I can't start something with you and not know for certain how I feel."

"I understand." I climb off the bed and ask, "How do we repair the damage done?"

"It doesn't sound right..." he holds up a finger and begins to move closer to me. He stops a couple of steps away and continues, "but thank you for loving me."

Oh, God.

Kill me now.

He must see the embarrassment on my face because he darts forward and takes hold of my hand. Holding it in both of his, he corrects himself, "I don't mean it that way. Fuck." He takes a moment to gather his thoughts, then says, "It means a lot to me, Mila. I want you to know I'll watch myself around you, so I don't hurt you unintentionally. I'll never take your love for granted, and… I just need time to figure out my own emotions because..." he pulls an awkward face, "there's an obvious attraction between us. I won't deny that, but I just don't want it to split our group right down the middle."

Everything he says makes sense, and even though my chest is filled with disappointment, I have to face the fact that Jase is right.

The risk is too significant if he doesn't love me back. It's either everything or just friendship.

"So let's just go back to being friends minus the flirting," I offer.

"That would be great." He hesitates for a moment, then asks, "Can I hug you."

I force a smile to my face. "Of course, dumbass. Don't start being weird around me now."

When his arms wrap around me, I struggle to hold my tears of disappointment back but somehow manage.

At least you didn't lose him. Count your blessings, Mila.

For a moment, I allow myself to cling to Jase as I force my love for him back into the deepest part of my heart.

He tightens his arms around me and whispers, "I'm sorry I lost control earlier."

I nod against his shoulder, swallowing hard.

"And I do care for you. You're one of my favorite people."

I nod again, and pressing my lips together, I breathe deeply through my nose.

God, this hurts so much more than I thought it would.

Jase pulls back, and his eyes search over my face, then he asks, "You want to go have dinner? You didn't eat earlier because I was an asshole."

I let out a burst of air, and the chuckle sounds hopeless. Shaking my head, I point to my laptop. "I have work to finish."

"Okay." He hesitates again but then turns around and walks out of my room.

Why did he have to take my heart with him?

Chapter 8

JASE

Even though I've spoken with Mila, everything keeps feeling like an epic clusterfuck.

It's been three days since the explosion, and I'm nowhere near getting any clarity on my emotions. I can't deny the attraction I feel for Mila, but damn, it's just not enough.

'Do you love her?' my heart whispers.

"It's not worth risking everything," my mind warns.

I shut my eyes for a moment, and once again, I push the question to the farthest corner of my mind.

Fuck, this is hard.

"You okay?" Hunter asks, and it makes my eyes dart to him.

We're supposed to be watching Jeopardy on TV and betting on the winner, but somewhere along the line, my mind returned to Mila.

I clear my throat before I answer, "Yeah, I'm just tired."

Luckily it's a believable lie seeing as we went out last night and only got back in the early hours of the morning.

It's the first time Mila didn't go with us because she spent the weekend at her parents' place.

And she's not back yet.

Getting up, I stretch out and say, "I'm going to bed. Catch you tomorrow."

"Night," Hunter answers, and then he reaches for Jade, where she's asleep against his side so he can carry her to bed.

Walking down the hallway, I glance into Mila's room, and the fact that she's not in there bothers me.

Usually, I wouldn't hesitate to message her to find out when she'll be home.

Fuck, will we ever get back to the point where I will feel comfortable doing that?

Entering my room, I shut the door, and then I yank my shirt off and drop down on my bed. I close my eyes, and in the privacy of my personal space, I allow my thoughts to turn to Mila.

'You're willing to risk everything for them.' My grandfather's words echo through my mind.

Am I?

God, it's such an impossible question to answer. I don't know if I'll be able to risk CRC Holdings for anyone. It will mean failing my family and closest friends.

Fuck.

I have my little sister, Carla, and my cousins' futures to think of. There's also Hana, Hunter, and his sister, Aria. The pressure of being the next CEO weighs so fucking heavy on me, it feels like I can't breathe.

But somehow, my grandfather and father managed to serve the position well, and they got to be with the women they love.

It's hard to separate Mila from my circle of friends. I'd die for any of them in a heartbeat, and yes, I love each one of them... but...

What's the fucking difference between loving a friend and loving the woman you want to spend the rest of your life with? Because that's the kind of love it will take for me to start a relationship with Mila. Nothing less.

She's not just another girl I can randomly date. Not with the business ties between our families.

I punch the damn pillow and turn onto my side. I will my mind to shut down so I can get some sleep, but the questions keep whirling, and the emotions keep nagging for attention.

Mila's gorgeous as fuck. She's intelligent, and her sass is everything.

Yeah? But...

She fights me at every turn, and I love the challenge.

And? Is that enough?

Fuck, it feels like there's some weird tango going on inside of me. One step forward, two steps back.

Yeah, I'd die for any of my friends, so I can't use that as a measuring stick. I let out a frustrated growl as I keep trying to find the difference between loving a friend and being in love.

The attraction is definitely there, but that can't be the only difference. Right?

Is she home yet?

I get up and go to check, and still seeing her door open with no sign of her, I begin to worry.

Fuck this.

I go back to my room, and grabbing my phone, I type out a text.

Jase: Are you okay? Will you be home tonight?

I fucking stare at the phone, and as the minutes tick over, I keep tapping on the screen so it will light up, hoping to see her read it any second.

When it finally shows she's read it, I let out a heavy breath.

Thank fuck.

And then it shows she's typing.

Mila: I'm staying the night. My first lecture isn't until 11. I told Jade.

I stare at the message wondering why the hell it bothers me.

It's because you were worried.

Now that I know she's okay, I toss my phone to the side of the bed and go back to staring at the ceiling.

Sleep keeps evading me until I get up and go to the kitchen for a bottle of water.

I chug half of it down and walking back to my room, I stop in front of Mila's.

Knowing she won't be back tonight, I step into her private space and shut the door behind me. Leaving the light off, I go to sit down on her bed and stare at the shadow of the half-full bottle in my hands.

You miss her.

Yeah, but I'd miss any of my friends if they were gone for three days.

Right?

I'd miss Hunter for sure. Fallon and Hana as well. Hell, I'd even miss Kao and Noah.

My thoughts get stuck on Jade.

Would you have noticed if she weren't here this weekend?

I'm sure I would've noticed, but with her being Hunter's girlfriend, I wouldn't miss her. That would be... weird.

A while back, when Hunter and Jade were fighting, I didn't bother checking in on Jade. I was focused on Hunter.

Everything in me begins to still as I latch onto the differences between Jade and Mila.

Fuck. Could that be it?

I try to imagine kissing Jade and instantly pull a weirded out face. God, no. Never. The thought alone is enough to traumatize me.

Also, Hunter would kick my ass if he knew I just thought about it.

"Go to fucking sleep, Jase," I grumble at myself. Getting up, I leave Mila's room and head back to mine.

Falling down on the bed, I let out a groan as I try to find a comfortable position.

MILA

Late for my class, I sprint across the lawn. I slip into the auditorium and slump down on the first available seat. Crap, that was too close. Serves me right for oversleeping.

Not your fault you were up half the damn night, thinking about the text Jase sent you.

I let out a sigh and remove my laptop from my bag. I try to focus on the lesson as it starts, but my thoughts keep going back to the fact that Jase now knows I love him.

I should have kept my big mouth shut.

I spent the weekend with my parents because I needed time to process everything. It didn't help at all, though.

I've been alternating between feeling upset that I messed things up with Jase and dying of embarrassment because he knows my secret.

I'm also avoiding Jade, Fallon, and Hana, knowing my friends will want to talk about the fight between Jase and me. At least the part they saw in the restaurant.

My thoughts keep spinning around the mess my life has become, and I don't even notice the lecture is over until Jade taps me on the shoulder. "Hey, you look like you're miles away. What's wrong?"

I pack my bag again, and getting up, I shrug. "I'm just tired. I didn't sleep too well last night and totally overslept this morning."

We walk out of the auditorium, and with an hour to wait until our next class, I say, "I haven't eaten yet? Want to grab something with me?"

"Sure."

Fallon catches up to us and shoots me a questioning look. "You okay?"

"Yeah." I smile widely at my friends. "Just tired. I'll go to bed early tonight, but right now, I need food."

Walking across the lawn, I hear Jase's familiar laugh, and my head snaps in his direction. He's standing with Jessica and her friends. Jessica is practically hanging on his arm, and I quickly glance away from the sight.

I hear Jessica giggle, and then she asks, "Will you go with me to Nate's party this Friday?"

I walk faster, not wanting to hear his answer. Who Jase dates has nothing to do with me.

"Mila!" Justin catches up to me and smiles. "I haven't seen you around campus this past weekend."

"I went home."

He falls into step next to me and asks, "Are you on your way to the restaurant?"

My eyes go to his face, knowing what his next question will be. The poor guy's been trying really hard the past week.

Maybe I should give him a chance?

I nod to his question. "Yeah. I'm starving."

"I know you said you aren't dating right now, but would you consider eating with me?"

What do I have to lose?

"Sure." I turn my gaze to Fallon and Jade's, who both stare at me with wide eyes. "You don't mind if I skip lunch with you today?"

"No." Fallon's answer bursts over her lips.

Jade shakes her head, her eyes darting between Justin and me, then she says, "Don't mess with my cousin, or I'll kick your ass."

Justin lets out a burst of laughter. "It's just lunch, Jade."

89

"Yeah." She continues to give him a look of warning until Fallon pulls her away.

Walking into the restaurant with Justin, I gesture to a random open table. "Want to sit there?"

"Sure." He pulls a chair out for me, and once I've taken the seat, he sits down next to me. "How was your weekend with your parents?"

I smile because I love spending time with them. "Good. I got to go for a manicure with my mom."

Justin's eyes drop to my hands, and I hold them out for him to see.

"Black nails. Kinda looks cool on you."

"Thanks." I scrunch my nose. "I like it."

Justin hands me a menu, then glances at one. "Are you in the mood for anything specific?"

Without looking at the selection, I answer, "I'm going to have a gourmet chicken sandwich."

"Sounds good, actually." He signals for a waiter and places our order, then glances at me. "Anything to drink?"

"A coke, please."

When the waiter leaves, Justin turns his attention back to me. "Mind if I ask you why you're not dating?"

My eyes dart to the table where Fallon and Jade are sitting, and my gaze collides with Jase's. He looks pissed off and only glances at me for a moment longer before his eyes turn away from me.

Owing Justin an answer, I say, "I want to focus on my studies."

He nudges his shoulder against mine and smiles. "Yeah, but you should make time for fun as well."

"I suppose," I reply.

This time I can feel someone staring at me and know it's Jase. My eyes snap to his, and I give him a look of warning to stop it. He shakes his head, and getting up, he leaves the restaurant.

What's his problem?

Justin glances over his shoulder. "What are you looking at?"

"Nothing." Focusing on him, I ask, "How was your weekend? Did you do anything fun?"

"We went to Studio 9 on Saturday. I saw Jase and the rest of the group there."

"Oh yeah, Jade told me they went."

"She's dating Hunter now, right?"

"Yes."

Justin lets out a chuckle. "It doesn't look like Jase will be settling down any time soon."

The smile drops from my face. "Why do you say that?"

91

Justin shrugs. "He was partying pretty hard. He had a swarm of girls around him."

I let out a hollow-sounding chuckle. "That's nothing new."

And still, it hurts like a bitch.

Our food comes, and I focus on eating half the sandwich even though my appetite has been missing in action since the fall out with Jase.

Chapter 9

JASE

I've been walking around like a bear with a sore tooth ever since I saw Mila having lunch with Justin on Monday. It's been one hell of a long week, and with the exam tomorrow looming over my fucking head, I haven't been able to study.

When I stalk into the suite after my last class, Hunter's eyes fly to me from where he's making coffee in the kitchen.

"What's wrong?"

"Everything," I snap.

I go to stand by him, leaning back against the counter and crossing my arms.

Hunter raises an eyebrow at me. "Are you finally going to tell me what's been eating at you since last week?"

I let out a sigh and admit, "I got into a fight with Mila."

Hunter finishes stirring the caramel liquid, then leans against the counter opposite from me, and says, "I know. Wanna tell me what it was about?"

My eyes lock on my best friend. "She was upset because of all the flirting, and then I kissed her."

Hunter chokes on the sip he just took, and I move forward. Patting his back, I stay next to him as I explain, "There's a spark between us, but damn, after talking with my grandfather, I'm even more reluctant to start anything with her. I can't risk pissing off Mila's father."

Hunter stares at me as he clears his throat. "Do you care about her?"

I give him a don't-ask-me-a-stupid-question look. "Of course."

"No, I mean, are you in love with her, or do you care for her as a friend?"

The million-dollar question.

Or, in my case, billions.

"I'm still trying to figure that out."

Hunter nods and takes a sip of his coffee before he asks, "And Mila?"

I shake my head. Even though we don't keep secrets from each other, I'm not about to betray Mila's trust by telling Hunter she loves me. That's between her and me. Instead, I say, "There's a mutual attraction."

"But you're not going to act on it?" Hunter's gaze sharpens on me.

"Not at the moment. I first need to figure out how I feel about her. I won't play with Mila's emotions."

"Good, because I won't be able to stop Jade when she kicks your ass if you mess with her cousin."

I frown and ask, "How did you know you loved Jade enough to risk your friendship with her?"

"Our friendship was nothing like yours and Mila's."

I give him a look. "Still, how did you know?"

"I just knew," Hunter answers. He stares at his coffee then adds, "I couldn't give up on her or lose her. I think that's when I realized. Not having Jade in my life is not an option."

"Yeah, but you'd fucking die without me as well," I argue.

Hunter lets out a chuckle. "Fucking arrogant ass." He places his hand on my shoulder. "It's different with Jade. I sure as fuck don't want to see you naked."

I shove his hand away. "Don't even joke about shit like that."

"Okay, seriously, though," Hunter comes to stand in front of me and locks his gaze with mine, "You'll know she's the one when you can't go a day without thinking of her. She's the one who's more important than anyone else." He gives me a grin. "Yeah, you've been downgraded to number two."

"Fuck you." I let out a chuckle then say, "I understand, though." I give Hunter a grateful smile. "I need to go study, or I'm failing tomorrow's exam."

"Are we still going to Studio 9 tomorrow for Nate's party?" Hunter calls after me.

"Yeah." I walk into my room and get settled behind my laptop. I begin to read over the work, but every couple of seconds, my thoughts drift off, and I catch myself thinking of what Hunter said.

You'll know she's the one when you can't go a day without thinking of her. She's the one who's more important than anyone else.

Mila's been on my mind twenty-four-seven, that's for fucking sure.

Is she more important than Hunter, though?

Can I imagine her not being a part of my life?

I shake my head and focus on my laptop screen. I only manage a couple of minutes before I get distracted by my thoughts.

Fuck, at this rate, I'm going to fail.

Focus, Jase.

After another thirty minutes of struggling through the study material, I throw my head back and let out a frustrated groan.

I can't get Mila out of my mind, and it's driving me crazy. Seeing her with Justin on Monday almost made me lose my shit.

You know what that means… right?

I close my eyes as I admit I do have more than just friendly feelings for Mila.

A lot more.

My heart begins to beat faster as I allow myself to accept the truth.

So? What are you going to do about it?

MILA

This week has been exhausting, and honestly, I just want to crawl under my covers and sleep, but instead, I'm getting ready with Jade so we can attend Nate's party.

I haven't seen much of Jase, and it's helped a little. I don't feel like I have to walk around on eggshells.

"A penny for your thoughts," Jade says as she reaches past me for some lipgloss.

"I'm just tired."

"You've been tired a lot lately. Is everything okay?"

Needing someone to confide in, I admit, "I told Jase I love him."

Shock ripples over Jade's face. "When did this happen? What did he say?"

"Last week, and we're sticking to just being friends," I give my cousin the short version.

Jade sits down on my bed. "Are you okay?"

I shrug. "I wish I never told him, but it's done, so I have to move on."

"With Justin?"

I shake my head. "No, he's just a friend. I'm in no hurry to date."

Jade nods then proceeds to put on her boots.

Fallon comes into my room, and the second I see the dress in her hands, I begin to shake my head.

"Please, I don't want to be the only one wearing a dress," Fallon begs.

I can never say no to Fallon, and getting up, I take the black dress from her. "The things I do for you."

"It's because you love me," she teases.

"Yeah, as long as you know that." I strip out of the jeans and shirt I was going to wear and slip on the dress. It's tight-fitting and practically becomes one with my curves.

Fallon's eyes glide over me, then she rushes from the room. A couple of seconds later, she's back with a pair of heels. "Nothing like a pair of Louboutin's to round off an outfit."

I grin at her as I take the heels, and stepping into them, Fallon gives me an approving look. "My work here is done."

I let out a chuckle as I go to pick up my purse. I slip my phone into it, then turn to Jade. "You ready?"

She rushes over to my dressing table and grabs a bottle of perfume, then comes back and holds it out to me. "So, you smell all pretty as well."

I squirt some on and place the bottle back on the table.

"Are we going or not?" Jase yells from the front of the suite.

Jade rolls her eyes. "Let's go."

I take my phone from my purse and pretend to check something as I follow behind her. I should suck it up and act like nothing happened, but it's still too hard, so instead, I find ways to avoid Jase.

We leave the suite, and when a hand settles on my lower back, I look up, thinking it's Noah or Kao, but when I lock eyes with Jase, I instantly feel flustered.

"Just wanted to say you look beautiful."

My first thought is that Jase never walks at the back, but always with Hunter, Fallon, and Hana at the front. It's something they've always done.

"Ah... thanks."

Luckily, we don't have to wait for the elevator, and we all bundle inside. I get stuck next to Jase, and the ride down is torturous as I stand with my whole left side plastered against his.

Deep breaths, Mila.

When we step out of the confined space, I hang back with Kao and Noah. Glancing at my cousin, I ask him, "Where have you been? I haven't seen much of you."

Noah grins as he answers, "I've been studying my ass off."

We head out of the dorm, and I let out a burst of laughter. "We both know that's a lie. You don't have to study with your damn high IQ. So unfair."

Noah lets out a chuckle. "I still study, Mila."

As we approach the cars, the smile drops from my face when I realize Hana and Fallon are riding with Kao and Noah. That leaves me stuck with Jase.

Not wanting Jase to think I planned it, I give him an apologetic smile as he opens the passenger door for me. I slip inside and take another deep breath.

This is going to be such a long night.

The drive to the club is filled with silence, and it begins to feel suffocating. By the time we stop at the venue, I feel a little nauseous. I get out of the car and suck in the chilly air.

Crap, I forgot to bring a jacket. I'm going to freeze my butt off later.

We all walk into the club, and half the people here already look drunk. Nate spots us, and with an alcoholic beverage in his hand, he stumbles closer to us.

Someone's had too much to drink.

"Jase!" Jessica's shrill voice can be heard above the music. "You made it."

I let out a sigh as Jessica throws her arms around Jase's neck, and having seen enough, I make my way to our usual table in the VIP section on the upper floor.

Sitting down next to Jade, I say, "I'm ready to go home."

She lets out a chuckle. "Let's go dance. You'll be in a better mood in no time."

I glance down at the lower floor, and seeing Jase talking with Jessica has me standing up and saying, "Yeah, let's go dance. I need to get rid of some tension."

I wait for Jade to kiss Hunter as if she'll never see him again before we head to the dance floor. The music is electric and dancing with Jade is always fun.

I let the music sweep me away from all my worries. We stay on the dance floor for a couple of songs, and then Jade leans over and says, "Justin's behind you."

I glance over my shoulder just as Justin takes hold of my hips and moves to the beat with me. When he leans into my back, the acidic smell of alcohol drifts to me as he says, "You look hot, Mila."

Not liking him behind me, I turn around. "Thanks. Are you enjoying the party?"

He nods, and a wide grin spreads over his face. "It's even better now that you're here."

Shoot. Not wanting Justin to think I'm into him, I say, "Listen…" I lean closer to him, so he'll hear me, "We're just friends, Justin. I'm really not interested in dating you."

Suddenly someone grabs hold of Justin and then punches him. I let out a shriek as my gaze darts to the guy.

My eyes widen even more when I see it's Jase. He wraps an arm around my waist and yanks me against him, then growls at Justin, "I said she's off-limits. You should've fucking listened the first time."

Oh, God. Not this again.

Chapter 10

JASE

With my arm tightly wrapped around Mila's waist, we stand motionless on the crowded dance floor. My gaze drops to hers, which is filled with shock.

One minute I'm still talking to Jessica, and the next, I'm punching Justin.

I'm losing my fucking mind over her.

Since yesterday I've been trying to think of a way to approach her, and then tonight, she looks like a fucking goddess.

I also picked up on the vibe that she's trying to stay away from me, and I don't like it one bit.

We're the only ones not dancing when Mila begins to pull away, her gaze narrowing at me.

Her eyes dart around us before they lock on mine again, and then she says, "Seriously, Jase? What the hell?"

She's managed to put a couple of inches of space between us, but I tug her back against my chest and wrap both my arms around her.

Her mouth opens, but I shake my head, which has her glaring at me. The closeness of our bodies makes a current of electricity flare to life.

The ever-fucking-present spark I can't get rid of.

Loosening my grip slightly, I let one of my hands brush down to the curve of her ass, so I can keep her locked against me.

I feel Mila's breath hitch, and then a burst of warm air fans over my neck. We might give each other shit, but in moments like this one, it's clear as fucking daylight Mila's more than just a friend.

Slowly, our bodies begin to move to the beat of the music while our eyes never break contact.

I watch as Mila's expression turns from pissed to unsure.

Yeah, babe, me too. I have no fucking idea what I'm doing. All I know is I can't stop.

Her green irises draw me in until I'm imprisoned by them.

Hesitating for a moment, Mila lets out a sigh, then lifts her hands to my shoulders. I can feel the warmth from her touch seeping through my clothes.

Her gaze scans over the other dancers, and when her hips move with mine, I know she can feel my cock growing hard because her eyes snap up to mine.

Right now, I'm itching to drag her back to the suite so we can fuck this… whatever this electric feeling between us is… out of our systems.

But I know the instant we get naked, our friendship will be over. Mila knows it too, and that's why she's been doing her best to keep me at a distance.

If only I had the self-control she has. It would make this so much easier.

I want Mila in a way I've never wanted another woman. I want to touch her, taste her, and make her mine.

Again, dickhead, if shit goes sideways, then you won't have her in your life at all.

With my mind running circles around Mila, my movements grow more seductive.

Yeah, my mind is definitely not the one in charge at this moment.

Ever since I admitted the truth to myself, I've been overwhelmed by the need to be close to her.

My hands are on a mission of their own as they brush up and down her back before slipping over her hips and following the natural curve to her ass.

My palms drink in the feel of her perfect ass, and I tug her as close to me as I can. A breath of air rushes from Mila, and then her hands slip behind my neck as her eyes drift shut.

She fucking loves my hands on her.

Fuck.

Heat sizzles up my spine, and it cuts all access to common sense as desire takes over.

My right hand brushes back up, over her hip and waist, until I reach her ribs. I tighten my hold on her, my fingers reveling in feeling how feminine her curves are. Tentatively my thumb brushes under the curve of her breast, and when her lips part, it sends my heartbeat into overdrive.

I keep stroking the swell of her breast, wishing we were in the privacy of my room so I could strip her naked and fuck her.

Fuck. I'm going to shoot my load right here on the dance floor.

Images of Mila naked, her legs spread wide while I pound into her wet pussy, bombard me. My lust is fueled by thoughts of my teeth closing around her nipple while I suck a moan out of her.

Fuck. Calm down, Jase.

A tremble ripples through Mila's body, and it echoes into mine. Her eyes open, and when I see heat radiating from them, it takes every ounce of strength I have to not throw her over my shoulder and carry her out of here.

Christ, I want to kiss and fuck her until I'm so deep inside her, she won't be able to get me out. This last week has been absolute hell. I missed flirting with her. I missed hearing her sass me.

My other hand joins the torture fest, my fingers digging into her ass as I grind my aching cock against her.

I fucking missed you, babe.

She inhales sharply, her eyes becoming hooded with lust.

Lowering my head, my mouth skims over her jaw until I can feel the warmth of her breaths fanning over my ear. It sends goosebumps spreading over my body at the speed of light.

My new favorite feeling in the world – Mila's breath on my ear.

My cock weeps to be buried inside her. My fingers itch to rip her clothes off. My fucking body wants hers more than it's next breath.

My hand on her ribs inch a little higher, and then my thumb brushes over her hard nipple. Our breaths grow faster, and it makes me let go of her ass so I can lift my hand to her jaw. My thumb grazes over her bottom lip, and immediately her tongue darts out.

"Fuck," I groan, almost in pain from wanting her. "You're killing me."

I'm standing on the edge of a cliff, and all it will take is a nudge from Mila to send me over.

Her teeth scrape against my thumb, and the edge dangerously begins to give way beneath my feet.

"Fuck this. We're going home right now," I growl.

'Don't move too fast. You first need to talk to her,' my mind whispers.

'I don't fucking care! I want her now,' my body rages.

My jaw brushes against hers as I bring my mouth closer to her lips.

I don't fucking care anymore.

I want Mila.

I need Mila.

Someone bumps into us, and it knocks me back to my senses. In a daze, I turn to whoever it was.

"Jase, why are you making me wait?" Jessica's hands take hold of my jaw, and then she pulls my head down. I'm shocked out of my mind when she lays a kiss on me.

MILA

Holy shit.

My mind is clouded, and my self-control is missing in action when someone bumps into us.

Jase glances to our right, and then my jaw drops as I watch Jessica grab hold of him. She proceeds to kiss him as if I'm not here.

His hands are still on me, and it takes a solid couple of seconds for my mind to catch up with what I'm seeing.

What. The. Fuck?

Anger begins to lick at my insides, and I snap, "I'm not into threesomes." Yanking myself free from Jase, I rush into the sea of bodies around us.

I can't believe I let that happen.

Again.

What's wrong with me? Am I such a glutton for pain?

Seriously?!

How could Jase do that to me?

And better question yet, why did I let him?

With my heart and mind a total mess, I stop by Jessica and Nate's table, and not caring two shits, I take Jessica's drink and down it.

"Looks like the high and mighty Mila West has been replaced," Justin sneers. "How does it feel to be toyed with?"

I glare at him, not in the mood to get into a fight. I'm done with this epically screwed-up night.

I battle my way to the door while my heart keeps sinking. What was I thinking? That Jase would finally stop his whorish ways and realize I'm the one?

Ha! Stupid, Mila.

How could I be so gullible to ever think Jase would want more with me?

Yeah? The only more he wants with you is a quick fuck.

Or a freaking threesome!

I let out a disgusted growl as my anger keeps growing, and in all honesty, I'm more upset with myself than with

Jase. I shouldn't have allowed myself to get swept away while we were dancing.

Stupid!

For a moment, I remember my purse is upstairs, but not wanting any of our friends to see me in such a state and asking questions I'm not ready to answer, I disappear out the doors and into the cold night air.

Even the coming winter chill does nothing to lessen the anger burning through me.

I actually feel a little sick. That drink of Jessica's was potent. Just wanting to get home so I can take off this stupid dress and heels, I make my way through the parking area.

Pissed off, I stop and lean with one hand against a random car to take off the damn shoes. I lose my balance, but then a pair of hands grip hold of my hips. I almost sprain my damn neck when I quickly glance over my shoulder, and seeing Justin, I continue yanking the other heel off.

"I'm good, thanks," I mumble to Justin.

When he doesn't let go of my hips, I try to turn, but then his arms wrap around me, and lifting me from my feet, he carries me in between two parked cars.

My heels fly to the side as I try to slap at his arms. "Put me down!"

Then his alcohol-drenched breath is hot on my ear. "You've fucked with me for long enough, Mila. It's time to back up all that flirting with some action."

"What?" I try to glare at him again, but he pushes me forward and over a car's front. When his hand slips up the back of my dress, my heart all but stops, and realization knocks the breath right from my lungs. "Justin! Stop!"

He lets go of me and tries to cover my mouth, and it gives me a chance to yank free and make a run for it. Running barefoot on ice-cold bricks is not the wisest thing I've ever done.

Justin quickly catches up to me, and wrapping an arm around my waist, he yanks me off my feet. His free hand slaps over my mouth, and then I'm dragged back.

Deeper and deeper between the luxury cars gleaming in the moonlight.

"Stop fighting, bitch," Justin growls darkly, and it only makes my heart beat faster while I struggle against his hold.

You need to get out of here, Mila.

Panic bleeds into the darkest part of my soul. My breathing speeds up until it's all I can hear. My eyes are wide, even though I can't focus on any of my surroundings.

Justin drags me to the side of the club where the dumpsters are. Knowing I'm in deep trouble, I let out a scream, but it's muffled by his clammy palm. I taste the salty sweat from his skin, and it almost makes me gag.

The music is nothing but a muted beat as pure terror grips my hammering heart. Justin throws me to the cold ground, and I quickly push to my hands and knees, but then he's on top of me, shoving me to my side. My hip hits the ground with a splintering pain, and Justin uses his body to force me onto my back. It rips another frightened scream from me.

He moves fast, slapping his palm over my mouth, and it snaps my head back against the hard ground with brutal force, which makes me bite my tongue as my teeth clatter. The blow stuns me, and my vision begins to blur until all I can see are shadows.

Dread makes the dark reach at me with claws. It makes the air thin, and time eerily slows down. The horror of my situation makes my insides quiver and my mouth dry.

Justin's dark frame towers over me as he rips at the fabric of Fallon's dress. I no longer feel the bite of cold air.

"No!" I try to cry against his palm.

All I can feel is Justin's fingers as he grabs hold of my breast and squeezes until I scream against his hand.

"You owe me, Mila. You think you can tease me and just walk away?" Justin's voice is a vicious growl that agitates my nerves and leaves my insides quaking with fear.

Sinking my teeth into the palm of his hand, I bite down as hard as I can. It draws a roar of pain from Justin, but at least he yanks his hand away from my mouth.

I suck in a breath of air, and I'm just about to scream for all my life's worth when there's a blow against my cheek. It makes bright dots explode in my vision, dazing me.

The blows keep coming engulfing me in a world of pain, but I don't stop struggling, hitting at anything I can as I wildly try to free myself from under him. Dread takes over every part of me, and in this terror-filled moment, one thought is crystal clear – I have to survive this. Somehow.

The music from the club suddenly gets louder, and I hear *Halsey* sing, *'I've tasted blood, and it is sweet. I've had the rug pulled from beneath my feet.'* And then her voice is muted again.

There's a blow to my side, and it feels like my ribs shatter. My breath is knocked from my lungs, and I'm unable to draw in another. Fire spreads through my side and licks at my lungs, and I don't have time to process the pain as a harsh bite sinks into the sensitive flesh of my breast.

Daddy! Ryker!

Desperately my soul cries for my father and brother to save me from this hell. It only fills me with a devastatingly desolate feeling because I know they won't come to help me.

Jase.

Jase, I need you.

An anguished cry tears through me, and I wish I had stayed and fought with him. At least I would've been safe.

Wildly, my eyes keep darting around for something I can use as a weapon. My nails claw at Justin in my desperation to get free while I keep sending up silent prayers that someone will come to help me.

Instead of my prayers being answered, all I get is another slap, another bite, another punch until I feel like nothing but broken shards of pain.

Blood fills my mouth, dribbling out the side and down my aching jaw. The excruciating pain all over my body begins to drag me into a bottomless pit filled with nightmares and soul-destroying horror.

Justin yanks at my panties, making a tsunami of frightening terror crash over me, and I drown in it. It sucks the fight from my body.

I feel his hand slip between my legs, and I let out a despairing cry as a demoralizing feeling engulfs me, erasing all the light and color from my world.

My mind shuts down, and my soul escapes to the farthest corner of existence in an attempt to flee from what's coming.

And then there's nothing.

No muted music from the club.

No light shining down from the moon and stars.

No dreams of a bright future.

No hope of ever being with Jase.

There's nothing but Justin as he hurriedly tries to position himself between my legs.

This is not how my first time was supposed to be. I wanted Jase to have my virginity, but all that will be left is a piece of trash, discarded where I belong – right by the dumpsters.

Emptiness stretches and grows inside of me, consuming every part that makes me human. What's the use of having dreams and hopes when my will to live is being crushed.

"Fuck!" Someone shouts. It's familiar, and I try to latch onto the voice. "What the fuck are you doing?!" And then Justin's weight is dragged off of me, and he's flung to the side.

The sound of punches and pain-filled grunts seeps through to me, and I manage to weakly turn my head in the direction of the fight.

My sight focuses on Jase, where he's beating up Justin, and it makes a suffocating relief bleed through me. My throat tightens until I can't suck in any air. Tears blur my vision as I watch Jase deliver punch after punch, pummeling Justin into a bloody mess.

Through my tears and the consuming fire in my chest, I gasp for air. The sound makes Jase's head snap in my direction, and our eyes lock for a moment.

I want to tell him how relieved I am that he found me.

I want to tell him I'm sorry I didn't stay to fight with him.

I'm so sorry.

Jase lets go of Justin's unconscious body and darts over to me. He sinks to his knees as he pulls his phone from his pocket.

There's a buzzing in my ears, and I can't hear what he says. When he drops the phone next to me, I begin to struggle to focus on his face.

The most beautiful face I've ever seen. It's been the reason for my every heartbeat the past three years.

Those golden-brown eyes. God, those golden-brown eyes give me life.

Jase's trembling hands hover over me as his face distorts with emotion I've never seen before. It almost looks like he can feel my pain.

I keep my eyes locked on his face until his features begin to blur, and they fade into the dark night around me.

Chapter 11

JASE

A frenzied rage takes over my body as I repeatedly slam my fist into Justin's face. I can feel the skin over my knuckles tearing, but there's no stopping my furious craze.

I hear a wheezing breath, and it yanks me out of my moment of madness. My head snaps to the girl Justin was attacking, and then all the air is sucked from my lungs. I rush to her side and drop to my knees as all life flows from them, my body numb with shock and horror.

Mila.

My Mila.

I somehow think to call 911 for help before the phone drops from my hand. Leaning over her, my hands tremble, and I don't fucking know what to do.

"Mila," I choke on her name. Frantic, my gaze sweeps over her body, and my heart fucking shatters as the realization sinks in like hot lava.

Justin hurt Mila.

Despair seeps through every part of my body as I watch her gasp for air, every breath sounding painful.

My eyes take in the torn fabric of her dress, exposing a peach-colored bra with red stains bleeding into the silk. The dress is pushed up, and her panties are torn, bunched around one thigh.

Anguish and horror darken every part of me as an unspeakable thought shudders through me.

Justin raped Mila.

Oh, God.

I pull her dress back down and shrug out of my jacket so I can wrap it over her, not wanting anyone else to see her like this.

For an instant, there's a faint hope that I might have found Mila in time and that Justin didn't manage to…

My eyes take in Mila's state, and one thought drowns out all the others.

The one moment Mila needed me most, I wasn't there for her.

White-hot anger rages through me. "Where the fuck is the ambulance," I growl. I glance around us, a desperate feeling mixing with uncontrollable fury. I have to do something.

My gaze goes back to Mila's, and when her eyes drift closed, my world fucking explodes into a million distorted pieces.

"Mila!" I gasp through my panic. "Baby, stay with me!"

Her breathing becomes slower, and the bleakest emotion I've ever felt paints what remains of my world in black.

"Mila," I groan. I carefully move my hand under her neck, and with my other, I take hold of her shoulder and lift her limp body to me. I press her face into the crook of my neck as the air begins to explode over my dry lips.

I feel her weak breaths fan over my skin, and it shreds my soul into an unrecognizable mess. My heartbeat speeds up as my vision blurs, and when I still can't hear any sirens, I shout, "Fuck!"

My breaths explode in white puffs into the dark night as I struggle to my feet, and I raise Mila's body against my chest.

I can't fucking wait. I have to do something.

My legs are drained of their strength, but I force them to move.

I have to get her help.

I'm halfway to my car when sirens get through to me, and it makes me change my direction. I break out into a run toward the road, and as I reach the pavement, an ambulance pulls up to the club.

One of the emergency personnel jogs toward me, and my legs give way. I sink down to the cold ground. "Help her." It's the only words I can manage.

"Put her down," he instructs.

I quickly lay Mila back down. The man begins to ask me one question after the other, and the night spins into chaos.

Every vital sign he checks offers meager comfort.

I feel a hand on my back, and in a daze, I glance at Fallon's tearstained face. It's only then I notice all our friends crowding around us and the police asking them questions, and it rips me back to the present.

Pushing to my feet, I pull away from Fallon, and I run toward the side of the building where I left Justin.

"Jase!" Hunter calls after me.

The moment my eyes land on Justin, where he struggles to get to his feet, rage takes over, and it propels me forward. Grabbing hold of his shirt, I deliver one punch after the other. None of them offer me any satisfaction.

Someone grabs hold of me, and when Hunter darts between Justin and me, I can only manage an incredulous look.

"He fucking hurt Mila," I shout in disbelief that my best friend would stop me and not fucking help me kill the piece of shit.

"Sir, you need to calm down." Feeling feral, my head snaps in the direction of the voice.

Hunter steps right up to me and grabs hold of my face. His eyes bore into mine as he says, "You can't get arrested. Mila needs you now. Let the police handle Justin." I begin to shake my head, needing to wipe Justin from the face of the planet. He doesn't get to breathe the same air as Mila after what he's done to her.

Hunter wraps his arms around me in a deadlock and begins to repeatedly say, "Mila needs you. We'll make sure Justin pays, but right now, Mila needs you."

The words break through the cloud of rage around me, and when I nod, Hunter relaxes his hold on me enough to only keep his one arm wrapped around my shoulders.

Not happy that I won't get to kill Justin tonight, I watch as two officers read him his rights.

Another officer picks up my phone from the ground, and it has me snapping, "That's mine."

Before the officer hands the device back to me, he first takes down my statement. With a warning that they will be in touch with me, Hunter steers me toward his car.

Right now, everything is hard. Talking. Breathing. Thinking. Just fucking everything.

It's in the early hours of the morning that I get to the hospital they took Mila to.

"You should get cleaned up," Hunter mentions and gestures to my hands that are covered in blood.

I stop at the restroom and washing my hands, I watch the blood mix with the water. When I'm done, and my gaze meets my reflection in the mirror, I see the bloody stains on my shirt, and once again, the ground is ripped from beneath my feet.

It's Mila's blood.

The sight is devastating, and it tightens my chest until it feels like I'm going to implode. I have no idea how Mila's doing.

I suck in a couple of breaths of air, trying to find my bearings.

I rush to dry my hands and jog to the waiting room. Sitting down next to Hunter, I ask, "Any news?"

He shakes his head and gives me an encouraging smile. "I'm sure they'll come to tell us soon how Mila's doing."

Fallon thinks to have a nurse look at my hand, and I sit impatiently through the examination and while she wraps a bandage around it. Luckily it's nothing serious.

We have to wait for what feels like endless hours before Mila's older brother, Ryker, comes to the private waiting room.

I get up, my eyes glued to Ryker's distraught face as he says, "Mila's stable. My parents are with her."

I want to see her. I want to hold her. But I can't, and it's fucking killing me.

"What did the doctors say? Will she be okay?" Hunter thinks to ask.

"She..." Ryker swallows hard, and for a moment, it looks like he might puke, but then he says, "Mila has two cracked ribs, some soft tissue damage, and a concussion. She'll have to stay a couple of days. All we can do is wait. You all might as well head home. I'll call if anything changes."

I shake my head and drop down on the plush couch. My eyes focus on my bandaged right hand.

I should've killed Justin while I had the chance. Now the fucker is sitting safely in a cell.

Flashes of Mila's smiling face keep alternating with the sight of her broken body.

126

Everything feels muted, and my surroundings look dull as if all life has been drained from it.

Mila's the brightness behind every color around me. She's the rhythm to the beat of my heart. Her smile lights up my world, and her sass spices up my mundane existence.

Without Mila...

What's left to live for?

"Jase." Hearing Mr. West call my name has my head snapping up, and I dart back to my feet. His features are dark with worry as he comes to take hold of my arm, saying, "Mila just came to, and she's asking for you."

I nod and hurry down the hallway to the private room she's in. When I walk inside, and my eyes land on her, the pressure in my chest eases up a little.

"Jase," she croaks, and her bruised face crumbles.

I dart forward, and sitting down on the bed, I lean over her. "I'm here, Mila. I'm here."

She manages to lift one hand and grabs hold of my shirt, pulling me closer to her. When she ducks her face into my neck, I wrap my arms around her and hold her as she cries.

That fucker will pay for every tear she sheds.

"I'm here, Mila," I keep whispering.

Holding my broken girl, I vow to never leave her side. I don't know how I'm going to do it, but I'll help her through this nightmare.

I have to cling to the hope that I'll see her smile and hear her sassing me again.

Chapter 12

MILA

It's a struggle to get my eyes to open, and when they finally do, it's to see Dad's worried face and Mom's tears.

For one blessed second, I'm filled with confusion.

But then, flashes of the night begin to bombard me. My heart almost jumps out of my chest as fear drags me back to the nightmare my life has been thrown into.

I see Justin's demented face.

I feel his hands on me.

Then it all swirls into blackened chaos when I remember the feel of him between my legs.

Nausea overwhelms me, and through my panic and despair, I can't take in any of the words spilling from my parents' lips.

I can't focus. I can't deal with any of it.

Crushed, my mind latches onto a safe thought. *Jase.* Every ounce of love I have for Jase wars against the terror I'm engulfed in.

"Jase," I whimper, and my desperate gaze latches onto my father's. "Jase."

He nods and rushes out of the room. I can't tear my eyes away from the exit, and the moment Jase appears in the doorway, it feels like some of the darkness retreats with his presence.

"Jase," I croak as the relief from the sight of him overwhelms me.

He darts forward and sits down on the bed. "I'm here, Mila. I'm here."

His voice acts as a soothing balm to my shattered soul. With Jase in reaching distance, I try to lift my left arm, but a wave of sharp pain has me stilling, and I try to move my right instead. When the ache isn't as intense, I manage to grab hold of his shirt and pull him closer.

I bury my face in his neck, and feeling some semblance of safety, my tears begin to fall. I cry because of the nightmare I survived, but also for everything that was stolen from me.

I feel so small and fragile in Jase's arms. It feels like there's nothing left of the person I once was, and it makes me cry harder.

"I'm here, Mila," Jase repeatedly whispers until I nod against his neck. My movement makes him pull back. His features are tight with anguish and rage. When our eyes lock, and I get to see his golden-brown irises again, it makes me feel a little safer.

In the span of a single night, everything between us has changed. Right now, I don't care whether we're friends or more. I care about nothing but how safe I feel when he's close by. Jase has become a shelter for my ruined soul and wrecked heart.

"Don't leave," I whisper. As long as Jase is with me, the gruesome memories can't sink their claws into me.

Without Jase, they'll drag me so far under, there won't be any way of getting out of the darkness.

"I'm not going anywhere," Jase says. He brings his hands to my face, and his touch is careful as his eyes drift over me.

With my hand still gripping a fistful of Jase's shirt and my eyes locked on his face, I drift off to a world filled with jagged edges and dark shadows.

JASE

Mr. West made sure I can stay with Mila because my presence helps to keep her calm.

She hasn't woken up long enough to tell us what happened. But whenever she regains consciousness, her hand tightens its grip on mine, and her eyes frantically search until they lock on mine. Only then does she relax enough to fall asleep again.

I must've nodded off because I'm startled awake when someone places a blanket around my shoulders. My head snaps up, and when I see Mrs. West, I relax.

"I've brought you something to eat, Jase," she whispers.

I can't stomach anything right now. "I'll have it later."

"At least drink something then," she says hopefully.

I reach for the bottle of water on the bedside table and take a sip, so Mrs. West will stop fretting.

She gives me a weak smile as she sits down on the opposite side of the bed, and her eyes scan over her daughter. I watch as every bruise on Mila's snowy skin slams a painfilled blow into her mother.

She reaches for Mila's hair and lovingly combs her fingers through the black strands. "At least you got to Mila before he could…" She swallows hard, and tears spill over her cheeks.

It takes a moment for her words to sink in, and for the first time since this nightmare started, I feel hopeful. "He didn't rape her?" I ask, a desperate need to know filling me.

Mrs. West shakes her head. "No." Reaching across Mila, she places her hand on mine and gives it a squeeze.

I'm filled with overwhelming relief that Justin didn't rape Mila. My eyes scan over her, and the relief quickly evaporates.

Mr. West walks into the room, and coming over to me, he places his hand on my shoulder. "Your parents are in the waiting room. You should go and set their minds at ease."

My instant reaction is to say no, and my eyes dart back to Mila's sleeping face. I can't even bring myself to let go of her hand.

"It will give me some time with Mila. You should actually go home and get some sleep. Mila's peaceful right now. Go shower and sleep so you can be rested when you come back later."

After warring with myself for a minute, I answer, "I'll only shower then come right back." I lean forward and press a kiss to Mila's hand, and it feels wrong as I let go of her. I almost give in and grab hold of her again, but instead, I force myself to my feet. Looking at Mr. West, I ask, "Do you have my number?"

He nods as we swap places, and he takes the seat I just vacated. "I'll call the moment she wakes up."

"Please." My eyes dart back to Mila, and they linger on her for a while before I turn and leave the hospital room.

The echo of my steps on the tiled floor is too loud as I pass by the other VIP rooms. The white walls gleam too bright. All my senses feel like they're stuck in overdrive, and when I walk into the waiting room, and my eyes land on my father, it feels like something snaps inside me. It releases a tidal wave of emotions, and Dad must see it all on my face because he darts forward and wraps me up in a tight embrace. I grab hold of the shirt on his back as my world once again spins out of control.

"God, son," he breathes. "I'm so sorry." He pushes me away, and his worried gaze searches over me before he yanks me back to him.

After a moment, he lets go of me so Mom can have her turn. The moment I feel my mother's arms around me, my throat tightens to the point of cramping, and my eyes begin to burn.

Mom pulls back and lifts her hand to my cheek, where she places it in a lovingly soft touch. "How are you holding up?"

I can only shake my head, which has her embracing me again. "I'm here, my baby," she whispers, and it gives me the comfort only a mother's touch can provide.

"I have to shower," I finally manage to utter.

Mom nods and goes to grab her bag, where she left it next to a chair.

Dad immediately places his arm around my shoulders. "We'll go with you and wait while you shower."

Mom comes to take my hand, and then the three of us leave the hospital. Outside the entrance, we run into Ryker, Jade, and Mr. Daniels.

While our parents greet each other, Jade gives me a hug. Feeling numb from the constant bombardment of emotions, I can't bring my arms up to hug her back.

Before she pulls away, she whispers, "Thank you."

I manage to nod.

Ryker places his hand on my shoulder, giving it a squeeze.

I feel like a ghost, just going through the motions.

Because my soul is up in that room with Mila.

As Ryker, Mr. Daniels, and Jade go to check on Mila, my family and I leave the hospital. We make our way over to Dad's car. I slide into the back and stare out the window as Dad drives us to the academy.

Not wanting to inconvenience my parents, I say, "You can just drop me off. I know you have work to get back to."

"We're not leaving you alone," Dad grumbles from the front.

"Hunter will be there," I argue.

When he brings the car to a stop in front of the dorm, Mom gets out and opening my door, she reaches inside and takes hold of my hand, as she says, "We have to go talk with the dean. Let's just get you to the suite and see if Hunter is even home."

As I step out of the car, I notice how students freeze in place. Everyone's eyes are on us, and it makes my anger detonate, wreaking havoc inside me.

A shout rips from me, "What the fuck are you looking at?"

Mom's hand flies to my chest. "Let's go inside, Jase."

I yank free from her and take threatening steps closer to the students, but then Dad's there, blocking my way. He grabs hold of my shoulders as he barks at everyone, "Go to your dorms!"

Everyone scatters, finding a place to hide.

Dad locks eyes with me. "Calm down, Jase."

I shake my head, needing to hurt something as much as I'm hurting. I need an outlet for everything I feel.

Keeping a tight hold on me, Dad forces me inside the dorm. When we step into the elevator, Mom's arms come around me. For a moment, I struggle against her hold, but then the ground gives way beneath my feet, and I sag into her embrace, unable to keep the heartache from shredding me into an unrecognizable mess.

They usher me out of the elevator and into the suite. Hunter's coming down the hallway, but the moment he sees us, he turns around and jogs to my room. He opens the door and then follows us inside.

I love my parents with all of my heart, but the moment Hunter takes a step in my direction, I break free from them and rush to him. Without hesitation, he takes the full brunt of my body hitting his. Hunter locks his arms around me, and I fucking break into a million pieces.

"Let it out," he whispers. "I've got you."

I give Hunter all the tension and uncontrollable emotions that have been weighing so heavily on me.

"Hunter, will you make sure he showers while we talk with the dean and get Jase something to eat?" Dad asks.

"Yes, Uncle Julian," Hunter answers, and he begins to move me toward the ensuite bathroom.

I let him help me out of my clothes and the bandage around my hand. Stepping into the shower, my whole fucking body is a trembling mess.

If you're such a mess, how bad must it be for Mila?

The thought clears my mind instantly, and I rush through my routine so I can get back to her.

After drying myself, I quickly brush my teeth before I go to my walk-in closet. I don't have the patience for buttons, and grabbing a pair of black jeans and a t-shirt, I yank the items on.

"Hey, slow down," Hunter says.

Shaking my head, I quickly step into my shoes and grab a jacket. While shrugging it on, I say, "I have to get back to Mila."

"You need to eat first," Hunter argues.

My eyes lock on his. "I can't fucking eat."

Hunter places his hand on my shoulder. "You need to stay strong, Jase. You can't make yourself sick by not eating and sleeping."

Hunter's right, but I still can't bring myself to stay away from Mila for a moment longer. "I'll grab something at the hospital. I just need to get back to her."

The ringtone from my phone interrupts us, and I rush over to my discarded pile of clothes. I dig in the pants and yank the device from the pocket.

Not recognizing the number, I answer, "Jase Reyes."

"It's Logan," Mr. West's voice comes over the line. "Mila woke, and when she didn't see you, they had to sedate her. She should be calm for a little while, but I was hoping you could come back sooner?"

"I'm on my way back," I answer. Cutting the call, I shove the phone in my pocket and look at Hunter. "Can you pack an overnight bag for me? I'm going to stay at the hospital until Mila's better." I walk to the door, then remember I left my car at the club and turn back to Hunter. "Is my car still at the club?"

"No, but I really don't think you should drive," he says as he walks out of the door with me. "Let me take you, and then I'll come back to pack your clothes."

"Okay," I agree.

"Will Mr. West be okay with you staying with Mila?" Hunter asks as we leave the suite.

"Yes, and with it being a VIP suite, the hospital won't dare give us any shit."

Hunter lets out a chuckle. "I'd like to see them try."

"Let's hurry," I say, desperate to get back to Mila. I don't want her waking up to my not being there a second time.

Climbing into the car, I dig my phone out and call my parents, so they'll know I've gone back to the hospital.

Chapter 13

MILA

It's a struggle coming to, but when I open my eyes and focus on the white ceiling above me, I hear voices murmuring somewhere in the room.

"We can take turns staying with her," Dad whispers. "That way, you won't fall behind with your classes."

"I can do my work here. My parents already cleared it with the dean, so my professors will email the assignments to me," Jase grumbles.

Jase.

My eyes drift shut as calmness washes over me.

"We'll be here at night so the three of you can get a break," Mom says.

"We don't have classes at the same time," I hear Noah. "We need to at least attend some of the lectures, Jase. Between Jade, you, and me, we can cover the day shift. Uncle Logan, Aunt Mia, and Ryker can handle nights."

Shifts. Days. Nights.

This is what my life has been reduced to?

Everyone I love has been severely affected by what happened.

The thought stirs the shadows to life, and flashes of the horrible night begin to bombard me. Helplessness settles hard in my stomach as I remember how Justin dragged me toward the dumpsters.

My heart begins to thump faster, and I shut my eyes tightly against the vile images, my hands curling into fists.

I feel the vicious blows, the angry bites.

It's like I'm watching a broken horror movie, only seeing bright flashes of terror.

The urge to run overwhelms me, and I dart up into a sitting position. Pain sears through my chest from the sudden movement, tearing a cry from me. My breaths are shallow, each one feeling like a sharp stab to my lungs.

I'm tired, not just physically. I'm shattered to the bone. It feels like my soul weighs a ton, dragging me under the wave of emptiness that keeps crashing over me.

I feel a hand on my back, and the unexpected touch has my eyes flying open as my body instinctively flinches away. Realizing I just yanked away from Dad, a sob breaks through my feeble barrier, and I quickly cover my mouth with the back of my right hand. One tear slips from my left eye and rolls down to my neck. I gulp in breaths, fighting for control over the devastating feelings.

There's a frantic panic bleeding into what's left of my soul as my eyes dart around the room.

Dad. Mom. Jade. Noah. Ryker.

And then… Jase.

Desperately, my eyes latch onto his.

It's because Jase is the one who stepped right into your hell to fight off the monster.

Lowering my hand to my lap, I say, "Can…" My voice is hoarse, and I first clear my throat before asking, "Can I have a moment alone with Jase?"

I just need a minute to ground myself. I don't want my loved ones seeing me like this.

"Sure." My eyes fly to Dad's, and when he leans down to press a kiss to my forehead, I have to force myself to keep still.

I've lost the comfort of a simple touch.

My eyes blur from realizing I've lost so much more than I thought, but I fight back the tears, not wanting to upset my parents even more.

When everyone has left the room, leaving me alone with Jase, he sits down on the side of the bed and tilts his head to catch my eyes.

Meeting his golden gaze, I soak in the feeling of being safe before I say, "Thank you." A puzzled look flashes over his strong features, and it has me explaining, "Thank you for helping me last night."

Jase begins to reach for my hand but quickly stops and pulls back. It brings a frown to my forehead, and he's so damn perceptive he instantly picks up on it. "You flinched earlier when your dad touched you."

"I was just caught off guard," I try to set his mind at ease. I lower my gaze to Jase's hand, and seeing the broken skin over his knuckles, I lightly brush a finger near the bruises.

Slowly Jase turns his hand over, holding his palm up for me, and I don't feel any hesitation as I rest my hand on his.

Not all simple touches are gone.

Because of Jase, I haven't lost everything, and this time I'm unable to keep the tears from rolling down my cheeks as I lift my eyes to meet his. My voice is hoarse with emotion. "Thank you for stopping him."

When Jase shifts closer to me, I lean forward, and the moment I smell his comforting scent and I get to bury my face in his neck, my world doesn't feel so utterly devastated.

144

Jase wraps his arms around me, his touch still careful, and it has me whispering, "I'm okay with you hugging me."

"Good," he murmurs against my hair, and then he jokes, "'Cause you know me, I'm all about love."

A smile tugs at the corner of my mouth, but a stinging sensation from my bruised lip has me stopping. Still, hearing Jase crack a joke has never sounded so good before.

When he begins to pull away from me, my right hand darts up, and I grab hold of his shirt. "Just a moment longer."

His arms tighten around me again, and my eyes drift shut from the relief I feel.

"Do you want to talk about what happened?" he whispers.

Quickly, I shake my head. I never want to talk about it. I just want to forget it ever happened.

This time when Jase pulls back, I force myself to let go of him, knowing I can't keep clinging to him.

Jase brings his hand to my face and gently brushes his thumb over my jaw. My eyes lift to his, and when I see how tight his features are with something akin to rage, I ask, "Do I look that bad?"

His eyes meet mine, and then the corner of his mouth lifts. He keeps staring at me until I feel a flutter of something familiar.

Love.

"You'll always be beautiful to me, Mila."

It's not his words that get to me, but the tone of his voice. It's like a cleansing rain shower on my dirtied soul. It washes some of the stains away, and for a moment, my world is not quite so dark.

JASE

My gaze drifts over her face, taking in the dark bruises around her left eye all the way down to her jaw, where the swelling looks painfully feverish.

Jade must've packed Mila's clothes because she's wearing her own sweatpants and t-shirt.

Every couple of seconds, I'm lulled into a false sense of peacefulness, but then it vanishes, and the chaos inside me returns like a destructive tornado.

I see the same emotions flashing over Mila's features. One moment she seems calm, and the next, panic and fear darken her eyes.

I've never dealt with anything like this before. I'm stumbling around in the dark, but the need to make everything better for Mila has me asking, "What can I do to help?"

Her eyes lower to her hand on her lap. "You've already done so much, Jase. I just need time. I'm sure everything will be back to normal soon."

Her words are a total contradiction to her body language. Her shoulders are hunched forward, and she still hasn't moved her left arm from where it's wrapped around her waist.

Fear fucking radiates off of her, and it makes me inch a little closer. I move slowly as I reach for her, and when she doesn't flinch away, I wrap my arm around her and pull her back against my chest. I feel the tension ease from her shoulders as she leans against me, and when she lets out a breath as if she's been holding it for hours, I tighten my hold on her.

"I'm not going anywhere. If you need me to hold you until you feel safe again, then I'll hold you for as long as it takes."

Mila shakes her head, and pressing her forehead against my shoulder, she whispers, "This thing has disrupted everyone's lives enough."

My stubborn girl.

The thought makes the corner of my mouth lift slightly.

"Okay, then I'll just hold you because I need to. Deal?"

Mila lifts her head, and pulling back, she looks up at me. A frown mars her forehead, and there's a flash of heartache on her face. "I'm sorry. I didn't even think of how you must feel." She places her hand against my chest, concern tightening her features. "Are you okay?"

How do I answer that question? I'm not okay because she's not okay.

Knowing I can't say that to Mila, I smile at her. "I'm fine, Mila. I just need to be here for you. Will you let me do that?"

Her eyes start to shine, and her chin quivers, and it has me leaning into her until our foreheads touch. When she nods, I let out a breath of relief.

I pull back and press my lips to her forehead. My eyes drift shut, and I can't bring myself to pull away yet.

The door behind us opens, and glancing over my shoulder, I see Mr. West come into the room, followed by a policewoman and a doctor.

I begin to get up from the bed, and my moving out of the way has Mila's eyes falling on the two women. I watch as Mila's whole body shrinks while she slowly sucks in a deep breath. Pain flashes over her face, and then she starts to shake her head. "No." Her breaths are shallow as they rush over her lips while she struggles to climb off the bed.

The doctor immediately stops walking. "Miss West, I'm Doctor Kelly Bower. I'm one of the psychologists here at Ojay Valley Memorial."

Mila frantically glances at the window as if she's actually considering using it as an exit. I rush around the bed, and the instant I take hold of her shoulder, she darts forward and slams into my chest. Feeling Mila cower against me strips me of the last of my restraint.

Mila's the only one that matters now. I'll do everything in my power to protect her and make her feel safe.

I wrap my arms tightly around her, and glancing over my shoulder, I shake my head so they don't come closer. "Does she have to talk to you now?"

The doctor gives us a comforting smile. "No, we can come back later. She should talk to Officer Lane as soon as possible, though."

"I..." Lifting her head, Mila gives me a pleading look, her voice filled with desperation, as she whispers, "Not now. I can't remember much anyway."

"I'll leave my card, and you can contact me as soon as you're ready," Officer Lane says. "The sooner, the better. Every detail will help in the case against Mr. Green." She hands the card to Mr. West before they all leave the room.

When we're alone, Mila's whole body is trembling, but she still lets go of me. She wraps her arms around her waist, and ducking her head low, she takes a step backward.

"I'm going to use the restroom," she whispers.

Knowing I can't follow her, I wait for the door to shut behind her before I rush out of the room.

Stepping into the hall, I hear Dr. Bower say, "...another factor that impacts the degree of trauma is how helpless the victim felt. For some individuals, memories of the events are fragmented and disconnected. It takes time for the victim to be able to place the pieces of the traumatic event into a chronological narrative. We have to be patient. It's a long process."

Victim.

The word grinds against everything inside of me, but I know it won't help if I lose my shit right now. Stepping closer to the group, I ask, "Do you need Mila's statement? Won't mine be enough to prosecute Green?"

Officer Lane turns to me, and I remember my manners. Reaching out a hand, I shake hers as I explain, "I'm Jase Reyes. I was the one who found Mila. I gave my statement at the scene."

"Mr. Reyes, yes, I've read your statement. I have some questions for you to answer." Officer Lane flips open her notebook and asks, "Is now a good time?"

"Yes." I want to get this over with, so I can get back to Mila.

"Is there someplace private we can talk?" Officer Lane asks Dr. Bower.

"Yes, just down the hall."

Mr. West takes a step closer to me, and addressing the two women, he says, "I'll be with my daughter while you question Jase."

Officer Lane and I follow Dr. Bower to an office. She offers us both a seat, and I'm surprised when she sits down as well. When she sees my questioning gaze on her, she explains, "I'm also here for family and friends, Mr. Reyes. The experience must've been traumatizing to you as well."

Traumatizing is the understatement of the fucking year.

I nod and turn my attention to Officer Lane, which has her asking, "Can you tell me again, in your own words, what happened the night of the attack?"

I didn't expect that specific question, and it hits me square in the gut. I've managed to block the memories of last night from my thoughts so I could focus on Mila, but the question rips the scab off the fresh wound, and it fucking gushes through me.

After searching inside for Mila, I push through the exit door and step out of the club into the cold evening air.

This night went to shit, so fucking fast. It was like a speeding train derailing. One minute, things are finally at a good place between Mila and me, and the next, fucking Jessica happened.

While I lost my shit with Jessica, Mila disappeared. I wanted to follow after her immediately but knew I had to clear things up between Jessica and myself before trying to fix things with Mila.

"What a fucking mess," I grumble as my eyes scan over the parking area. I walk a little forward when something catches my eye. Moving closer, I crouch down and frown at the random pair of heels.

Suddenly a desperate cry pierces the night, and it instantly makes the hair on my body rise. Darting to my feet, I search between the cars, thinking the owner of the shoes might've injured herself.

A hopeless wail comes from the direction of the side of the building, and it sends my heartbeat into overdrive. I break out into a run, instinctively knowing someone needs help.

When I round the corner and see a guy on top of a girl, my worry explodes into anger. The fucker's white ass gleams in the moonlight as he moves on top of the girl.

Darting forward, I grab hold of his shoulders and yank him away from her. When I get a good look at his face and see that it's Justin Green, I lose all my self-control and begin to beat the ever-loving shit out of him.

The fucker's been nothing but trouble.

A gasp for air from the girl grabs my attention, and the moment I look at her, Justin's limp body drops from my hands.

Mila.

The split second of recognition feels like an eternity of torture as the horror sinks into my bones.

Those cries belonged to Mila.

Justin was on top of Mila.

I manage to make it to her side before my legs give way, and taking in the sight of how brutally Justin has hurt her, it feels as if someone just dug into my chest, ripping my heart right from it.

The pain is excruciating, paralyzing me.

"Mr. Reyes?" Dr. Bowes' voice yanks me out of the dark thoughts. She reaches over to me, giving my hand a squeeze. "Are you okay?"

Clearing my throat, I say, "I'm fine." I turn my gaze to Officer Lane. "Sorry, what was the question?"

Officer Lane gives me a sympathetic look. "Can you relay the happenings of last night in your own words?"

My heart sinks into a dark pit as I repeat my statement. With every word spilling from my lips, it feels like a chunk of my soul is being shredded until there's nothing left but the turbulent mess of emotions whirling inside me.

If it's so hard for me to talk about, I can't even begin to imagine what it must be like for Mila.

The thought has me sitting upright, and I pay more attention to every detail I remember. I'll answer the questions a million times if it means Mila doesn't have to.

Chapter 14

MILA

I feel like a caged animal. Helplessness weighs so heavily on me, I can't make my body move from where I'm standing in the middle of the bathroom.

Endless torture-filled minutes pass before I can finally lift my eyes to the mirror. My reflection shocks the breath right out of my lungs, and filled with horror, I take in every bruise on my face. Each one is a reminder of what happened, and I quickly lower my eyes again. Tenderly, I lift my shirt and look at the dark bruises around my ribs.

I let the fabric fall over me, and my arms drop limply to my sides.

This place that's become my life is … a wasteland. There's nothing significant left. Every heartbeat feels futile.

I'm devastatingly empty, but at the same time, I'm filled with merciless turmoil. So many words to describe what I feel, but none of them really fit.

Fear? Can this really be fear? Every sound has me jumping. Every touch has me convulsing. It's as if every single thing around me has the potential to hurt me.

The sheltered safety I always had is now gone.

Empty? No, not emptiness. I'm brimming with emotions, all hopeless, all dark, all brutal – and they're stripping away the last of my sanity.

Tainted?

I lift my eyes to my reflection again, and the gruesome sight makes a sob escape. I cover my mouth with my right hand.

I'm ruined.

Distraught, I try to keep quiet as I cry.

There's a knock at the door, and then I hear Dad call, "Mila, are you okay in there?"

Not able to trust my voice, I grab a towel and press it over my mouth to mute the sobs. My family has suffered enough. I have to be strong around them, so they'll stop worrying.

I fight to push the rampant emotions down and clear my throat before I answer, "I'll be out in five minutes."

Turning on a faucet, I splash cold water over my face, trying to get rid of the evidence that I cried. I'm careful as I pat my skin dry and try to take a deep breath, but then the sharp ache in my chest reminds me to stick to shallow breaths. I hang the towel again and turn toward the door.

Knowing the sooner everyone goes on with their lives, the quicker I can forget this nightmare ever happened, I force a smile around my lips before I open the door and step into the room.

Mom's eyes snap to me, and Dad spins around. It feels like I'm under a microscope, and I widen my smile as much as I can with the split lip. "You should go home. I'm just going to sleep."

My parents keep staring at me as I gingerly climb back into the bed, then Mom says, "You look better. How do you feel?"

I shrug. The door to the room opens, and Jase comes in as I answer, "I'm fine, just bruised." I let out an empty-sounding chuckle. "I just need to sleep, and you've both had a crazy night. Go home and get some rest."

Jase comes to stand next to the bed, and knowing he must be tired as well, I say, "You should get some rest as well."

He tilts his head, and our eyes only meet for a moment before I turn mine back to my parents. It's really exhausting pretending to be okay, so they won't worry.

Carefully, I scoot down in the bed and pull the covers up to my chin. "Seriously, go already. You're all keeping me awake."

It's a struggle to turn onto my right side, but I grind my teeth through the pain.

Mom and Dad come to each press a kiss against my temple, and I grip the covers tighter. My smile falters, and it's becoming increasingly hard to keep up the front that I'm okay.

Finally, Dad says, "We'll be back in a couple of hours. Get some sleep."

"Okay." I close my eyes and bury my face in the covers.

It takes forever until I hear the door click shut behind them, and it feels like a reservoir wall breaks. I gasp into the covers, trying to smother the sound.

Then someone sits down on the bed, and Jase says, "Can you move over a little?"

Letting go of my death grip on the covers, I scoot back to make space for Jase. He lies down and pushes his left arm under my head. With his right, he pulls me against his chest.

I glance up at his face, and the comforting sight of him makes my tears fall faster as I admit, "It's hard."

He brings his right hand to my cheek and brushes tenderly over my bruised skin, giving me a look filled with a world of understanding and care. "I know, babe. That's why I'm not going anywhere."

I've never seen this side of Jase before. He's so ... he's a force of strength. He's solid and unwavering, where I'm a mess with no ground beneath my feet.

I know I can't cling to him and keep him from living his life, and it has me pressing my face to his chest as I whisper, "Jase?"

"Yeah?"

"You really don't have to stay. I know you have things you need to get back to."

I feel him press a kiss to my hair. "Nothing more important than you."

And again, it's not the words he says but the tone of his voice that gets to me. It smashes right through the feeble wall I tried to put up.

I smother the sob against his chest, and then his arms tighten around me, and he whispers, "Don't pretend to be okay around me, Mila. I saw what happened. Nothing you say will keep me from being here for you every step of the way. Let me help you through this."

I nod as my sobs grow harder, and this time I don't cry for everything that was taken from me, but for the one thing that remained. *Jase.* And I love him so much more than I ever thought I could.

JASE

Mila finally drifts off to sleep, and it gives me a moment to deal with my own wreckage left in the wake of her attack.

She feels fragile in my arms, and it makes me wonder how anyone could hurt her the way Justin did. How fucked up do you have to be to do something like that to another person?

But it wasn't just any person. It was Mila.

My Mila.

For weeks I've been flirting with her, skirting around the attraction I feel for her. I didn't dwell on the *why* I wanted to be with her as much as I did on the desire to have her.

Right now, the desire is MIA, and all that remains is the big fucking why. The *why* I managed to acknowledge but never got to share with Mila.

I love Mila. I love this girl so fucking much it scares the shit out of me.

I pull a little back so I can see her face. My eyes caress every inch of her, and the sight of the bruises grinds my heart to dust. Pressing a kiss to her forehead, I wrap her against my chest. I worry about the days ahead, and the pain Mila will still have to bear before she starts to heal.

I'll take it in a heartbeat. God, please. Just lay it all on me. I can't bear to see her hurting like this.

The silence of the hospital room weaves a cocoon around us until I'm focused on every breath she takes.

Mila's body jerks suddenly, and it rips me out of the bubble I'm caught in. Her eyes fly wide open, filled with terror. Her breaths speed over her parted lips as if she's just run a marathon.

"I'm here." The words rush from me, and at least my voice gets through to her, and recognition dawns in her green gaze.

"Jase." The sound of my name is filled with relief.

I move my right hand to the back of her head, and I press my forehead to hers. "I'm here, Mila."

When she slowly relaxes back against me, I ask, "Are you okay?"

She shakes her head. "I… I keep getting flashes. It's random and…"

I press a kiss to her forehead, and for a moment, her eyes drift shut. When I pull back, her face crumbles as she admits, "It feels like I'm stuck in a nightmare. Nothing stops. Not even for a second. Everything feels wrong and… just broken and empty."

My throat tightens until it cramps, but I bite my own emotions back as Mila opens up to me.

"Cry if it will help." I wish I knew the right thing to say. "Take it out on me if it will help."

Mila shakes her head and brings her eyes to mine. "You just being here helps so much." Her chin quivers as tears spill over her cheek, and I use my right hand to gently brush them away. Mila's voice cracks as she says, "You stopped it. I think that's why I… I feel semi-normal with you." A lonely look shadows her face. "Everything else feels foreign. It's as if I've been thrown into a world I don't recognize, and you're the only familiar thing."

I'm caught up in our stormy emotions as I admit what's been eating away at me, "I wish I'd gotten to you sooner. I…" I shake my head as regret and guilt take turns beating

162

the life out of me. "I keep going over last night and wish I had done a million things differently. I shouldn't have agreed that we go to the club. I should've pushed Jessica away and stopped you from leaving." I shake my head and locking eyes with Mila, I hate the words as they leave my mouth because they don't come close to how I feel about the part I played in her being attacked. "I'm so fucking sorry, Mila."

She lowers her eyes from mine and shakes her head. "None of it was your fault." A forlorn look settles on her face. "I remember thinking I should've stayed and fought with you."

Silence fills the room as our eyes meet again, and we stare at each other. There's a lot we need to talk about, but right now, all that matters is helping Mila through the storm.

"Let's talk about where we're going from here, so we're on the same page," I say. A frown forms on Mila's brow, which has me explaining, "I'm going to stick to your side and help you through this. Are you okay with that?"

"Yeah."

The next part is not an easy subject to broach, and I take a deep breath before I continue, "I noticed you flinch when anyone else gets near you. Even your parents."

Mila lets out a breath of air that almost sounds like a chuckle. "Who knew Jase Reyes could be so perceptive?"

A grin tugs at the corner of my mouth. "There's a lot about me you don't know yet."

The light-hearted moment is fleeting.

"I'm just jumpy right now. I'm sure it will pass, and everything will go back to the way it was," Mila says.

"But you're okay with me holding you?" I ask to make sure I don't do anything to upset her.

"Familiar, remember?" She nods. "It's calming... and it makes me feel safe."

Her words bring a smile to my face. "Good, 'cause I like holding you."

"Thanks, Jase."

Her words catch me by surprise. "For?"

"For not being weird around me."

Not fully understanding, I shake my head. "Weird?"

Mila's gaze meets mine, and for a split-second, her eyes shine a little brighter. "You treat me like... just me and not like I'm... damaged. I saw what I look like, and it..." she's unable to finish her sentence.

I bring my hand to her face and brushing my thumb over her jaw, I say, "The bruises will fade, Mila, and honestly, even with the added color, you're still fucking gorgeous."

A tear sneaks out of her eye, but her lips curve up as she says, "Such a freaking player."

A wide smile splits over my face. "Can't help it, babe. You bring out that side of me."

There's a thankful look on her face as she snuggles back against my chest. "Thanks for making me forget for a while. I think I can actually sleep now."

"Okay," I whisper as I press my mouth to her hair. I lightly brush my hand up and down the length of her back, hoping my touch will follow her into her dreams so she won't have another nightmare.

Chapter 15

MILA

The past couple of days, I've been lulled into a false sense of security because Jase practically moved into the hospital suite with me.

But now that I've been discharged and the exit of the hospital looms in front of me, panic tightens my muscles as my heartbeat speeds up.

Knowing my parents' eyes are on me, I force my feet to move. It took a lot of arguing to get them to allow me to go back to the academy. At first, they insisted I go home with them, but with Jase by my side, they finally agreed, as long as I start counseling sessions with Dr. Bower.

Stepping outside, a sea of camera flashes bombard me. Voices yell questions, and my frazzled mind latches onto one. *"Did Justin Green rape you?"*

And it opens the floodgates to other questions.

"Will you press charges?"

"Mr. Reyes, what's your relationship with Mila West?"

"Miss West, we heard you refuse to talk. Is that true?"

"Mr. Reyes, how do your father and grandfather feel about all of this?"

"Mila, is it true you and Justin Green dated?"

"Will this affect CRC Holdings' share price?"

"What is Trinity Academy going to do about this? Will Justin Green be expelled?"

Mom and Dad move between the reporters and me, and Jase wraps a protective arm around my shoulders, and with his other, he presses my face to his chest. He pulls me away and rushes us to where his car is parked. In a hurry, Jase bundles me into the passenger seat and straps me in before he runs around the back of the vehicle. Then the engine roars to life, and Jase speeds away from the parking area.

In a total daze, my eyes stare widely ahead of me.

'Did Justin Green rape you?'

Justin yanks at my panties, making a frightening terror close over my head, and I drown in it. It sucks the fight from my body. I feel his hand slip between my legs.

I gasp for air, and it makes the sharp pain in my chest pierce through my lungs. Nausea rushes up my throat, and I croak, "Stop the car."

Jase pulls over to the side, and I struggle to unclip the seat belt. Jase helps me, and the second I'm free, I hurry to open the door. I almost fall out of the car, but I'm just in time as my body begins to jerk. I sink to my knees as I empty my stomach. My lungs go up in flames, and tears stream down my cheeks.

God, this is too hard. I can't.

Then I feel Jase's hand on my back.

Shaking like a leaf in a shit storm, my body finally stops convulsing. The ache in my chest is too intense to take a full breath, making me feel dizzy.

Jase hands me my bottle of water I brought with me from the hospital, and I use it to rinse my mouth. Then his arms slip under me, and he picks me up as if I weigh nothing.

That's because I am nothing.

The thought is fleeting, but it packs a brutal punch. Jase sets me down on the passenger seat and frames my face with both his hands. Forcing me to look at him, he asks, "Are you okay?"

Am I okay?

I've been asked that question so many times over the past couple of days.

No, I'm not okay. Not even a little.

Instead of telling Jase the truth, I nod. "Yeah, just felt sick. I'm fine now."

I can see Jase doesn't believe me. "We'll be back at the dorm in five minutes, then you can rest."

I nod again and even manage to force a smile around my lips as Jase shuts my door. I wrap my arms around my waist and lean my head back against the headrest.

God, I'm exhausted. How will I get through this?

I only open my eyes when Jase brings the car to a stop in front of the dorm. My gaze scans over the students who've all stopped to watch.

Yeah, the freakshow's home.

Jase gets out of the car first, and then I hear him yell, "What the fuck are you all staring at?"

Students scatter in different directions, and I wait until the coast is clear before I push my door open.

In a flash, Jase hovers by my side as I climb out of the car.

"I'll grab our bags once you're settled in bed," he says as he wraps his arm around my shoulder and leads me into the building.

Once we're inside the elevator, I turn my body into Jase's and wrap my arms around his waist, pressing my face against his chest. I wish I could take a deep breath of him.

169

He brings his hands to my face and nudges it up until I'm looking at him, and then he gives me the most caring smile, whispering, "I'm so fucking proud of you."

Not following why, I shake my head.

"You're so brave, Mila."

I don't feel brave.

I try to smile as I say, "Nope, it's all you."

Jase leans a little down, his eyes boring into mine. I can see he means every word when he says, "You forget I've spent every day with you the past week, and I've seen how strong you are. Even at your own expense, you pretend to be fine, so others won't worry."

He saw right through my act?

As if he can read my thoughts, a grin pulls at the corner of his mouth. "Yeah, babe, so just remember, you can't hide anything from me, and I don't want you to."

The doors slide open, and Jase lets go of my face. He takes hold of my hand and pulls me out into the hallway.

Nearing the front door of our suite, I steel myself for whatever's on the other side. I'll have to work harder on pretending to be okay until this nightmare fades to the past because I won't let it affect my friends' lives.

It's destroyed too much already.

JASE

Mila's grip on my hand tightens as I push the front door open.

I mentioned to everyone we should go on with our regular routines, but I got a hell no to that suggestion.

Fallon, Hana, and Jade were adamant they were not going to hide what happened like a dirty secret, and hearing the girls say that made me feel like shit warmed over. I didn't mean that we forget. I just wanted to make things easier for Mila.

The instant we step into the suite, Fallon's there, and her arms wrap around Mila. When I try to pull my hand free from Mila's, she tightens her hold on me in a death grip.

Fallon pulls back, and her eyes search over Mila. "How do you feel? Shouldn't you still be in the hospital?"

A smile forms on Mila's face, but I notice it doesn't get anywhere near her eyes. "I feel good as new, and I'm ready to catch up on all the school work I've missed."

Moving half her body behind mine, Mila takes hold of my wrist with her other hand. Knowing she feels safe with me makes a feral protective feeling tighten my muscles.

"We have all the assignments ready, and Hunter had his dad's PA make sure the classes were recorded for you," Jade says.

Over the past couple of days, Jade has caught onto the fact that Mila doesn't like being touched, and I see how Jade struggles to hold back from hugging her cousin.

Mila shoots a quick glance in Hunter's direction. "Thanks, Hunter. The recordings will help a lot." Her eyes dart over our friends, not really stopping on any of them. "I'm just gonna sleep for a little while. I'll get started with the school work tonight, so I can catch up as quick as possible."

I talked with Hunter before I brought Mila home, and we agreed that I'd take care of Mila while he keeps our friends up to date with the progress she's making so everyone doesn't bombard her with attention and questions.

The girls are fighting us on that, feeling Mila needs us all, so it's going to be a rough couple of days to adjust to the new normal.

My eyes meet Hunter's, and he nods, immediately knowing what I need him to do. "Let's go grab some lunch, guys." Glancing at us, he asks, "Should we bring you something from the restaurant?"

I turn my head to Mila and softly ask, "How do you feel about pizza? I miss pizza."

She lets out a soft chuckle. "Pizza it is."

"Great," Hunter says as he wraps his arms around Fallon and Jade's shoulders, nudging them toward the front door.

Hana hesitates next to us. "I'm glad you're back, Mila. I know you don't want us to hover, but I'm here if you need anything."

Mila's lips twitch into a smile. "Thanks, my friend. I just need rest. I'll be back to normal in no time."

As soon as our friends leave the suite, I pull Mila down the hallway and ask, "Your bedroom or mine?"

She yanks back against my hold, and it has me stopping dead in my tracks and rambling, "Shit, I didn't mean it that way."

"Jase, no, I didn't even think that," she gasps. Her eyes dart to the floor. "I just don't want anyone, including you, changing your whole life for me. I'll stay in my room, and you go to yours. You can't sleep next to me forever. What will everyone think?"

Hell, yes, I can.

173

I close the distance between us. "I don't care what anyone thinks, Mila. Besides, our friends understand, and honestly, even if they didn't, I still wouldn't care. You're all that matters, and you're still having nightmares. I'm not leaving you alone to face them."

Mila's shoulders slump, and a frustrated look crosses her features. "I just don't want to disrupt your life. You've already done so much for me." Her tongue darts out, nervously wetting her lips. "And I don't want to get used to depending on you. It won't be fair."

Lifting my hand to her chin, I nudge her face up so she'll look at me as I ask, "To you or to me?"

Giving me a pleading look, she answers, "To you."

I've repeated the same words so many times over the past couple of days, and I'll keep repeating them until Mila believes them. "I want to be with you, Mila. This is not a chore for me. I worry my ass off when I'm not around you, so please just give me peace of mind and let me take care of you."

Mila surprises me by face planting into my chest and wrapping her arms around my waist. After a little while of hugging, she lifts her face to me and whispers, "You being here for me means everything. I'll never forget it, Jase."

"Good." Playfully, I raise an eyebrow and grin at her. "Chances are good I'll screw up again, and I'll need you to remember I'm not just another asshole."

She shakes her head, and for a moment, warmth seeps back into her eyes. "You can never be just another asshole."

Moving my arm around her shoulders, I repeat my question from earlier, "Your room or mine?"

This time Mila doesn't hesitate to answer, "Yours for now."

Chapter 16

MILA

I wake up to the smell of pizza hanging in the air and the soft tapping on a keyboard. I pull back from where my face is squished against Jase's hip.

My movement makes Jase stop typing, and he quickly sets his laptop on the side of the bed before he turns to me with a grin on his face. "You slept for five hours."

Wow, it's afternoon already?

He looks so damn happy about the sleep I got, it makes a burst of warmth seep through my heart.

"Did you get some rest?" I ask, my gaze darting between the laptop and the half-empty pizza box.

At least he ate. That's good.

"I'll sleep later. I wanted to get some work done first." Jase begins to reach for the pizza box. "Are you hungry? I'll go warm a couple of slices for you."

"Thanks," I answer. I move gingerly into a sitting position. "I'm going to shower first." I shift off Jase's bed and begin to walk to the door, then pause to add, "Afterward, I'm going to catch up on some work. I'll see you later."

Without looking at Jase, I slip out of his room and head to my own. Once I'm inside, I shut the door behind me and take a moment to just breathe before I turn around to glance around my room.

Everything feels different... like none of the personal belongings are mine.

There's a tap on my door, then Jase comes in and places my hospital bag at the foot of my bed. He walks to me, and lifting his hand behind my neck, he presses a kiss to my forehead before he leaves again.

Wanting to keep my mind busy so it won't dwell on the dark memories, I empty the hospital bag into the laundry basket. I grab a clean pair of sweatpants and a t-shirt from my closet, along with underwear, and turning, my eyes land on the purse on my bed.

One of the girls must've brought it home from the club. I walk closer and opening the purse, I take my phone from it. The battery's died, and I plug the device in to charge, then walk into the bathroom.

I let the water run in the shower while I brush my teeth and strip out of my clothes. Everything feels automatic

177

until my gaze lands on my reflection in the mirror. All the bruises have faded to a yellowish-green, and most of the swelling is gone.

A memory stirs in the back of my mind, and I shake my head, suppressing it.

Focusing on the present, I step under the spray of warm water and wash my hair. It's a struggle only using my right hand because I still can't lift my left arm too high.

I'm going back to classes on Monday, and I hope the bruises will fade even more before the weekend is over, so I can cover any evidence of the attack with makeup.

When I wash my body, I don't look at myself, not wanting to see the ugly bite marks and bruising on my ribs.

I keep my eyes trained on the tiled wall until I'm finished rinsing off. Unable to lift my arms high enough to wrap my wet hair in a towel, I pat it dry as best I can, then get dressed.

Once I'm covered, I walk out of the bathroom but come to a halt when I see Jade sitting on my bed.

"Oh… hey."

Jade shoots up, and her eyes first scan over me before she says, "You washed your hair. Want me to help you dry it?"

I nod, not wanting to alienate myself any further from my family and friends. No matter how hard it is, I have to get back to how things were.

I grab my phone and charger and go to plug it in at my dressing table so I can check my messages while Jade dries my hair.

I sit down on the little stool, and instead of looking at myself in the mirror, I watch as Jade rubs a towel through my hair. She keeps shooting me smiles, and not wanting my cousin being weird around me, I ask, "Can we pretend it never happened?"

Jade's hands freeze in my hair, and her eyes slowly lift to meet mine. "If that's what you really want?"

I swallow before I explain, "I know it's been hard on you. I really can't remember much, and I just want to forget the whole mess."

Jade gives my shoulder a squeeze, and for a moment, my body freezes.

"Whatever you need." She scrunches her nose as she looks at my hair. "And right now, we need to dry this rat's nest."

I give her a thankful smile and switch on my phone. The device starts to beep and vibrates like crazy as all the messages come through. I set it to silent and go into my messenger.

Uncle Carter: We're taking care of it all, Sweetheart. Just get better. We'll see you soon. Love you.

Uncle Jax: I'm only a call away. Let us know as soon as you're ready for some company.

Uncle Marcus: My ass isn't with you right now because your mom threatened my life. Love you.

Uncle Rhett: I'm here. Always. xxx

Mamma G: My god-baby. I'm sorry I'm stuck on the other side of the planet. Let me know when I can call you. Love you with all my heart. xoxoxoxoxox

My sight blurs at all the messages, especially the last one from my godmother. I haven't seen her in a while because she's on vacation with her husband in Taiwan.

I have to blink the unshed tears away as I read the texts from my aunts.

Everyone's rallying around me, and yet I've never felt more alone.

There's a message from an unknown number, and I hesitate to open it, but then click on it.

Hi, Mila. It's Jamie Reyes. I just wanted to reach out to you. I've been through something similar and

wanted you to know I'm here if you need to talk to someone who will understand how you feel. All our support and love.

My body begins to tremble from keeping back the tears. I didn't know Jase's mom has been through something like this.

With the first signs of hope blooming in my chest, my hands tremble as I press reply. For a moment, I hesitate again, then I type, **Hi, Mrs. Reyes. It's Mila. I didn't know, and I'm sorry to hear. I appreciate the offer, but I don't even know where to start.**

It shows that she reads the message immediately, and then three dots begin to jump on the screen.

You start by accepting you didn't do anything to deserve this. It should never have happened to you. There's no time limit to your healing, Mila. Just focus on the now. What happened to you was a horrific act of violence. Allow your loved ones to be there to help you through this.

How can anyone help me through this? I don't want to think about it, never mind talk about it. Besides, my family and friends are already awkward enough around me.

Not knowing what to reply, I type a generic message.

Thank you, Mrs. Reyes. I'll keep your advice in mind.

I keep going through the messages, deleting the random ones from students I'm not exactly friends with.

Jade switches off the hairdryer and pulls a brush through my black strands. "There, now you look human again."

"Thanks, Jade." I get up as I go to the voice messages and say, "I'm just clearing all the messages, then I'm going to catch up on some work."

"Want me to sit with you and explain the assignments?"

"Yeah, that will help a lot. The sooner I catch up, the better."

"I'm just going to grab my laptop."

Jade darts out of my room as I bring the phone to my ear.

All the voicemails are along the same lines. Everyone's sorry to hear what happened and hope I'll get better soon.

Then a voice comes over the line, and my entire body freezes.

"Mila. I know I'm not supposed to contact you, but I just want to say how sorry I am. Fuck, I have no idea what got into me." Justin's breaths are harsh and panicked.

Then his breath is hot on my ear. 'You've fucked with me for long enough, Mila. It's time to back up all that flirting with some action.'

My breaths start to rush over my lips as my mouth dries up.

"What I did to you... I... fuck... I'm so sorry. I'm so fucking disgusted with myself. I'm out on bail, but my dad says there will be a court case. I'll take whatever sentence they give me. Fuck, I deserve the worst."

Justin throws me to the cold ground, and I quickly push to my hands and knees, but then he's on top of me, shoving me to my side, and he uses his body to force me onto my back.

"I just... I can't believe I hurt you like that. I'm a good person. Fuck, I thought I was. I'm so fucking confused, and I regret that night so fucking much."

'You owe me, Mila. You think you can tease me and just walk away?' Justin's voice is a vicious growl that agitates my nerves and leaves my insides quaking with fear.

JASE

A cry from Mila's room has me dropping the plate of pizza and breaking out into a run. I burst through the door and don't see her immediately. Moving forward, I catch sight of her cowering body, where she's sitting in a small ball next to the dressing table.

"Mila," her name explodes over my lips, and I go to crouch by her. "What happened?"

Her eyes are wild with fear, and I suppress my first instinct to hold her. I sink to my knees and move a little closer. "Mila?"

Her eyes dart over me, and it takes longer than usual before recognition washes over her face. She scrambles to her knees and darts forward, slamming into me. My arms wrap around her, and I hold her tightly as she begins to cry while rambling, "I... remember. He... called. I... remember when he... dragged me to... the dumpsters."

"Shhh... you're safe now," I say, trying to comfort her as best I can.

Mila pulls back and shakes her head, then points to something behind me and says, "He called. He left a voicemail."

I glance over my shoulder, and seeing the phone on the carpet, realization hits. I reach for it and unlocking the device, I go to the voicemails and press the phone to my ear.

"Mila. I know I'm not supposed to contact you, but I just want to say how sorry I am."

Hearing the fucker's voice makes rage explode through me. It's more intense than any anger I've felt before.

"I'm going to fucking kill him," I growl as I get up and shove the phone into my pocket before I rush to the door.

Mila hurries after me and grabs hold of my arm. "Don't, Jase!"

I pull free from her and stalk toward the kitchen. I grab my car keys from the counter, and it has Hunter getting up from the couch in the living room. "Where are you going?"

"To kill Justin Green. The fucker called Mila," I shout, enraged that he dared to fucking say he's sorry.

He's fucking sorry?

Before I can take another step, Hunter darts in front of me and grabs hold of my shoulders. "You can't go beat him up, Jase."

I shove Hunter away from me and shout, "That's the second time you've stopped me instead of fucking helping me kill that fucker."

Hunter doesn't get out of my way but instead steps right up to me and roars, "You need to fucking calm down." He points to behind me. "Look at Mila!"

My head jerks around, and seeing the panic on Mila's face while Jade holds her makes the anger take a backseat as worry for Mila washes over me.

I stalk back to her and framing her face with my hands, I press my forehead against hers and say, "I'm sorry." I suck in a deep breath of air and lay a kiss on her temple. Wrapping my arms around her, I pull her away from Jade. "I'm calm. I'm sorry."

I'm so fucking far from calm.

Mila's arms wrap around me, and she clings to me. "Please don't do anything."

My heart is beating out of my chest, and it's the hardest thing I've been asked. I want Justin Green six feet under, but what I want doesn't matter. Nodding, I say, "I'm sorry I lost my shit."

Keeping my arm around Mila, I glance at our friends and see that Hana picked up the pizza and broken plate from the floor. "Thanks, Hana."

"No problem." She goes to stand by Fallon.

Noticing the worried looks on all their faces has me saying, "I'm sorry I exploded."

186

My eyes meet Hunter's, and it has him saying, "You know I'll have your back with everything, but I won't stand by and watch you land your ass in jail. We need you here."

"I understand." I smile at my friends, hoping to put them at ease, then say, "We're going to take a nap." Keeping Mila close to me, I steer us back to my room.

Once I have the door shut behind us, I wrap my arms around her and press a kiss to the side of her head. "Sorry for reacting like that."

Mila shakes her head, and pulling a little back, her eyes search over my face. "But you're okay now, right?"

I smile down at her and nod. "How about you?"

"You kinda scared me out of the panic attack I was having." She even smiles a little, but it only makes me feel like shit. Knowing I just made that call all about me and not about her eats at my worn gut.

Mila pulls back and glances at the bed. "I'm not ready for another nap, though."

That makes two of us, but it was the only excuse I could come up with, so I could get Mila alone in my room.

"Want to watch a movie?" I offer. Hell, I'll do anything she wants right now.

Mila nods. "One movie to relax, and then I have to work on my assignments."

I hold a finger up. "Give me a second." Rushing out of my room, I go to Mila's. I grab her laptop and school bag and jog back to her. I place the laptop on the bedside table and the bag on the floor, then point to the bed. "Get comfortable. What do you want to watch?" I walk to the entertainment system across from my bed, and grabbing the remote, I turn on the TV. "I've got everything from action to that sappy shit women like to watch."

"I want sappy shit," Mila says, and hearing her chuckle brings a smile to my face.

"As long as I get to complain about men not really doing all that shit in real life."

"Deal." I glance back to where Mila is sitting with her legs crossed on my bed. Her black hair shimmers, and there's color in her cheeks. When I stare for too long, Mila asks, "Why are you staring?"

I shrug and pay attention to the TV as I go to the romance section. "Cause you're so beautiful. Sometimes it catches me by surprise. Which one do you want to watch?" I walk to the bed, and sitting down on the mattress, I lean back against the headboard with my legs stretched out in front of me.

When Mila doesn't answer, I glance at her and seeing her staring at me, I tease, "Are you staring at me 'cause I'm pretty too?"

Mila scrunches her nose and shrugs. "Nah, it's because you're not half as bad as I thought, and sometimes it catches me by surprise."

I chuckle as I gesture at the TV. "Which movie do you want to torture me with?"

Mila grabs the remote from me and scrolls twice through the whole damn list before settling on '*The Vow*'.

She lies back against the headboard and places the remote between us. "I'm warning you, no bad-mouthing Channing Tatum, or I'll have to throat punch you."

Raising an eyebrow at her, I pretend to be offended. "Seriously? What do you see in that guy?"

Mila gives me a disgruntled look, and I have to say I missed seeing that expression on her face. "For one, he gives a much better strip dance than you."

Taking hold of her arm, I pull her closer to me while I joke, "Just wait. One day I'll blow your mind with my sexy moves."

Mila lets out a burst of laughter and cuddles into my side. When she rests her cheek on my chest, I bring my hand to her hair and play with the strands while watching the start of the movie.

Halfway through, Mila dozes off, and I make sure she's fast asleep before digging her phone out of my pocket. I send Justin's number to my own phone before I block his number and delete the voice clip. I listen to the others to make sure there's nothing else that can upset Mila before I switch off her phone. I drop hers on the bedside table then take hold of my phone.

Pressing dial on the fucker's number, I wait for him to answer. It goes to voicemail, and I grind the words out, "Don't fucking phone her. Don't even think of her. I'm going to make sure you fucking pay."

Cutting the call, I take a deep breath before I bring up the number for Preston. He's Mr. Chargill's PA and just the person I need right now.

"Preston Culpepper speaking," he answers.

"It's Jase. I need a favor, please."

"Oh… sure," I hear something in the background, and then he asks, "What can I help with?"

"I need you to erase someone."

"Everything?" he asks, not even questioning why I'm asking him to do this.

"His name is Justin Green. He was a student at Trinity until recently. I want everything erased. Social security, bank accounts, every single thing you can find on him." Knowing how thorough Preston is, I quickly add, "Just not the police records. That's all I want to remain, so he's only known for what he did."

There's a moment's silence, then Preston asks, "Is he the one that attacked Mila West?"

"Yes."

"Consider it done, Jase."

"Thanks, Preston. Keep this between us."

"My lips are sealed."

Cutting the call, I drop my phone next to Mila's. I let my eyes drift over her face, and a smile tugs at the corner of my mouth.

One way or another, I'm going to destroy Justin Green.

Chapter 17

MILA

I can't believe I dozed off again. Staring at Jase's sleeping face, I keep still, not wanting to wake him.

My thoughts return to earlier when he got angry. I've never seen him like that, and I find it weird, I wasn't scared of him. I was more worried he'd do something that would get him into trouble.

My eyes drift over every inch of his face. He hasn't shaved the last couple of days, and the stubble makes him look older.

I've seen a different side to Jase, not just the usual joker and player. It makes me wonder what else I don't know about him.

He stirs, and his arm tightens around me.

Even in his sleep, he doesn't let go of me.

With my eyes not leaving his face, my thoughts turn to the blow-up this afternoon, and I know I have to do something. I have to take back control of my life. The attack has affected my loved ones too much, and seeing how worried our friends were was a wake-up call.

As the sun begins to set, I allow myself to think about what's happened the past week. The attack wrecked my life into something unrecognizable, but through it all, my feelings for Jase have never changed. If anything, I love him even more now.

Where I feel painfully aware of my surroundings and those around me, it's different with Jase. I know he saw me at my worst, and I thought it would fill me with shame.

Maybe it's because I saw how much the attack upset him that it didn't?

That's right, Mila. Count the blessings in your life and focus on them.

After today and the voicemail, I know I won't be able to hide behind Jase much longer. I'll need to give my statement. I'll have to talk about the incident so things can proceed, and I can get closure when Justin is dealt with.

So Jase can get closure.

I'm careful as I pull free from Jase, but the movement still wakes him, and he mumbles, "Where are you going?"

"I'm just going to call my dad," I whisper, and leaning closer to him, I press a kiss to his cheek. "Sleep some more."

Spotting my phone next to the bed, I grab it before I get up and sneak out of the room.

I slip into my own room, and switching on the phone, I bring up Dad's number.

"Mila, are you okay?" his worried voice comes over the line.

"I'm fine, Daddy. Can you let Officer Lane know I'm ready to give my statement?"

"Yes. I'll call her right away and bring her to you."

"Thanks, Daddy."

"How are you feeling?"

"Much better. I got a lot of sleep today," I answer to set Dad's mind at ease.

"That's good to hear. I'll see you in ten minutes."

"Okay." I cut the call and suck in a deep breath until the pain in my chest from my cracked ribs reminds me to not push my luck. I still have a lot of healing to do, but the call to Dad is a step in the right direction.

You're not ready.

Panic tightens my muscles for a moment, but I force the thought away, and adamant to ignore my inner voice, I quickly pull a brush through my hair. Before I leave my room, I take a couple of breaths, then walk out and head toward the living room.

I fist my hands next to my sides, and the moment Jade catches sight of me, she worms herself free from Hunter's hold and jumps up.

"I'd like to talk to everyone," I say.

I go sit on the nearest couch as Jade yells, "Get all your asses to the living room! Family meeting."

Kao's the first to appear, and the second he sees me, he darts forward to take the seat next to me. He hesitates for a second, then asks, "Can I hug you?"

I bring a smile to my face and force myself to lean into him. The hug pushes my limits, and my body begins to tremble.

Kao's one of your best friends, Mila. He'd never hurt you.

Glad no one else tries to hug me, I watch as all my friends take a seat. I'm about to start talking when Jase walks into the living room. He taps Kao on the shoulder. "Move over." And then he squeezes in between us and places his arm around me, asking, "We're having a meeting?"

I place my hand on his thigh. "Yeah, I want to get this over with so I can move on with my life."

And so you can move on.

I pull my hand back from Jase's leg and suck in a deep breath until my healing ribs ache. Letting the air out, I say, "I know the last week has been hard on everyone. Thank you for all the support." I glance at each of my friends. "I'm fine. Everything's healing, and I'll soon be back to kicking everyone's butts." I let out a chuckle. "Figuratively. I'll leave the actual kicking and punching to Jade."

My comment draws chuckles from everyone.

"My dad's coming over with the police so I can give my statement. After that, I don't want to talk about what happened ever again. I just want everything to go back to the way it was, so please don't be weird around me. Just go on with your lives as if it never happened."

There's a wave of expressions on everyone's faces, and I can see Fallon's struggling to keep quiet. Giving her an encouraging smile, I say, "Get it off your chest, Fallon."

She shakes her head, her features tightening with heartache. "I can't forget what I saw, Mila."

Her admission has every muscle in my body tightening, and apprehension ripples through me. "You saw?"

When she nods, shame pours over me like boiling hot water. My voice is hoarse when I ask, "Did you all see?"

Kao gets up, and coming to crouch in front of me, he tilts his head. "Look at me, Mila." My eyes dart to his for a second before they drop to my hands on my lap. He places his hand over both of mine, and my whole body jerks, which has him pulling back. "Look at me, please."

I shake my head but lift my eyes anyway.

There's a caring expression warming Kao's blue eyes. "I love you, Mila. You're one of the most important people in my life. Don't feel embarrassed around us. We only saw when they loaded you into the ambulance. We hate what happened to you, and... God, I wish I could turn back time and stop it, but none of it will ever change the way I feel about you or how I see you. You're still badass. You're still my go-to person whenever I need someone to slap me upside the head. You're still our Mila."

My chin begins to tremble, and there's one hell of a big lump in my throat, but refusing to cry, I swallow the emotion down and whisper, "Thanks, Kao. That means a lot to me."

Jase pulls me closer to him and presses a kiss to the side of my head. "Yeah, we all love you, and nothing will change that."

There's a sad twinge in my chest as I nod.

I need to put the attack behind me so I can deal with my feelings for Jase. They're stronger than ever after everything he's done for me, and I'll have to put distance between us, so I can get over him once and for all.

We're just friends, and that's all we'll ever be.

Maybe if I focus on that, I'll be able to get through the next couple of weeks.

JASE

Listening to Mila while she gave her statement to Officer Lane was fucking hard.

I can see the relief on Mr. West's face after it's all done. "Can I make an appointment for you to start meeting with Dr. Bower?"

Mila shakes her head. "No, but don't worry. I am going to talk to Mrs. Reyes." Her eyes dart to mine. "Your mom offered, and I'm going to take her up on it."

Mr. West seems to know more than me because he says, "Oh, that's good. She'll be able to help you a lot. Knowing that makes me feel better."

How will Mom be able to help Mila?

I get up and shake Mr. West's hand before I excuse myself and go to my room. Shutting the door behind me, I pull my phone from my pocket and dial Mom's number.

"Hey, my baby, how are you holding up?" her voice comes over the line.

"Better." I pause then say, "Mila mentioned she's going to take you up on your offer to talk about what happened."

"Oh, good. I'm glad to hear that."

I take a deep breath then continue, "Mr. West said you'd be able to help her? Is there something I should know?"

"Yeah, but not over the phone. Come to the house and bring Mila along."

"Okay." I shove my phone back into my pocket, and walking out, I run into Mila as she comes down the hallway. "Did your dad leave?"

She nods. "Yeah." Letting out a breath, she says, "It's been one hell of an intense day."

"Listen," I reach for her hand, "I'm heading over to my parents', and my mom asked for you to come along. Are you up for it?"

Mila glances down, looking at her clothes, then says, "Yeah, but I'll need to change. I can't go to your house in sweatpants."

"I'll wait." I wink at her, then walk to Hunter's room. Since he and Jade started dating, I don't risk just walking in. God only knows what position I might find them in, so I knock first.

"Yeah?" he calls from the other side of the door.

"Are you decent?" I call back.

I hear a chuckle. "We are now."

Shaking my head, I push the door open. Jade's snuggled against Hunter's side, and they're watching a movie on the entertainment system he recently had installed.

"I'm heading over to my parents. Mila's coming with me."

"Okay, send them my regards."

Before I can close the door, Jade says, "Jase, thanks for being there for Mila."

"Always." I shut the door and don't have to wait long before Mila comes out of her room, dressed in jeans and a soft cashmere sweater. She's even managed to put on some make-up. Taking hold of her hand, I link our fingers and say, "Let's hit the road, beautiful."

The corners of her mouth lift in a thankful smile.

I grab my car keys, and opening the front door, I wait for Mila to walk out before I follow, drawing the door shut behind us. I keep holding her hand as we walk to the elevator, and the doors slide open immediately. Stepping inside, I press the button for the ground floor then let go of Mila's hand so I can wrap my arm around her.

"Are you ready for this?" I ask.

Glancing up at me, a small smile plays around her lips. "Yeah."

When the doors open and we step out into the foyer, I tighten my hold around her shoulders and pull her into my side. My eyes keep darting around us as we leave the dorm, and whenever I see a student look in our direction, I scowl at them.

Reaching the car, I open the passenger door, and once Mila climbs in, I grab the seat belt, and pulling it over her, I clip it in.

There's a questioning look on Mila's face, and it has me asking, "Is something wrong?"

She shakes her head. "No, but I can put on the seat belt myself."

"I know." Pulling back, I shut the door and jog around the front of the vehicle. Getting in, I start the engine and strap myself in before I steer us out of the campus.

It's a short and quiet drive to my parents' house, and my mind keeps alternating between wondering if Mila is really up for this visit and what my mom's going to tell us.

Maybe she wants to talk about when Aunt Kingsley almost drowned? Or perhaps it's about what my grandmother did to Aunt Layla? My mind runs circles around all the possibilities. I don't have any contact with my grandmother, but I know she served a sentence for almost murdering Fallon's mom.

Figuring that must be it, I pull up the driveway and park behind my father's car. I unclasp both our seatbelts, and getting out, I dart around the vehicle and open the passenger door for Mila.

After she's out of the car, I take hold of her hand, and we walk into the mansion. "Mom," I yell, so I'll know where she is.

"In the sunroom," Dad shouts. He comes out of the kitchen and smiles when he sees Mila with me. "Hi, Mila. How are you feeling?"

"Much better, Mr. Reyes."

"Mom said she has something to tell us?" I ask as we walk with Dad to the sunroom. Last year, Mom converted the entertainment room into an indoor garden and replaced that part of the ceiling with glass. Since then, she spends all her free time there.

"Yes." Dad doesn't say anything else as we walk into the room.

A smile instantly forms around Mom's lips when she sees us, and she gets up from the plush couch to hug me.

"You look pretty," she compliments Mila, only giving her shoulder a squeeze.

"Jase, let's give the ladies some time alone," Dad says.

What?

My eyes dart to Mila, and she quickly says, "I'll be fine. Go catch up with your dad."

Dad takes hold of my shoulder. "Come on."

Letting go of Mila's hand, I hesitate until Mom gives me a comforting smile. Walking out of the room, I glance back and watch as Mila sits down next to Mom.

I follow Dad to the living room, and he pours us each a tumbler of whiskey. "Let's sit."

I take the drink from Dad and sit down on the couch. When he takes the seat next to me, I start to frown.

"There's something I need to tell you," Dad begins. "First, you need to know we didn't tell you because we felt it wasn't something you needed to know."

I take a deep sip from the amber liquid as my heartbeat begins to pick up its pace. I have a feeling whatever Dad's about to tell me is bad.

Dad sets down his own glass before he turns his body toward me. His eyes scan over my face before he says, "While your mom attended Trinity, she was stalked by a serial killer."

What. The. Actual. Fuck.

"She was what?" I snap, stunned to hell and back by what my father just said.

Dad shifts closer to me and places his hand on top of mine. "You need to know your mom is fine, son. We've kept it quiet so the media wouldn't get involved. Only a handful of people know about this."

"Hold up." I pull my hand from under my father's and frown at him. "Let's go back to the part about the serial killer. What happened?"

"The man stalked your mother, and he managed to abduct her, but we got to her in time. That's all you need to know."

That's all I need to know? Seriously?

"How can you say that?" I explode. "You can't drop this bombshell on me and say that's all I need to know!"

I dart up from the chair, my muscles tense as the residual shock from what I just learned ripples through me.

Dad rises to his feet, and taking hold of my shoulder, he says, "Do you really need to know the details, Jase? It won't change anything, will it? Your mom's fine now. It's all that matters. She survived, and she dealt with it. We've all dealt with it. We just thought you should know the reason for your mom reaching out to Mila."

Fuck, Dad's right. I don't think I can handle hearing the details. I'm barely hanging on as is.

Needing confirmation, I ask, "But Mom's okay? She's really fine?"

Dad pulls me into a hug. "Yes, your mom has fully recovered from the ordeal. Let's focus on helping Mila."

I nod and wrap my arms around Dad as I admit, "It's hard. How did you cope?"

We sit down again, and Dad lets out a chuckle. "I didn't. Honestly, I was beside myself. I went into overprotective mode until I nearly drove your mother insane."

His comment makes me think of when Mila said she can put on her own seat belt, and I say, "Overprotective is

205

an understatement. It's tough leaving Mila alone just so she can take a shower."

The corner of Dad's mouth curves up. "I felt guilty and blamed myself for what happened to your mom. I think I tried to make up for it by showing her I'd never leave her alone again."

Realizing Dad went through the exact same thing I'm going through offers me some relief. "So, what should I do?"

Dad's eyes lock on mine, and there's so much love in them as he stares at me. "You can only be there for her. Help her get back into a normal routine." Dad pulls me into a hug. "And as for you, I'm here whenever you need to talk. Don't go through this on your own."

When we pull apart, I confess, "I used to tease Mila a lot. It was our way of communicating, but since the attack... I'm just scared I'll say something wrong."

Dad gives me an understanding smile. "From what I've heard, Mila's kept everyone at a distance except for you."

"Yeah, but she's starting to open up to the group. She met with the police tonight and gave her statement as well. I'm scared she's going to start pulling away from me."

"Jase, she feels comfortable with you. That's very important for her right now. Just be yourself. Mila's made it clear it's what she wants by turning to you when she needed someone the most."

I nod as Dad's words sink in. When Mila woke up, she called for me. She never shrunk away from me or asked me to leave, and it makes me think.

What if?

Bringing my eyes back to Dad's, I ask, "How were things on the romance front while Mom was recovering?"

A huge grin spreads over my father's face, "Things were always good. We didn't let what was happening drive a wedge between us. If anything, it brought us closer together."

"Yeah, but…" I pull an awkward face as I admit, "We weren't exactly dating before the attack."

Dad's one eyebrow pops into the air. "Shit, you could've fooled me. I thought you were a couple already."

"Well, we're not. I was going to talk to Mila, but then she was attacked," I state.

"I'm afraid you'll have to bite the bullet and tell Mila how you feel."

Not exactly the advice I wanted.

"With my luck, she'll tell me to go to hell."

Because I already upset her enough when we had the fight. I don't want to do that to her a second time. Especially not now.

Dad gets up and chuckles. "Or she might surprise you. What's the worst that can happen?"

"Our friendship can die a sudden and horrible death," I grimace.

Dad shakes his head. "Never. Tell her how you feel and if she doesn't feel the same, then so what? You care for the girl. There's nothing wrong with that."

Not wanting to go into detail about everything that's happened between Mila and me, I agree, "Yeah, you're right."

Chapter 18

MILA

After hearing about Mrs. Reyes' ordeal, I stare at her with wide eyes.

"You're…" I struggle to search for the right words and say, "so brave."

Oh, my God. There's so much I have to be thankful for. At least I wasn't stalked and drugged to the point that my loved ones thought I was losing my mind.

Mrs. Reyes leans over and places her hand on mine. "You're brave, too, Mila. But it's up to you whether you let what a sick man did define who you are. You're not responsible for what happened. That's all on your attacker. You're Mila West, a beautiful girl with a bright future ahead of her."

Holy shit. What she says rings so true. I got stuck in my head, thinking my life was ruined.

That I was ruined.

But that's not true. The life that was ruined was Justin's. He's the one with no future, and I won't let him take mine as well.

Still worried, I ask, "Did you have nightmares?"

Mrs. Reyes nods. "The first two weeks were the hardest, but with my husband and family's support, I got past it."

I gnaw at my bottom lip, then admit, "I'm returning to classes on Monday. Everyone on campus knows what happened."

Mrs. Reyes' expression turns stern. "And it has nothing to do with any of them. If someone approaches you, make it clear your life is not open for discussion." Giving me an encouraging smile, she adds, "And honestly, even if they whisper behind your back, don't let it get to you. It doesn't matter what anyone thinks, Mila. I kept reminding myself only the opinion of my loved ones mattered. Surround yourself with your friends. They'll take good care of you. And you have us. We won't tolerate anyone making this harder for you."

I nod as I listen to her advice. Still, I know it will be challenging, but it helps to hear I have the Reyes family behind me. No one would dare go up against them.

Just then, Jase and Mr. Reyes walk into the room. Jase goes to hug his mother and wanting to give them some privacy, I move to the side and glance around at the plants.

"Mila," Mr. Reyes says as he comes to stand by me. "I've spoken with the dean. If anyone gives you any trouble, report them, and they'll be dealt with swiftly. Or tell Jase, and he'll take care of it."

Smiling at Mr. Reyes, I say, "I'm sure everything will be fine but thank you for caring."

"You ready?" Jase asks as he walks toward me.

I nod, and I'm about to thank Mrs. Reyes when she comes to give me a hug, and she whispers, "Call me whenever you need to talk."

"I will. Thank you so much for everything." Feeling more comfortable around her after hearing what she's been through, I tighten my hold on her for a moment before I pull back.

We say goodbye to Jase's parents, and I wait until we're in the car before I glance at Jase and say, "No wonder you're so damn good with me. Gosh, I never knew your Mom went through something like that."

Jase doesn't start the engine but instead slumps back against the seat, shaking his head. "I didn't know before tonight."

"What?" The word explodes from me, and my hand darts out to take hold of his.

His face is filled with disbelief as he looks at me. "My dad just told me while my mom was talking to you."

"Crap, I'm sorry, Jase." If I had known, I would've been more sensitive about mentioning it to Jase.

He shakes his head and smiles at me. "All that matters is that my mom's okay. And I got some good advice from my dad."

"Yeah? What did he say?"

Jase starts the engine, and placing his right hand on the back of my seat, he looks behind us as he reverses the car. Before putting the car into drive, his eyes lock on mine, and he grins, "My dad said I should go back to flirting with you. The sooner things are normal again, the better."

I pull a disgruntled face. "Don't you dare. I'm so over fighting with you."

Steering the car down the road, Jase reaches for my hand, and picking it up, he brings it to his mouth so he can press a kiss to the back of my hand. "Nah, you love flirting with me."

"Fighting," I argue, but I can't stop the smile from tugging at my lips.

"Flirting, fighting, it's the same thing," Jase says, his sexy grin back.

Damn, I missed seeing that grin.

When we get to the dorm, Jase practically drags me to his room.

"I have to work on my assignments," I warn him.

"I know," Jase says as he sits down on the bed, dragging his own laptop closer. He glances at me and pats the space beside him. "Sit your sexy ass down so we can get some work done."

Shaking my head, I grab my laptop and make myself comfortable on the bed while grumbling, "Should've known you'd be back to your old self in no time."

Truth be told, I'm glad. Jase seems more at ease after the visit to his parents.

JASE

When I'm done creating the graph and filling in the details needed, I glance over at Mila. She's frowning at the laptop like it grew two heads.

"What's wrong?" I ask as I lean over to see what she's working on.

"I'm struggling with the depreciating cost."

I glance over what she's done, then explain, "You need to deduct the total cost, but instead of doing it all in one year, you write off a certain percentage over five years."

She frowns at me. "But it's a laptop. The thing won't last two years. At least, mine doesn't."

"Okay," I shift closer and point to the excerpt she was given to work off. "In this case, you need to work out the depreciating cost based on what the IRS requires, which is five years as per the example they gave you."

She scrunches her nose. "I freaking hate accounting."

"No, you're just stubborn," I joke. "You can't apply what you would do in real life to your studies. Facts are facts, babe."

Mila frowns at me. "Why do you call me that?"

"Huh?" Now she's lost me.

"Babe. Why do you call me that?"

Tilting my head, my own frown forms on my forehead. "Does it bother you?"

"No." She pushes her laptop to the side and turns to me, crossing her legs. "I just want to know why you call me babe."

"Because you're my babe," I answer the only way I know how to. I don't think now is the right time to tell her I love her. I want to wait until she's better.

"Ugh," she huffs as she grabs her laptop again. "You're even more impossible to understand than accounting."

I let out a burst of laughter. "What's so hard? I'm all about love."

She lets out a snort, then flinches with pain. "Ooh, I need to take a break and put an ice pack on my ribs."

Closing my laptop, I set it aside and get up. "I'll go get one."

I jog to the kitchen and grab an ice pack from the freezer, and walking back into the room, I say, "Lie down. I've seen the nurse help you with this enough times to be an expert."

Mila lies on her right side, and I sit down behind her. Taking hold of her shirt, I lift it just enough to place the cold compress over her injury. Keeping my hand on the pack so it won't slide, I lie down and rest my head on my right arm.

After a couple of minutes, my eyes drift over Mila's profile. "Does it feel better?"

She nods. "Thanks."

Wanting to get more comfortable, I push my right arm under Mila's neck, and lying down with my head on the same pillow as hers, I wrap my arm under her chin.

We lie in silence for a moment, and then I ask, "Will you be okay to return to classes on Monday?"

Bringing her hands up, she takes hold of my forearm and answers, "Yeah."

"When we're done with the ice pack, remember to show me your schedule," I say.

"Why?"

"I'm not letting you walk around on campus by yourself."

She turns onto her back and stares at me. "I'll be with Jade and Fallon."

I adjust the pack on her side, then raise an eyebrow at her. "So?"

"So, they'll be with me. You can't attend your own classes and follow me around on campus. That's just crazy."

"Mila, I'm not going back to classes yet. You're stuck with me until I'm sure no one will give you shit."

She sits up and gives me a you-must-be-joking look. When I see the sparks begin to fly in her eyes, a grin pulls at my lips.

216

God, I missed those sparks.

"You're not missing any more classes because of me," she says, her voice sharp with incredulity that I'd even think of doing such a thing.

Sitting up, I lean over to her until our faces are only inches apart. "Yeah, are you going to stop me?"

She lets out a frustrated huff. "You're impossible, Jase." Then she pulls a face as she mutters, "And you think I'm the stubborn one in this relationship."

I tilt my head as my grin grows broader, and catching her eyes, I ask, "Relationship?"

"Ugh, you know what I mean." She rolls her eyes and begins to scoot off the bed, then she says, "I meant our friendship."

"Nope, I heard you clearly say relationship," I tease her.

She walks around the bed and grabs the pillow behind me, then whacks me with it. "Stop teasing me."

With a scowl on her face, she walks out of my room, and I jump up. I laugh as I run after her. "Where are you going?"

"All the arguing made me hungry," she grumbles as she stops in front of the fridge.

"Sit down." I steer her to a kitchen stool before I go to take the leftover pizza from the box. I plate a couple of

217

slices for us, and while it's warming, I ask, "What do you want to drink?"

"Water is fine," she says.

I glance at Mila, and when I catch her eyes on me, I wink at her.

It earns me a huff as she rolls her eyes and slides off the stool. "That's it. I'm choosing another romance to torture you with."

I laugh as I watch her disappear down the hallway.

Dad was right. Since I started treating her like nothing's wrong and teasing her again, she's been much more relaxed and almost back to her old self.

Chapter 19

MILA

With Jase back to his old flirty self, and all my friends going about their everyday routines, I started to feel like my old self until I woke up this morning.

It's my first day back at classes since the attack and my chest is filled with apprehension. I carefully do my makeup, so none of the fading bruises will be visible.

When I'm done getting ready for the day, my eyes glide over my reflection in the mirror. I look the same as I did before the attack.

But I don't feel the same.

The nights have gotten much better, but that's because I've been sleeping in Jase's bed.

My gaze goes to my own bed. From tonight, I plan on sleeping in my room. I haven't told Jase yet, but I'm sure he'll be more than happy to have his space back for himself.

I've been trying my best to move forward, but I still feel... broken. I'm holding my breath like I'm waiting for the other shoe to drop.

I let out a huff, and getting up, I leave my room so I'll get out of my head.

Walking to the living room, I hear Jase say, "You can head to class. I'll walk with –" Seeing me, he stops talking, and his eyes drift over me.

He stares at me so long, I glance down at the jeans and sweater I'm wearing. "Is there something wrong with my clothes?"

Jase shakes his head, and a grin tugs at his mouth. He walks to me, and wrapping his hand behind my neck, he pulls me closer and presses a kiss to my forehead.

I hear him take a deep breath, then he murmurs, "Mhhh... you smell good."

He's been doing that a lot. Making comments about me looking beautiful and how he likes the perfume I'm using.

I don't think I'll ever get used to this side of Jase. And, honestly, it makes it a whole lot harder to get over him.

Taking my bag from me, Jase says, "Let's get you to class." I watch him check something on his phone, then he says, "We have ten minutes. Want to grab a coffee or something to eat on the way?"

I try to take my bag back from Jase, but he grabs hold of my hand and link our fingers.

Scowling at him, I say, "You're not walking me all over campus, Jase."

"It's not open for discussion." Jase drags me to the front door, and I give Jade a look asking for help.

She just joins us and says, "I've tried talking to him, but he won't listen. Let's go, or we'll be late."

Taking the elevator down to the ground floor, I free my hand from Jase's and cross my arms over my chest, mumbling, "I don't need babysitters."

Jase ignores my comment, reading something on his phone. I inch closer to him and glance at the screen, then I instantly wish I hadn't as I read the text messages Jase is scrolling through.

Summer: My family is hosting a benefit function, and I'd love to have you there. It's Saturday at six pm. xoxo

Rachel: Hey, Jase. Just wanted to let you know I'm thinking of you. All my hugs & kisses.

Jessica: I miss you!!!!! Let me know when you're done babysitting so we can hang out. Promise to make it worth your time.

Ugh, I should've known better.

221

The doors open, and I dart out of the confined space, then I remember Jase has my bag and swinging around, I grab it from him before walking away as fast as possible.

My heart splats somewhere at my feet. Angry at myself for even caring, I cross my arms over my chest and storm out of the building.

"What's the hurry?" Jase says as he catches up to me.

Stopping, I glare at him. "You obviously have things to do. Hell, all those messages alone should take you the whole day. I'll be fine on my own. Go freaking service your harem."

I stalk away, more adamant than ever to put distance between Jase and myself. This has to stop, or I'll end up losing my damn mind.

Jase grabs hold of my arm, and when he yanks me back, I slam into him. He takes my bag from me, and glaring at me, he snaps, "First of all, there's no fucking harem. Secondly, stop fucking fighting me on this. I'm walking you to class. That's the end of the discussion."

I scowl up at him, and for a moment, our angry gazes collide.

Shit, he looks unbelievably sexy when he's upset.

Shut up, Mila. Focus!

I try to free my arm from his hold, as I snap, "I don't need you."

Jase steps right up to me, and lowering his head, he keeps hold of my eyes as he says, "Are we back to lying to each other? Because we both know that's not true."

I become aware of students staring at us, and not wanting to make a bigger scene, I step away from Jase. "Let go of my arm."

He instantly let's go, and giving me one last glare, he grabs my hand and drags me to my accounting class.

JASE

Calm down, Jase. Just fucking calm down.

I keep repeating the words to myself as I pull Mila into the lecture hall. Jade catches up to us, giving us both a worried glance before she goes to take a seat. I place Mila's bag down on the desk before I turn to her. "See you in an hour."

Stalking out of the hall, I take my phone from my pocket and respond to the messages.

To Summer: Not interested.

To Rachel: Thanks.

To Jessica: Go to hell.

I glare at the text messages. Obviously, Mila saw them, and that's why she got upset.

Then a thought hits me, and I stop walking as a smile spread over my face.

Mila was jealous. I'm fucking sure of it.

Turning around, I jog back to Mila's class, and I walk to where she's sitting. She looks up at me with surprise flashing over her features. I frame her face with my hands and leaning down, I'm about to aim for her forehead, but at the last moment, I tilt lower, and I press a kiss to her parted lips. Before pulling back, I move my mouth to her ear and whisper, "Love seeing you jealous, babe."

I don't give her time to react and hurry out of the class, a huge-ass grin around my lips.

I know she's probably going to kick my ass as soon as the lecture ends, but I don't regret it. Yeah, I'm going to try my fucking best to take things slow with her, but in the meanwhile, I'm making sure she knows I'm done playing games. I don't want her seeing me as a player anymore.

I go grab some breakfast while waiting for Mila, the grin never leaving my face. I've just placed my order when

Nate approaches my table. The guy gives me an unsure look. "Can I talk to you?"

I shrug and gesture to a chair. "If it's important enough to interrupt my meal."

He takes the seat and leans closer to me. "There's something you should know."

Raising my eyebrow, I give him an impatient look so he'll get on with it.

Nate shifts uncomfortably in the chair, then leans even closer and whispers, "Jessica instigated the whole thing with Justin."

A frown settles hard on my forehead. "The attack?"

"Not the attack, but she kept telling Justin to go for Mila. She wanted Mila out of the way so she could date you."

This is news. Jessica has been pretty forward with me, but I never thought she'd go to such an extreme.

Nate sits a little back and shrugs, "I just thought you should know. Justin would never have tried anything with Mila if Jessica didn't keep telling him Mila was interested in him. Whenever Justin started to doubt whether Mila liked him back, Jessica would convince him Mila was head over heels for him. I just feel she's getting away with murder while Justin is the only one paying."

Not happy at all with the direction this conversation is going in, I growl, "I don't give a fuck about Justin. Don't ever mention him to me again. As for Jessica, I'll deal with her." I turn my attention away from Nate. "You can go."

He leaves the table, and I think over what he said while waiting for the food to come.

What part did Jessica play in the attack? Fuck, if I find out that she had anything to do with it, she's dead.

As anger simmers in my chest, my thoughts return to the night of the incident. Jessica was the reason Mila left the club. Was that her plan all along? To piss Mila off enough so that she'd storm outside where Justin could get her alone?

"Jase." My head snaps up to Hana. I didn't even notice her and Hunter sitting down. "What are you thinking so hard about?"

"Nate just told me something," I say. My food comes, and I wait for my friends to place their orders. Before the waiter leaves, I ask, "Can you prepare a coffee and bagel with cream cheese for when I leave?"

"Yes, sir."

When the waiter is out of hearing distance, I glance at my friends. "Nate says Jessica told Justin that Mila was interested in him."

Hana gives me an absurd look. "Mila made it clear she only considered him a friend." She leans forward, placing her elbows on the table. "Everyone knows Mila wasn't interested in dating anyone, Jase."

I nod. "Yeah, I know. I think Jessica had something to do with the attack."

Hunter's eyebrows shoot up. "You think? We need to be sure before we act."

"I know." I push the plate of food toward Hunter. "I'm not hungry. You have it."

"What are you going to do?" Hana asks, her eyes filled with worry.

"I'm going to find out the truth and deal with it."

"How?"

There's only one way, and I grimace because just thinking of talking to that fucker makes my blood boil. "I'm going to ask Justin if Jessica had anything to do with it."

"You're not meeting him alone," Hunter warns. "We don't need you being arrested for murder."

I shake my head. "I'm not going to meet with him. I won't be able to leave him breathing then." Taking my phone from my pocket, I bring up his number and press dial. When I get a generic message that the number is no longer in service, I let out a bark of laughter.

"What's so funny?" Hunter asks, giving me a worried look.

"I forgot I asked Preston to erase the fucker." I tuck my phone back into my pocket. "I'll have to find out another way."

"My dad's on the case against Justin. I could ask him to find out?" Hana offers.

Getting up, I give her shoulder a squeeze. "That would help a lot. Let me know as soon as you find out anything."

The waiter brings me the coffee and bagel, and I head out of the restaurant.

Pushing the worry about Jessica to the back of my mind, I steel myself for an ass-whooping from Mila for the kiss.

Chapter 20

MILA

I didn't pay any attention to the damn lecture. I've been too busy thinking of ways to get back at Jase.

He freaking kissed me? In front of all the students?

What the hell?

He's so dead. I'm going to freaking throat punch him.

I'm frustrated and hurt. Just because Jase took care of me the past week, it doesn't mean things can change back to how they were between us.

I can't handle the attack and Jase being hot and cold with me at the same time.

I pack my laptop back into my bag and shrug it over my shoulder.

I'm so upset, I don't bother waiting for Jade and stalk out of class. The second I step into the hallway, Jase straightens from where he was leaning against the wall, right outside the door. He holds a coffee and plastic-wrapped bagel out to me, and with a chagrined expression that makes him look too damn cute for his own good, he says, "Peace offering."

I glare at him as I take the coffee and bagel. "Don't ever do that again."

He pulls the bag from my shoulder, and placing a hand on my lower back, he nudges me to start walking.

"We have ten minutes for you to have breakfast before your next class."

I drink the coffee as we make our way through the sea of students around us. I'm painfully aware of every person who passes near me, and even though I'm upset with Jase, I can't stop myself from moving closer to him.

His hand moves up my back, and he wraps his arm around my shoulders.

Crap, this is going to be so hard. Jase is the only one who makes me feel safe, but being around him doesn't give me time to get over him. It's like being stuck between a rock and a hard place.

I finish the coffee and dispose of the cup in the next trashcan we pass. When we reach my next lecture, Jase again escorts me to my seat. He waits for me to sit, and then he places his hand on the desk and leans over me. I lower my head, so he can't kiss me on the mouth again, just in case it's what he wanted to do.

Jase presses his lips to the top of my head, and when he pulls back, I keep myself busy with taking my laptop from my bag.

Then I hear him growl, "Find somewhere else to sit."

My head snaps up, and I watch a guy rush away from us.

Jase sits down next to me, and it makes me frown at him. "You can't stay for the lecture."

He lifts an eyebrow. "Yeah? Who's going to stop me?"

"Jase," I hiss softly, not wanting to draw more attention to us than we already have.

Jade and Fallon come in and sit down next to Jase.

And before I can get Jase to leave, the professor walks in. The moment he spots Jase, his eyes widen. "Mr. Reyes? Are you joining us for today's lesson?"

Jase smiles. "Yeah, don't mind me."

I glare at Jase before turning my attention to my laptop. At this rate, I might as well not attend, seeing as I can't focus on anything.

I open a new document and type;

Me: You're distracting me from my classes!!!!

I shift the laptop toward Jase, and when he reads the message, he just freaking grins.

Jase: Yeah? I find it hard to concentrate with you sitting next to me as well.

Ugh, you're freaking kidding me.

Me: Leave.

Jase: No.

Me: I'm going to throat punch you in front of everyone.

Jase: Will you kiss it better afterward?

Me: #$%@&

Jase: Is that code for yes?

Me: Stop it!

Jase: Do you really want me to stop?

I stare at his question for too long, and giving up on this argument, I slap my laptop shut and pretend to focus my attention on the professor.

I hate admitting Jase's presence does help, even though he infuriates me with all the flirting.

———————————————————————

With every class, it gets harder.

The stares. The whispers.

On my way to my final lecture, I pull free from Jase. "I'm just going to the restroom."

"I'll be right outside," he says.

Walking inside, I keep my eyes downcast and dart into the first open stall.

I relieve myself and am busy buttoning my jeans when I hear someone else come into the restroom, and then I recognize Rachel's voice. "Have you seen her? She looks fine. They're probably just making a big deal of it all."

Summer comments, "Yeah, and now she has Jase walking around with her." There's a sarcastic chuckle. "She probably faked the whole attack to get Jase's attention. Things were going so well between him and Jessica."

God, I hate these girls.

"And poor Justin. What did he do to deserve this? She's ruined his life," Rachel snaps.

Poor Justin?

For a moment, I shut my eyes against the harsh reality that they think I made the attack up just to get Jase's attention. It makes me feel sick to my stomach, and a light sweat breaks out over my body.

My heart begins to beat faster, and not able to just stand here and listen, I yank the door open and don't look at the girls as I wash my hands. I grab a paper towel and quickly dab the water off.

When I open the door and walk out of the restroom, I bump into someone, and my head snaps up. Seeing Nate, my heart shoots to my throat, and I stumble backward to get away from him.

"Hey, Mila. I'm sorry about what happened."

Fear grips my insides, and I can only stare at him.

I expect to see Justin any second because they were always together. The thought makes my whole body tremble as terror ricochets through me.

Someone takes hold of my arm, and I shriek as I yank away.

"Mila." Hearing Jase's voice, my eyes dart to him, and I see him holding his hands up as he carefully steps closer to me.

All the thoughts about putting distance between us vaporize into thin air as my body darts forward, and I slam into his chest. I wrap my arms tightly around his waist and hide my face against his chest.

His arms engulf me, and his breath flutters over my hair. "You're safe. I've got you."

I just want to get away from the prying eyes and whispers. Lifting my face to Jase, I plead, "I want to go to the suite."

He nods and holding me close to his side, we leave the lecture building in a hurry. I keep my eyes down and cower against Jase's side.

My breaths rush over my lips as I fight to keep the memories from creeping back.

And everyone blames me.

I gasp through the shame the thought brings.

This is too hard. I was stupid, thinking I can pretend it never happened.

What do I do now?

JASE

Mila's been shooting me glares the whole day, but it's much better seeing her riled up because I'm flirting with her, than seeing the fear in her eyes.

I'm leaning against the wall outside the restroom, scrolling through my emails when Mila burst through the door next to me, and before I can reach for her, she slams into Nate.

Nate's eyes widen as Mila flinches away from him, and then he says, "Hey, Mila. I'm sorry about what happened."

I take hold of her arm, but she lets out a shriek and yanks away from me.

"Mila," I say so she'll look at me. Her eyes are wild as they fly to me, and the instant she sees me, she rushes forward into my arms. She grips me like I'm her only lifeline, and it fucking breaks my heart.

"You're safe. I've got you," I whisper, hoping the words will calm her a little.

My eyes snap to the students nearby, and they scatter away.

Then Mila tilts her head back, and the look on her face is wild with panic as she begs, "I want to go back to the suite."

I get her out of the building and back to our suite as fast as possible before I turn to her. Framing her face, I lift it so she'll look at me. "What happened?"

Mila shakes her head and pulling free, she pushes by me and walks to her room.

I follow her inside and shut the door behind us, then place her bag down. She stands with her back to me, her arms gripped around her waist.

I move around her and tilt my head to catch her eyes, but she keeps them trained on the floor. Her face is pale, and it only increases my worry.

"Tell me what happened," I say softly.

She lets out a breath of air and shakes her head. "Nothing."

"That wasn't nothing back there, Mila. Did Summer or Rachel do something to upset you? I saw them go in."

Her shoulders slump, and she finally brings her eyes to mine. "I just panicked. It's really nothing." There's a lost look on her face as she adds, "I'm sorry if I embarrassed you."

Inching closer, I wrap my arms around her, and I wait until she gives in and moves her own arms around my waist, then I whisper, "You didn't embarrass me at all, Mila. Remember what we agreed? It's you and me together in this thing. Stop trying to push me away and tell me what made you panic."

Mila presses her face into my chest and mumbles, "I just had a fright when I walked into Nate. Don't worry about it."

My gut tells me she's keeping something from me, but not wanting to push her, I change the subject, "You've only had the bagel today. Want me to order something?"

Mila pulls away and nods. "Yeah, please."

"Anything specific?" My eyes keep drifting over her face, and I'm relieved when I see some color returning to her skin.

She walks to her closet, saying, "Anything will do. I'm just going to shower, then work on my assignments."

"Okay." Thinking she'll come to my room when she's done, I leave to go shower myself. I need to wash this day off of me.

While I grab clean clothes, I quickly call the restaurant and order us each a filet with roasted vegetables.

I walk into the bathroom and open the water before I strip out of my clothes. Stepping under the warm spray, I rest my hands against the tiles and take a moment to just collect myself.

Seeing Mila have a panic attack was brutal, especially when she yanked away from me.

God, this woman has become my entire life in one week.

I now understand what my grandfather tried to tell me.

I'd do anything for Mila. I'd fucking burn this place down if it would help her heal any faster.

Chapter 21

MILA

Sitting on the floor of the shower, the water spills over me as my mind keeps going back to Summer and Rachel's conversation.

Is that what everyone thinks? That I'm faking this just to get Jase's attention?

Pressure builds in my chest, and I wish I could scream.

But instead, I gather myself off the floor and wash my body. I still can't bear to look at myself and keep my eyes trained on the tiles.

I rinse the suds from my skin and shut off the water before drying myself.

A knock has my eyes wildly flying in the direction of the door, and then Jase calls, "Mila, are you okay in there?"

I clear my throat as I rush to put on my clothes. "Yeah, I'll be out in a minute."

I almost forget to pull off the shower cap and just throw it in the basin. Opening the door, I don't look at Jase as he moves aside so I can pass by him.

I walk to the dresser and pick up my brush. I keep my eyes on the bottles scattered over the table while I comb my hair.

"Jase," Fallon calls. "Grandpa and Grandma's here."

"Shit," Jase curses, and instead of going to greet them, he walks to me. "Are you ready for company?"

Knowing I can't hide in my room with Mr. Reyes and Stephanie here, I say, "Sure."

I follow Jase out of my room and stay behind him as I try to steel myself, forcing a smile to my face.

"Jase," I hear Mr. Reyes' voice rumble, "how are you, son?"

"Good, sir." Jase shakes his grandfather's hand and hugs Stephanie, "Hey, Grandma."

I swallow hard as Jase turns to me, holding out his hand. I grab onto it like a drowning person and step closer. "Hi, Mr. Reyes, Stephanie."

Mr. Reyes' eyes settle on my face, and a grim expression darkens his features. "I'm so sorry about what happened, Miss West."

I nod and try to broaden my smile, but I fail miserably and just nod.

Stephanie gives me a sympathetic smile. "How are you holding up?"

"I'm okay."

God, this is so awkward.

"Is there anything we can do to make things easier for you?" Mr. Reyes asks.

I shake my head. "Jase has it all covered, but thank you."

"Good. Good," Mr. Reyes says. Then he turns his attention to Jase. "Take a walk with me, son." His eyes go to Fallon. "You too, my girl."

Jase places his hand on my lower back. "Will you be okay for a couple of minutes?"

I can see he doesn't want to go, so I put on a brave smile for his sake. "I'll be fine. I have things to do."

Jase's eyes meet mine, and I cling to the brave front until they leave the suite. I let out a breath and rush back to my room.

I forgo working on my assignment and climb into bed. I pull the covers up high and shut my eyes tightly.

This day has been too much. My nerves are worn and unable to stop it, the memories worm their way back to the surface. I still remember lying on the cold ground. I feel Justin's hands on me. I see all the glances from the other students. I hear their whispers.

My fragile grip on the control I've managed to regain slips. I press my face hard against the covers and try to focus on my breathing.

But it doesn't help.

I begged him to stop, and he didn't.

What did I do wrong?

Did I encourage him?

Was I too nice?

God, what did I do to deserve this?

I gasp as the thoughts start to flash faster through my mind, and soon I'm sucked back into the nightmare.

JASE

I glance at my grandfather as we slowly walk around the campus. I know what he's doing. He's here to show everyone he's aware of what happened, and he has my back with whatever decisions I make.

"Thank you for coming," I say.

"It's during trying times we need to show a united front, son."

"Hana told me Uncle Lake is working the case against Justin Green?" I ask.

"Yes. Lake will make sure everything goes smoothly," Granddad assures me.

"Good, good," I tease him by using the words that have become synonymous with him.

Granddad shoots me a scowl. "You're never too old for a spanking."

"You love me too much."

A grin spreads over his face. "More than you know."

He changes direction back toward the dorm. "I'll see you soon for our game?"

"Yes, sir. I just need to make sure Mila is okay before I leave her alone."

He nods. "Take good care of Miss West."

"I will."

He turns his attention to Fallon. "I'll see you tomorrow, right?"

"Yes, sir."

Fallon watches old movies with him once a week. That's their thing like chess is ours.

People can say what they want about Warren Reyes, but when it comes to his grandchildren, he always has time for us.

Fallon and I see our grandparents to their car, and we wait for them to drive off before Fallon asks, "How's Mila really doing?"

I shake my head. "Not good. I need to get back to her." Walking into the dorm, I say, "Something happened today. Mila won't tell me what. She was doing well until she went to the restroom. She came running out and bumped into Nate."

"Maybe it was just a panic attack?" Fallon asks as we step into the elevator.

"Could be." I'm not convinced, though.

"How are you holding up?"

My eyes lock with my cousin's, and even though we're close, I smile and lie, "I'm fine. I just worry about Mila."

I'm so far from fine.

Christ, it feels like I'll only be able to breathe again once Mila has healed.

"I'm here if you need to talk," she offers as we walk down the hallway.

Stepping into the suite, I grin. "Thanks."

I spot the food I ordered earlier on the counter as I pass by the kitchen and decide to check on Mila.

I look in my room first, and not seeing her, I go to hers. I knock on the closed door, and when there's no answer, I push it open and frown when it's dark inside.

"Mila?" She doesn't answer, and I switch on the light. Worry bleeds through my body when I find her room empty. I check her bathroom and then rush out of the room.

"What's wrong?" Fallon asks.

"I can't find Mila."

Jade peeks out of her room. "I saw her go into yours earlier. Have you looked there?"

I nod but still go back into mine. "Mila?"

I check my own bathroom, and my heart is pounding in my chest when I step back into my room… and that's when I hear her.

Muted sobs are coming from my walk-in closet.

I switch the light on and have to step inside before I see her cowering in the section where my shirts are hanging.

"Babe?" I crouch by her and place my hand on her knee.

She has one of my shirts in a death grip pressed against her face while her body trembles.

I slide my arms under her knees and behind her back and lift her out of the small space. Sitting down, I lean against the wall and pulling my arm from beneath her knees, I place it behind her head and hold her to me.

Fallon and Jade followed me inside, and they give us a look of concern before they leave, shutting the door behind them.

"I'm here. I've got you," I say until the trembling lessens. Slowly, I pull the shirt out of Mila's hands, and placing my finger beneath her chin, I lift her face. "Tell me what happened."

Her breaths are short little puffs. She shakes her head, then wraps her arms around my neck and buries her face against me. "Today was just harder than I expected."

I hold her for a little while longer, then say, "The food came. Do you think you can eat?"

She nods, and it makes a smile tug at my lips.

"Okay." I help her up before I rise to my feet. Framing her face, I raise it to me, and I wait until she lifts her eyes to mine. I see the fear and panic darkening her green irises. Leaning my forehead against hers, I whisper, "I won't let anyone hurt you again."

MILA

I feel rotten and depressed as I follow Jase out of his room. It feels like I've failed myself today. I so desperately wanted to be strong. I wanted to show Jase and my friends, I wasn't going to let this thing beat me.

But it did beat me.

And the only place I could find any sort of comfort was in Jase's closet. I needed to be surrounded by his scent.

I sit down at the island in the kitchen and watch as Jase plates our food. I don't have any appetite, but not wanting to cause him any more worry than I already have, I know I'll have to force it down.

He grabs two bottles of water then comes to sit next to me.

God, this is awful.

I hate that I fall apart the instant he leaves.

But I just can't handle being alone.

I force a smile to my face. "Thanks for the food."

"Sure."

I cut a carrot in half and shove it into my mouth. It's hard to chew and swallow, and I rinse it down with a sip of water.

I keep my eyes on my plate while I force all the dreadful emotions back into the furthest corner of my mind.

"It was nice of your grandparents to visit," I mention before I spear a piece of cauliflower and bring it to my mouth.

"It was."

I glance at Jase, and when I see he's not eating but just staring at me, I ask, "Aren't you going to eat?"

Jase rests his elbows on the granite surface and links his hands together. "Are you going to tell me what happened?"

I shrug and focus on cutting a piece of the steak. "It was just hard today."

I don't want to tell him about Rachel and Summer, because I know he'll lose his shit. Jase can't get rid of every student who whispers about me. I'll just have to find a way to deal better with everything.

My broken spirit can't bear a moment without Jase, but I still make the words leave my lips, "I think it will be better if you don't walk me from class to class. I don't want to draw more attention than I already have."

My eyes dart up to his. He stares at me for a couple of seconds, then shakes his head. "I don't care what anyone thinks, Mila."

But I do.

I don't want them thinking it was all an act to get Jase's attention.

I can't...

I take a deep breath, and for the first time, the aching stab in my ribs is welcomed. It gives me something to focus on. It's real.

And then something uncanny happens. I remember Mrs. Reyes' words.

'Even if they whisper behind your back, don't let it get to you. It doesn't matter what anyone thinks, Mila. I kept reminding myself only the opinion of my loved ones mattered.'

I set my cutlery down and slowly lift my eyes back to Jase's. Taking another deep breath, I let it out slowly, then ask, "Is this my fault? Was it because I had lunch with him?"

Anger tightens Jase's features, and he turns his body toward me. Placing his hands on the sides of my stool, he turns me until my knees are between his. "Listen carefully to me." My eyes never leave his as he bites the words out,

"None of this is your fault, Mila. None. Of. It. Do you understand?"

I nod and struggle to swallow down the lump in my throat.

"How many times have we flirted?"

I shrug. "Fought. We've fought a lot."

I was hoping to make him smile, but he remains dead serious. "And not once did I force myself on you."

True.

My heart begins to speed up as Jase's words get through to me.

"That fucker had no right to take what you refused to give."

I nod, and a tired smile tugs at my mouth. "Thanks."

"I want to hear you say it."

Frowning, I ask, "What?"

"That it wasn't your fault."

I lower my eyes to Jase's chest. "It wasn't my fault."

I shouldn't have left the club.

"Look at me," Jase says softly, his tone tender.

I clench my teeth together and force my eyes up to his.

There's a gentle expression softening his features. "Now, say it like you believe it."

I should've fought harder.

Jase lifts a hand to my cheek. "When I kissed you, you gave me shit for it, and you love me, Mila. This guy is nothing to you. Do you get it? He's fucking nothing, and he had no right."

He had no right.

I keep my eyes locked on the man I love with all of my heart. "It wasn't my fault."

The sexiest grin spreads over Jase's face, and he leans closer. "There's my girl."

The corner of my mouth lifts as I wrap my arms around his neck and hug him. "Thank you." When I pull back, I glance at our plates. "Let me warm them." When Jase begins to move, I give him a look of warning. "Don't you dare. Let me do this. I need to."

The grin never leaves his face as I place our plates in the microwave.

And it's at this moment I know I'll never be able to stop loving Jase. No man will ever compare to him.

Chapter 22

JASE

Mila manages to eat half of the food, and it makes me fucking happy.

After we're done, I clear our plates before I wrap my arm around her neck and playfully tug her against me. "Wanna torture me with a movie?"

"I'll never say no to that," she teases.

Walking into my room, I shut the door and get comfortable on the bed while Mila scrolls through the selection.

She picks 'Man Of Steel', and it has my eyebrow shooting up. "You seriously have a thing for Clark Kent?"

Mila wags her eyebrows as she comes to lie next to me. "He's hot and has abs for days. Plus, he's badass."

I drop my voice low as I murmur, "Sounds like you're describing me."

Mila lets out a burst of laughter. "Yeah, just add arrogant."

"You love my arrogant ass," I joke, and then realize my mistake too late. "Shit, sorry, I…"

"It's okay, Jase." Mila glances at the TV, and when she brings her eyes back to mine, I see the love in her eyes, and it makes my heart beat faster. "It's the one thing I'm not ashamed of. You're an incredible man. I don't regret loving you. Not at all."

It's on the tip of my tongue to tell her how I feel, but not wanting her to think I'm just saying it for the sake of repeating the words, I pull her closer to me, and I press a soft kiss to her mouth. "You make me want to be incredible."

Mila gets comfortable next to me and rests her head on my chest. It's become our position in bed.

Moving my left hand to her back, I draw lazy patterns over the length of it as we watch 'Man of Steel', aka me.

I grin at myself.

Yeah, I'll be her superman.

⸻

Considering what happened yesterday, we had a good night.

Mila doesn't argue when I walk with her out of the dorm, and I take it as a win. Fallon and Jade walk with us, and when we reach their class, Fallon says, "We'll be with Mila all day, Jase. You should get back to your own lectures."

"Yes," Mila instantly agrees. "I'll be fine." She even grins at me. "Besides, Jade can kick ass better than you."

My eyes dart to Jade's, and it has her nodding. "I'll take good care of her."

Fuck. This is hard.

Taking hold of Mila's hand, I pull her to the side and wrap my arms around her. "Call me the second anyone gives you shit."

She nods against my chest.

Over her head, I lock eyes with Fallon. "You let me know the instant anything happens."

"I will," my cousin promises.

I press my lips to Mila's hair and take a deep breath of her.

Fuck. Fuck. Fuck.

She begins to pull back, but I tighten my hold on her. "Just a second longer." Mila melts back against me, and I soak in the feel of her in my arms.

It feels like I'm abandoning her.

Christ.

I take a deep breath, filling my lungs with her scent before I pull back.

Mila gives me a warm smile and standing on her tiptoes, she presses a kiss to my cheek. "I'll be fine. Don't worry."

I clench my teeth as I watch her walk into the class with Fallon and Jade.

For a second, I close my eyes and thrust a hand through my hair in frustration as I turn around to walk away. I only manage two steps before I spin around and jog into the class.

Just like yesterday, Mila looks up at me with surprise on her face. Leaning down, I slip my hands over her cheeks and press my mouth to hers.

But unlike yesterday, it's not quick. I linger as I drink in the feel of her.

I fucking love you, Mila.

Letting go of her, I walk out, and I keep going until I walk into Hunter's room.

My best friend's eyes land on me, and it's all it takes for me to spill my guts, "I love her."

"I know," he murmurs as he closes the distance between us. He places his hand on my shoulder. "Did you tell Mila?"

I shake my head. "Not yet. I don't want her thinking I'm just saying the words because of what happened." Letting out a sigh, I walk to his bed and drop down on it. "I was so close to telling her last night."

Hunter sits down next to me, and the silence stretches around us.

"It's hard to leave her alone," I whisper. "I know Jade and Fallon are with her, but goddamn, it's fucking hard."

"They'll take good care of her," Hunter reminds me.

"I know."

It doesn't ease the pressure in my chest. Everything inside of me is screaming to run back to her.

"Fuck, Hunter, I just want to hold her and never let go."

Hunter places his arm around my shoulders. "You know it's not your fault, right?"

I let out an empty burst of laughter.

Ironic, isn't it? It's the same conversation I had with Mila.

But I should've protected her.

"It's my fault she left the club," I mutter, the pang of regret bitter on my tongue. I suck in a deep breath of air as

256

my guilt turns into a fist, taking blows at my heart. "I heard her scream twice before I got to her." I close my eyes against the painful memory. "I'll never forget the sound." I shake my head, trying to suppress the memory of Mila's hopelessly hollow wail.

"I'm sorry," Hunter says as he pulls me into a hug. "I'm so fucking sorry." After a little while, Hunter continues, "Mila's fierce. She's a fighter. She'll come back from this."

I nod. "I know she will."

"And so will you."

I let out a burst of air as I pull away from him. "Yeah, we'll find our way back."

And then, I'll love her like she's never been loved before.

The thought makes me square my shoulders, and getting up, I say, "We should get our assess to class."

Hunter rises to his feet, then exclaims, "Hold up." He slaps his hand over his heart. "Was that your way of telling me I've just been downgraded to second place in your life?"

"Shut up." I burst out laughing. "You downgraded me first, ass."

"Ahh." Hunter feigns hurt. "The blow."

"Fuck off," I grumble as I walk out of his room.

"Well," he sighs, "I'll just have to look on the bright side. At least I won't have you farting in my bed anymore."

"Yeah? You should've bottled that shit. I still think people would pay millions for a whiff of Eau de Jase."

MILA

Breathe, Mila. Just breathe.

"Finally, we get to eat," Jade croons as we walk into the restaurant.

"Yeah, I'm starving," I lie. I'll have to stomach the food somehow.

I grab a chair that will have my back to the other tables, and it gives me a view of the expansive bay windows overlooking the stretch of lawn between the dorms and the lecture halls.

My gaze darts over the students as they cross the lawn. Most have their eyes trained on their phones. Some laugh.

It reminds me to smile.

My lips lift automatically. It's one thing that's becoming easier to fake.

"What are you having?" Jade asks.

"A salad," I reply without looking at the menu. At least it will be a light meal.

My eyes land on Jessica and her friends as they walk toward the restaurant. Jessica's gaze meets mine, and a hateful look crosses her features as she slowly shakes her head at me as if she can't believe my audacity.

My eyes narrow on her until she's out of view.

Bitch.

Kao and Noah join us at the table, and not having spoken to them much, I widen my smile. "Hey, how are you?"

"I'm great," Kao answers from where he's sitting next to Fallon. His eyes dart to her before he glances at me again. "How are you holding up?"

"Much better."

Another lie.

A waiter comes to take our order, and after he leaves, Noah says, "You look much better."

"Thanks." I grin at my cousin.

"The Halloween Ball is coming up," Fallon mentions. "Any volunteers to help with the decorations?"

"Hell no," Jade instantly protests. "I saw how you suffered with the welcome ball. There's no way I'm submitting myself to that kind of torture."

Fallon turns her gaze to me, and I point to Jade. "What she said."

"Hey, Mila," Jessica suddenly pops up next to me. "I just wanted to tell you how absolutely horrified I was to hear what happened to you. I hope you feel better soon."

I struggle not to glare at her and fail miserably. "That's so sweet of you."

Bless your fucking heart, bitch.

For a moment, Jessica smirks before she turns her attention to Kao and Noah. "Hey guys, looking good as always."

Noah's eyes are sharp on Jessica, where Kao doesn't even bother to look up.

"Anyway," she drags the words out. "Fallon, I'll see you at the decorating committee meeting, right?"

Before Fallon can answer, Jade leans forward and says, "If you're done sucking up and ruining my lunch, you're welcome to leave. I'd like to salvage what I can of my remaining appetite."

The fake smile drops from Jessica's face, and she sucks in a deep breath. "Jade, it's always such a pleasure."

"Someone hold me back," Jade growls, and I quickly reach over to her and place my hand on her arm.

It only hits me a second later what I just did, and my eyes slowly turn to where I'm touching Jade. My lips part and an overwhelming sense of relief floods me.

I just gained something precious back.

Another simple touch.

My eyes dart to Jade's, and I see her watching me with a hawk eye.

A wide smile spreads over my face, and I give her arm a squeeze before I pull back.

I don't even notice Jessica leaving, and I couldn't care less about her as my eyes scan over my friends. They all saw the touch and have equally huge smiles on their faces.

Small wins, Mila. Each one counts.

Chapter 23

JASE

It's been four days since I've returned to classes, and Mila seems to be getting better every day.

She's smiling more, and her appetite is back. Every little step she takes back to being her old self is a win and makes pride grow in my chest.

I'm holding off for a couple of days before I start my weekly visits to my grandfather again.

With it being Friday, we'd usually hit the club, but that's the last place we'll be going back to any time soon. Instead, we decided to spend a quiet night at home and play Pictionary.

Hana is setting up the drawing board while Noah and Kao grab us snacks and drinks.

We've paired up in teams. Grinning at Mila, I ask, "How good are your drawing skills?"

She shakes her head. "I suck. Big time."

A chuckle escapes me as I wrap an arm around her neck, and pulling her against me, I plant a kiss to her temple. "We'll kick ass."

When everyone is ready, Fallon and Kao start. I turn the timer over, and Fallon begins to make a circle.

"Ball?" Kao guesses.

Fallon shakes her head and continues to draw various circles with bites taken from them.

"Dude, come on," I taunt Kao.

"Moon!" he yells like he's guessed the cure for cancer.

Fallon does a happy dance then hands the marker to Jade.

When it's finally Mila's turn, she stares at the board for a second, and then my eyes widen as she draws what looks like a cock shooting its load.

"Seriously?" I ask. I glance at the Pictionary box. "Is this the dirty version because all I can see is a cock shooting its load."

"What?" Mila shrieks. "Nooooo!"

She keeps adding more dots above the head.

I let out a chuckle. "Still just seeing an orgasm."

"Time!" Hana yells.

Mila looks at her drawing then gives me an incredulous look. "It's fireworks."

I let out a bark of laughter. "Same thing, babe."

Shaking her head with a wide smile on her face, she sits down next to me, mumbling, "You and your one-track mind."

Leaning closer to her, I whisper, "Yeah, and it keeps leading to you."

Mila's eyes snap to mine as I pull back, and I see the look of confusion on her face as she tries to figure out the meaning behind my words.

I've been getting that look a lot from her this week, like she's trying to put a puzzle together, but she's missing a piece.

Soon, babe. Soon.

The attraction has come back, a million times more potent than before the attack. Every time I touch her, I have to concentrate on keeping my grip soft. When I kiss her, it takes all my willpower to not give in to my need to devour her.

Light and sweet are killing me, but I won't give until Mila's ready.

MILA

It feels like I'm losing my grip on reality.

With everyone's eyes on me, it has a knot tightening in my chest, every day a little more.

It's getting easier to pretend, though, and it's working because my friends have returned to their old routines. Even Jase is back to his old self.

Kind of.

Instead of my forehead, he now kisses me on the mouth, and I don't know what to make of it. I don't want to read too much into it, but every kiss has me wondering if he's doing it out of pity.

I don't want Jase to pity me.

And the rest of Trinity? They keep staring and whispering. It's been a week since I've returned, and they still haven't gotten something new to gossip about.

It's exhausting.

And then there's Jessica with her glares and know-it-all smile on her stupid face.

I let out a sigh where I'm sitting next to Jase as we drive to CRC Holdings' head office to see Mr. Cutler, Hana's father. He's working on the case against Justin and needs to interview me.

The thought makes the knot tighten more.

Mom and Dad will be there. During their daily calls to check on me, I could hear their worry, and I've avoided seeing them.

Hopefully, I'll be able to fool them today into believing I'm fully recovered.

Jase brings his car to a stop in a VIP parking bay. I climb out and walk around the vehicle to him. He takes my hand, and I drink in the feel of his strong fingers gripping mine.

God, I'm going to miss this.

His voice has a way of getting through to me like no other. It has the power to chase the fear away.

Two weeks ago, I was adamant about putting distance between us, and now he's everything to me.

It will be so hard when I have to let him go because he'll probably return to his playboy ways soon.

We take the elevator up to the top floor. When the doors slide open, a receptionist greets us from behind her desk, "Mr. Reyes, Miss West, Mr. Cutler is waiting in the main boardroom for you."

Jase nods in her direction. He leads me down a stylish corridor and into a room with a large oval mahogany desk with chairs situated around it.

My dad instantly gets up from where he was sitting next to Mr. Cutler and quickly walks over to me. "My beautiful girl," he smiles lovingly as he draws me into a hug.

My heart kicks up a little faster, but with all the practice I've had, I don't let anyone pick up on my anxiety as I hug my father back.

"I missed you," I mumble against his shoulder.

When he pulls away and holds me at shoulder length so he can look me over, I smile a little wider.

I see the worry fade from his eyes, and knowing I've convinced one parent, I turn to my mom and hug her tightly.

My stomach shrinks, but I force myself to be as normal as possible. "Hey, mamma," I whisper.

She pulls back a little, and placing her hand on my left cheek, she presses a kiss to my right. "How do you feel?"

"I'm great," I lie. "I'm all caught up with school work."

Mom's eyes dart to Jase, and then he confirms, "Mila's much better."

I go to say hello to Mr. Cutler while Jase greets my parents, and then we each take a seat. I end up sitting between Mom and Jase while Dad and Mr. Cutler sit across from us.

Mr. Culter has a camera situated on the desk, and gesturing toward it, he asks, "Are you okay with us recording this meeting, Mila?"

"Yes, Sir." I shift in my chair while Mr. Cutler presses record.

"Can you state your full name to the camera, please?"

"Mila West." My tongue darts out, and I wet my dry lips.

Mr. Cutler gives me a comforting smile. He has the same calm nature as Hana, and it sets me a little at ease.

"In your own words, can you tell us what happened the night of September twenty-fifth?"

Sucking in a deep breath, I square my shoulders and grip my hands together under the table as I do my best to detach myself from my memories. I clear my throat before I robotically repeat what happened.

When I'm done, I suck in a slow breath.

Mr. Cutler glances at the papers in front of me and asks, "Did you consume any alcohol on the night in question?"

Shit.

My eyes dart to my dad before I nod. "I had one drink. I wasn't aware it had alcohol in it until I drank it." Feeling I need to explain more, I add, "It was an acquaintance's drink."

"Did you take any form of drug substance?"

I shake my head, and when Mr. Cutler's eyes lift to mine, I say, "No, I didn't."

The questions keep coming, and it's becoming increasingly harder to distance myself from the nightmare.

I reach for a bottle of water and swallow some down while I will my heart to remain strong.

I just need to get through today without anyone picking up on the fact that it's all an act.

You can do this, Mila.

You can do it for Jase and your family.

Hold out.

JASE

Mila looks calm as she answers one question after the other.

My eyes go to Mrs. West, and I see the relief written all over her face. Mr. West has a constant loving smile on his face where he sits across from us, his eyes not leaving Mila for a second.

Uncle Lake glances at me, and then he gives me a look that has me frowning. It's as if he's trying to convey something to me.

"Let's take a break," Uncle Lake says. He locks eyes with me before he excuses himself. "I'll be right back."

I push my chair away from the table and get up. "I'll be back in five minutes."

Mila nods and relaxes in her chair.

Once I step out of the boardroom, I follow Uncle Lake down the hallway until we're out of hearing distance.

"What's up?" I ask as he turns to face me.

"I've already spoken to the West's about it. The Greens and their attorney will be here soon. Justin has requested to speak with Mila. He wants to apologize."

"Fuck, no," I snap, then I realize I just cursed in front of my uncle. "Sorry, Uncle Lake, but no. There's no way I'm letting him near her."

Uncle Lake grips my shoulder. "Jase, it's not up to you. Logan and Mia are talking to Mila right now. It's Mila's choice to make."

"Is that why you called me out of the office?" I snap angrily.

I spin around and start to stalk back to the boardroom, but Uncle Lake darts around me, and pressing a hand to my chest, he forces me to stop. "It's Mila's decision, Jase. You need to calm down. This is not about how you feel." He lets out a deep breath. "And honestly, I think it would do her good. Not every victim gets an apology. It might help her find closure."

I glare at my uncle, not one bit happy.

Fuck.

But he's right. It is Mila's decision to make.

Walking toward the boardroom, I suck in a deep breath of air, and I don't know what I'm going to do if Mila agrees to see that fucker.

Entering the office space, my eyes immediately lock on Mila. She still looks calm, and it makes me wonder whether her parents spoke with her about Justin.

Sitting down, I reach for Mila's hands where they're resting on her lap, and I give them a squeeze.

Uncle Lake sits down, and looking at Mila, he says, "The Green's will be here in fifteen minutes. Have you decided whether you'll meet with them, Mila?"

"No, I haven't." She pulls her hands free from beneath mine and reaches for her bottled water.

She's actually thinking about it?

Leaning forward, I tilt my head to her so I can catch her eyes, and once she looks at me, I say, "You don't have to."

271

"I know." She gives me a reassuring smile. "But I want to put this ordeal behind me. Whether I face him in court or here, I'll have to at some point."

Fuck. This isn't right.

I shake my head and slump back in my chair.

Mila shifts in her chair, and lifting her chin higher, she looks like a powerful goddess as she says, "I'll meet with Justin."

And for the first time, I feel like the weak one.

Chapter 24

MILA

My heart has gone from thundering in my chest to nothing more than a whisper as my eyes lock onto Justin.

And I'm back, lying broken on the cold ground.

I draw in a deep breath of air and clench my teeth as I fight for control over my frail nerves.

Jase's hand covers mine, and he grips them tightly.

You're safe, Mila. Jase and your parents are here.

Justin can't hurt you again.

The Green's and their attorney take a seat, then the Attorney speaks, "I'm Adam Caruso, and I'm representing Mr. Justin Green." He rests his hands on the table, and looking at me, he offers, "In the light of what happened, we have a settlement we'd like to propose to you, Miss West."

Justin sits forward and places his hand on Mr. Caruso's arm, and my eyes get stuck on it.

I feel his fingers squeeze my breast. I feel them slip over the sensitive flesh between my legs.

And a blessed numbness cloaks me.

Feeling dead inside, I lift my eyes to Justin as he says, "Can I please have a moment before you start discussing business?"

Business? That's what my pain has been reduced to?

Everyone turns their eyes to me.

Breathe, Mila. Just breathe.

Not removing my gaze from Justin, I reply, "You have one minute."

"Thank you," Justin says. "I want to apologize to you, Mila."

For almost raping me? Do you really think there are any words on this planet that will make up for that?

"I know nothing I say will make it better. What I did to you was nothing short of vile."

Justin clears his throat, and it looks like he's struggling to keep his composure, and it has a frown forming on my forehead.

"I never imagined my biggest mistake would be your greatest trauma. I want you to know I'm receiving counseling. To be honest, I tried to deny any memories of attacking you the day after it happened. I couldn't face the horrendous fact that I hurt you. I've done something immensely wrong, and I'll forever live with the guilt."

274

And I'll live with the shame. The looks. The whispers.

Jase pries my trembling hands apart and links his fingers with my right hand. His grip is firm, and I let myself draw strength from him.

Justin takes a moment, and then a tear slips down his cheek, and his voice is hoarse as he continues, "I'm not asking for your forgiveness. I want you to know how much I regret my actions of that night. I'm willing to accept whatever punishment is dealt to me. I'll continue receiving counseling."

Justin's eyes lock with mine. "You were nothing but kind to me. You made it clear you weren't interested in a relationship with me. I forced myself on you and repeatedly chose to ignore you when you told me to stop. I won't blame being drunk that night. I'm taking full responsibility for my actions."

Silence follows Justin's words.

My mouth is dry, but I can't bring myself to reach for the water.

Instead, I manage to force one word over my lips, "Why?"

Justin shakes his head. "Because I wanted you, and I made myself believe you were interested in me, as well."

The need to get up and walk out is overwhelming, but I know it will only prolong the inevitable, so I stay.

I sit and face the man who reduced me to nothing.

I hear his words, and instead of them making me feel better, they rip the scabs off and pour salt over the wounds.

A part of me knows I should forgive Justin, not just for him, but for my own peace.

But I can't. Not yet.

JASE

I can't believe Mila accepted the settlement. Probation? Counseling? Speaking at colleges around the country in a campaign to stop violence against women?

That's it?

For all the hell Mila had to endure, I feel the fucker should die in prison.

But I don't have a say in the matter.

I'm struggling to contain my rage as I drive us back to Trinity.

Mila just stares out of the window, and I only manage to keep it in until I park the car.

Slumping back against the seat, I grumble, "He deserved so much worse. Why did you accept the settlement?"

Mila unfastens her seatbelt, and opening the door, she says, "I did it for myself, Jase. It's my way of getting closure."

We climb out of the car, and I wait until we're in the elevator before asking, "And? Did you get closure?"

Mila nods and looks up at me with a smile. "Yeah, I feel like I can move forward now and leave the whole ordeal in the past."

My eyes scan over her face, and even though she's smiling, I can't see any signs that she's not dealing. Something still bothers me.

Maybe it's because I feel it's too quick?

As we step into the hallway, Mila drops a bomb on me, "I should start sleeping in my own room."

I start shaking my head before I can even form the words. "No, there I'm putting my foot down."

"But – "

"No, Mila." Not wanting her to think it's because I don't think she's ready, I say, "I'm not ready yet. Just give me some more time."

We stop outside the front door, and Mila takes hold of my hand. "Jase, I have to move back to my room at some point."

"Yeah," I grumble as I push the door open and walking to my room, I say, "That point is not happening today."

Mila follows me inside and shuts the door behind her.

I go to my walk-in closet and shrug out of the suit jacket, then yank the tie free from around my neck. Unbuttoning my shirt, I glance at Mila.

"We can talk about it again a week from now. Deal?"

She shrugs, and her eyes drop to my chest as I pull the shirt off, then she whispers, "Yeah, I suppose."

I did some reading and learned, sometimes sexual assault survivors struggle with intimacy. Mila's been pretty comfortable with me and needing to know if she's okay with seeing me naked, my hands drop to my belt, and loosening it, I pull it free from the loops.

A grin begins to tug at the corner of my mouth when her lips part, and she keeps staring at me. Her lashes lower, and then she bites her bottom lip and tilts her head as if she's trying to get a better look.

Taking it a step further, I unbutton the pants, and I'm an inch away from giving Mila a full show when I drop my voice low, "Enjoying the view, babe?"

"Huh?" Her eyes snap back up, and when she sees the smirk on my face, she gets all flustered.

Mila reverses into the door and fumbles for the handle. "Ahh... sorry." And then she darts out and slams the door shut behind her.

I'm not.

There was definitely desire on her face, and I'm reveling in it because it shows she's comfortable with me, not just as a friend, but as a man.

I quickly step out of the pants and grab a pair of sweatpants, pulling them on. I yank a t-shirt out of the closet and shrug it on as I walk to Mila's room.

I only knock once then let myself in. I'm greeted with a shriek, and then Mila ducks into her closet. "Jase! I'm half-naked. Get out."

I shut the door and lock it so no one will disturb us, and with my heart in my throat, I walk to the closet.

Mila's eyes grow huge at the sight of me, and she holds her blouse to her chest as if it will save her from a threat to her life.

I almost give in to her request but then push through. "Don't be shy around me. The bathing suits you wear cover less."

She gives me a what-the-fuck look.

I take a step closer to her, and it has her sputtering. "Jase… ah…" and then she just shakes her head and lowers her eyes to the plush carpet.

I close the distance between us, and placing my finger under Mila's chin, I lift her face to me. "Why do you want me to leave?"

"Ah…" She cowers back from me, and it makes my eyes sharpen on her. "I don't want you seeing me half-naked."

"Why?"

She swallows hard. "Because I'm not comfortable."

"With what?" I keep pushing her.

If she can get through this, I'll believe she's healed.

Her jaw clenches, and then she grinds out, "I don't want you seeing me."

Tilting my head, I lift her chin again and catch her eyes. "Why?"

"Jase," she groans, and it sounds desperate.

Not giving in, I whisper, "Tell me why, and I'll leave."

Mila shakes her head, and tears begin to shine in her eyes.

I move a little closer, and it makes her tighten her grip on the fabric in her hands.

Then she shoves me back with one hand and shouts, "I can't even look at myself." She gasps for air, and anger tightens her features. "There, I said it. Are you happy now?"

Not at all.

My eyes hold her angry gaze. "You've been pretending to be okay all along, haven't you?"

"I am fine!" she snaps, and pushing by me, she rushes to the bathroom.

My gut kept telling me she wasn't dealing, and it was right. Mila's been putting on an act all along.

I go to sit on her bed, and a couple of minutes later, the door swings open. She's put on the blouse again.

Her gaze flits around the room, and she looks uneasy.

Getting up, I close the distance between us and wrap her up against my chest, and it's all it takes for her to give in.

Her hands go to my back, and she grips hold of my shirt as her body begins to jerk. She smothers her sobs against my chest.

Closing my eyes, I press kisses to her hair and whisper, "Why did you keep it all in?" Another kiss to her cheek. "Why did you push yourself so hard?"

"I... just... wanted everyone... to be normal... around me," she cries, and it fucking breaks my heart.

"Even me?"

She nods, and a soft sob escapes her, then she whispers, "Especially you."

I bring my hands to her face and pull her a little back to see her eyes. "Mila, don't pretend around me. I know you're fucking fierce and strong. You don't have to prove that to me."

She pulls her face free and slams back into my chest. "I don't want you to pity me."

"Oh, babe," I let out on a breath. I lower my mouth to her ear and whisper, "That will never happen."

Chapter 25

MILA

No. No. No. No.

What have I done?

I fought so hard to put on the brave act, and now it's all for nothing.

Shame burns through me, and in its wake, it leaves only the ashes of who I once was. The girl I've been pretending to be.

I'm pathetic.

It's been two weeks already, and I even got an apology from Justin, but for some sick reason, I can't let go of the nightmare.

Jase lets go of me, and I use the back of my hand to wipe the tears from my face. "Put on something comfortable, then we'll talk. I'm waiting right outside your door."

I watch him leave, hating myself even more for causing him more worry.

Drained and out of strength to fight, I walk to my closet and strip out of the blouse and skirt I wore for the interview. I pull on a pair of comfy sweatpants and a t-shirt and then suck in a deep breath. The ache in my chest is once again welcomed as I walk out of my room to face Jase.

He doesn't say anything until we're sitting on his bed. With my legs crossed, I wrap one hand around my waist and use the other to draw random patterns on the covers.

"Why can't you look at yourself?" Jase asks.

I squeeze my eyes shut as another wave of shame hits. After a couple of seconds, I whisper, "I don't want to see the scar and bruises."

Jase reaches for me, and he pulls me onto his lap. He leans back against the headboard and presses a kiss to my temple, then asks, "But the bruising will fade on your ribs."

I shake my head and press my face into his neck. "The bite mark."

Jase is quiet for a moment, and it makes my whole body tense. I startle when he turns me to face him, and keeping my eyes on his chest, I straddle him.

"Look at me." His voice is soft as his hands settle on my sides.

I lift my eyes to his, and when I see the caring expression on his face, it makes the lump return to my throat.

"You trust me, right?" he asks.

"Yeah," I breathe.

He leans closer, and then his breath skims over my jaw and flutters on my ear. "Remember when we were dancing?"

How can I forget?

I nod and lift my hands to his chest. Nerves tighten my stomach when his mouth drifts over my skin, and then he pauses an inch away from mine, "Remember how it felt when I touched you?"

My hands fist his shirt. "Yes."

Jase's hand lifts to my face, and his thumb brushes over my bottom lip.

God.

When he does it again, my lips part, and my tongue darts out.

"Still fucking kills me, babe." His voice is low and hoarse, and then his mouth is on mine.

'Wait,' my mind groans.

'No,' my heart growls. 'I need this. I want this.'

I know I will regret it later, but right now, I don't care.

My hands move to the back of Jase's neck, and my fingers get lost in his hair as I open my mouth, begging him to come inside. The moment his tongue touches mine, my heart rockets into the sky and explodes like the fourth of July. Tingles rush over my skin, waking parts of me I never knew existed.

And then nothing else exists.

Only Jase.

A moan drifts up my throat from how extraordinarily intense it feels kissing him.

His hand slips behind my neck, and his other moves to my back, and then he pulls me flush with his chest. His tongue strokes mine, and it sweeps me away until it feels like I'm flying and free-falling all at once.

My breaths speed up, and I can't get enough of Jase.

But then he slows the kiss down, and leaving my mouth wanting more, he feathers kisses down my neck.

"I'm addicted to the taste of you," Jase murmurs against my racing pulse, and it makes goosebumps explode over my body.

He moves his hands back to my sides, and when he grips hold of the shirt, I pull back and grab hold of his wrists.

His eyes find mine. "Trust me, Mila."

God, this is hard. I don't want him seeing the bite mark. Shame douses the fire Jase has ignited in me.

Jase presses a soft kiss to my lips and pulling back, his gaze locks with mine again, and I know he's waiting for permission.

"I can't," I whisper. "I don't want you looking at me like I'm... damaged."

His eyes fill with a look I haven't seen before, and it makes them turn to liquid gold. "That will never happen, Mila. Trust me."

Trust Jase.

I nod, and when he starts to lift the fabric, I shut my eyes, not wanting to see his reaction.

Jase stops, and his voice is soft. "Look at me, babe."

I suck in a couple of breaths and pry them open.

Jase keeps his gaze on mine as he lifts the shirt over my head.

Apprehension fills me as I watch his eyes lower to my breasts. But then something happens, I never in a million years expected. Jase places his hand on my ribs, and his thumb brushes against the swell of my breast.

His eyes come back to mine, and then he growls, "You're so fucking beautiful, Mila."

My heart is nothing but a frantic flutter in my chest as he leans in and presses a kiss to my breast.

And then he lifts his head. "Look at me, touching you."

His thumb brushes over my nipple, and I'm torn between how good it feels and doing what Jase asked of me.

I lower my eyes to his neck, then his chest, then his arm. I slowly follow the map of veins on his golden-tanned skin until his hand comes into view.

And then Jase's thumb traces the outline of the light mark.

In my mind, it looked so different. So stark.

But it's already fading.

My eyes dart back to Jase's face, and when I see him smiling, I throw caution to the wind and grabbing hold of his face, I lift myself a little higher and slam my mouth against his.

And then I kiss him with every ounce of love I feel for him.

Loving Jase is the best thing I've ever done.

JASE

I manage to stay in control. Then Mila looks at me with so much relief right before she kisses the ever-loving shit out of me.

And all my good intentions crumble like a house of cards.

My hands drop to her waist, and lifting her off me, I push her back onto the bed until she's lying beneath me. The kiss grows desperate and hot, and it burns me up until I feel feverish with want for her.

I finally get to express my love for Mila, and it's wild and all-consuming. My hand finds the snap of her bra, and I unhook it. Pulling the lace from her body, I throw it to the side.

For a second, I break the kiss, and gripping the fabric at the back of my neck, I yank my shirt off and drop it next to us. I'm careful as I lower myself to Mila so I won't put pressure on her ribs, and I let out a moan when I feel her soft skin against my chest.

My cock turns to steel in a matter of seconds, and for the first time, I pull away from a girl.

Not just a girl.

I'm breathless as I say, "We have to stop. I don't want to push you."

Mila looks up at me with her eyes dark with lust, her lips parted as breaths rush over them, and it's fucking erotic.

God, now is not the time to test my self-control.

"You're not pushing me," she says. Her hands tighten their grip on the back of my neck. "I want this."

And then my fucking traitorous eyes drop to her breasts.

Christ.

My cock swells impossibly hard, and it doesn't help that my gaze drinks in every inch of her skin over her taut stomach.

Mila's fucking breathtaking.

When I bring my eyes back to her face, and I see the need etched into her gorgeous features, the little restraint I've managed to regain vanishes into thin air.

My body melts back against Mila, and my mouth greedily finds hers. I drown in the taste of her as my hand covers her breast. Feeling her nipple against my palm sends ripples of pleasure racing down my spine.

Our tongues battle for control, and then a moan drifts into me from Mila.

Holy. Fucking. Shit.

Her hands move down the length of my back, and her touch is electric, sending my heartbeat into overdrive.

When her fingers dig into my ass, more pleasure shudders through me. My hand glides down her body, her skin so fucking soft, I can't get enough of touching her.

I pause at the band of her sweatpants, but then Mila breathes into me, "Don't stop." And it's the only permission I need.

My hand slips under the fabric, and I palm her lace-covered pussy.

And I swear fireworks explode behind my eyes. Everything is brighter. Color so fucking vibrant fills every part of my life.

Separating our mouths, my eyes lock with Mila's, and the words are on the tip of my tongue, but it doesn't feel right saying them in the heat of the moment.

I shift the lace aside, and when my fingers brush over her clit, Mila's lashes lower over her eyes, and she gasps for air. I'm so fucking focused on her reaction to my touch as I push a finger inside her the whole fucking world could go to hell, and I wouldn't notice.

MILA

Oh, my God.

There are no words to describe the sensations Jase is making me feel.

Being with him, in this intimate moment, is overwhelming, addictive... it's everything and so much more.

I get to explore every muscle. Every hard dip and swell of his body.

Jase moves my panties to the side, and when his fingers brush over my flesh, my stomach free-falls into nirvana. Slowly, he pushes a finger inside me, and the moment is so intense, I struggle to breathe. I'm left gasping as Jase brings me to a state of ecstasy I never knew existed.

I've made myself orgasm before, but it's nothing compared to the sensations I'm experiencing right now, and I haven't even reached my release yet.

"Fuck, Mila," Jase breathes. His mouth claims mine while his fingers work their magic between my legs.

I feel a tightening in my abdomen, and it's the only warning I get before my body shudders beneath him. He instantly breaks the kiss, and his eyes are on fire as he watches me orgasm.

It's so freaking powerful, I can't even breathe.

A look similar to awe settles on Jase's face, and he's never looked hotter.

Vehement. It's the only word I can think of to describe Jase Reyes, and it doesn't do him justice.

When I come down from the orgasm, Jase fixes my panties before pulling his hand out of my sweatpants. My eyes widen as I watch him suck my release off his finger.

My ovaries can't take more explosion worthy moments.

They need to recover first.

Jase shifts himself until he's lying next to me and grins proudly. "Well, that was… wow." He wraps his arm around my waist and pulls me against him.

My eyes dart to his face. "What about you?" I ask, even though the only experience I have is from the sex scenes I've seen on TV.

Thank God for Game Of Thrones sex scenes.

"What about me?" he asks, the sexy grin never leaving his face.

I've never been one to hold back, and even though it's embarrassing, I say, "I want you to orgasm as well."

His grin stretches wider. "Watching you come was enough to get me off."

My jaw drops open. "For real?"

He nudges his nose against my cheek and then presses a lazy kiss to my lips. "Yeah. You were fucking hot."

A weird sensation of pride fills my chest, and I'm left smiling like an idiot.

Chapter 26

MILA

Even though it's hard keeping eye contact with Jase because I feel a little self-conscious after the intimate moment we shared this afternoon, I find myself smiling more.

We haven't spoken about what happened between us, and if it were up to me, we never will. But still, Jase gave me something back I thought I'd lost forever. A sense of worth. My inner beauty that was deformed in my own mind.

For once, we're sitting in the living room, watching *The Hangover* with Kao and Noah. I'm hardly paying any attention to the comedy because I'm too conscious of Jase.

Damn, just having him breathing next to me is enough to distract me from anything.

Jase's phone starts to ring, and he gets up and disappears down the hallway.

My eyes go back to the television, and I let out a chuckle when something funny happens.

Jase comes back, and leaning down, he says, "I'm going out for an hour or two. Will you be okay?"

"Sure." I nod. I almost ask him where he's going at seven on a Saturday night, but not wanting to sound possessive and needy, I bite the question back.

Jase rushes out of the suite, and it catches Kao's attention. "Where's Jase going?"

I shrug as I get up, figuring I'll go get a cappuccino from the restaurant and then come back and paint my nails. The black I have on looks horribly chipped off.

I go to my room and slip on a pair of shoes. Grabbing my wallet and keycard, I head to the front door.

I hear Noah chuckle, "Probably to get laid."

Kao lets out a burst of laughter. "Nothing like a booty call."

I shake my head as I leave the suite.

Jase wouldn't do that. Not after what we shared today.

With it being a Saturday, the campus isn't too crowded with most students out for the night. Walking into the restaurant, I head over to the barista and place my order.

I have to wait a couple of minutes and go to take a seat at an empty table.

Hearing a familiar laugh, my eyes go to the entrance as Summer and Rachel walk inside.

At least Jessica isn't with them.

The two girls go to the counter to place their order, and I hear Rachel ask, "Where's Jessica?"

Summer chuckles. "She just left for a date. She was so excited, and if you ask me, it's about time they got together again."

"Yeah, the past two weeks have been stressful for her."

"Mila," the barista calls for me. I get up and not looking at the girls, I take my order and leave.

'Jase wouldn't do that,' my heart whispers.

'Are you sure?' my mind questions.

I hurry back to the suite, and rushing into my room, I shut the door and lock it before I place the beverage, my wallet, and keycard on my dresser.

Only then do I allow myself to think about what I overheard.

He wouldn't.

My mind begins to torture me with memories of Jase and his playboy ways. All the times I've seen him with other girls and whenever he hooked up with a girl at the club.

And it spirals out of control as my breaths speed up.

An awful thought shudders through me.

Does he think he fixed me this afternoon, and now we can go back to the way things were?

You were the one pretending everything was fine, remember?

But…

This is what you wanted, Mila. You wanted Jase to go on with his life.

Yeah, but after today I didn't expect it would be without me.

He never said he wanted to be with you.

I close my eyes against the reality because it hurts too much. The disappointment and rejection remind me of what happened the night of the attack.

Jase and I never talked about him and Jessica lip-locking right in front of me while he was dancing with me.

It brings back the old anger and pries open a door I thought I had managed to shut tightly.

I kick off my shoes as I try to force the memories of the attack back. Climbing into my bed, I pull the covers over my head.

You don't need Jase to hold your hand every day.

You can do this on your own.

The worst is over.

Right?

The bruises have mostly faded. My ribs are much better. I even got an apology today and closed the chapter on it all.

You're fine.

I grip my pillow tightly and bury my face in it as the past three years of unrequited love and the horror of the attack flood me.

Exhausted from the meeting, and warring with myself for what feels like hours, I finally drift off to sleep,

I'm surrounded by darkness, but I can feel something behind me. It's monstrous. My heart begins to beat in my throat as I run, searching for any kind of light.

Jase!

My lips form his name, but no sound comes out.

There's only silence. The night is black as ink.

Something claws at my back, and then I fall. I keep falling, my mouth wide open in a scream, but again there's no sound.

And then I hit the ground, and ice pours through my veins, freezing my body.

I feel broken, and I'm barely breathing, knowing this is how I die.

Slime coats my skin, and I see a shadow tower over me. There's insanity gleaming from its eyes. I feel it claw at me as if it's trying to tear me open.

Paralyzed and mute, horror crash over me.

Jase doesn't come, and the monster tears through my flesh.

JASE

"I almost beat you," I joke.

"There's no such thing as almost in chess, son," Granddad chuckles.

He called earlier and feeling that Mila was in a good place, I decided to come over for a quick visit.

The game took a little longer than I expected and glancing at my watch, I see that it's just gone past ten pm.

"I should get back," I say as I rise to my feet.

"It was good seeing you again. I've missed you for the past two weeks but understand why you couldn't visit."

I give my grandfather a hug then walk to the front door. "I'll see you next week. Maybe I can beat you then."

"Don't get your hopes up," he chuckles, seeing me off.

I walk to my car and getting in, I strap on the seat belt before starting the engine. The drive back to campus is quick, and I wonder what Mila did while I was gone as I take the elevator up to our floor.

Walking into the suite, I'm greeted by absolute fucking chaos.

"Call Jase!" Fallon screams, and it makes me break out into a run.

"What – " My question is cut short when I see someone broke down Mila's door, and I hear Jade crying, "It's me, Mila. Open the door."

My heart slams against my ribs as worry burns through me.

Hunter sees me and explains, "Mila was screaming, and I had to break down the door, but then she locked herself in the bathroom."

"Why didn't you call me?" I dart into her room and see Jade and Fallon in front of the closed bathroom door.

They move out of the way as I knock on the door. "Mila, it's Jase. Open up."

When she doesn't answer, I use my shoulder and throw my full body weight against the door. Breaking through, she's lying on the floor, curled in a small bundle.

I drop down next to Mila, and the moment I touch her, she convulses and lets out an agonizing cry that rips right through me.

Flashes of that fucking night tear through me.

Grabbing hold of Mila's shoulders, I pull her up and lock my arms around her. She struggles against my grip, and her hand connects with the side of my neck.

"I'm here, babe. I've got you. You're safe."

Her fist slams against my chest, and then all the fight leaves her body, and she smothers a cry against my shirt.

"I'm here." I keep repeating the words, and sitting flat on my ass, I pull her onto my lap and tighten my arms around her.

Her sobs are broken, and each one shudders through her body.

I shouldn't have left her alone. God, what have I done?

Mila's voice is hoarse as she cries, "You didn't come."

"I'm here now," I say, and bringing a hand to her face, I have to force her to look at me. All the light has been dimmed in her eyes, and it has me asking, "What happened?"

The question has Mila trying to pull free from me, and when I don't loosen my grip on her, she shoves at me, screaming, "Let go of me!"

It's the first time I'm unable to calm her down, and it makes panic rip through me like a hurricane.

I let her go, not wanting to upset her even more. A helpless feeling settles hard in my gut.

Mila struggles to her feet, and as I rise to my full length, anger begins to radiate off her. "How could you?"

"I'm sorry I left," I say again.

Mila shakes her head hard. Her body's tense, and she wraps an arm around her waist. "Why did you go out with her?"

Say what?

Confused as fuck, I tilt my head, and a frown forms on my forehead. "What are you talking about?"

"I know you went out with Jessica," she snaps. "I was stupid to think this afternoon meant anything."

My eyes snap to Jade and Fallon and the rest of our friends watching as the night continues to unravel into chaos, and I bark, "Can we have some privacy?"

They quickly leave, and I turn my gaze back to Mila. "I wasn't out with Jessica. I went to my grandfather's."

I see how my words stun her and needing her to believe me, I yank my phone from my pocket and pull up my call list. Holding the device to her so she can see, I say, "He

303

called and asked that I come over. That's where I've been for the past three hours."

Mila shakes her head, and her eyes dart from the phone to me. "I thought..." she shakes her head again, as if she still can't believe the evidence.

"Why did you think I was out with Jessica?" I ask.

Mila's shoulders slump, and she looks defeated as she admits, "Before the attack, you were always out with a girl, and tonight I overheard Rachel and Summer say that Jessica was out on a date. I... I assumed."

"You still think I'm fucking around?" Hurt blooms in my chest.

Christ, haven't I proven myself over the past two weeks?

Mila closes her eyes and whispers, "What was I supposed to think? It's not like we're in a relationship." And then she begins to ramble, "And it's okay. I'm sorry I overreacted, and I know I can't cling to you forever."

I move forward, and when I frame her face, and she doesn't pull back, the tension in my body eases a little. I lift her face to mine. "Mila, you can."

She tries to shake her head, whispering, "You have your own life to live."

Not able to hold it in anymore, I lean down until I'm eye level with her. "You are my life."

I see the disbelief on her face, and stepping as close to her as I can, I say, "I love you, Mila."

Shock ripples over her face, and her lips part, but then the disbelief settles back in her eyes.

"I love you." I lean in and press a kiss to her lips. "I'm sorry it took me so long to say it."

x

Chapter 27

MILA

Jase loves me?

I keep staring at him while uncertainty and hope wars in my aching chest. It feels like I'm standing on an edge, and if the words aren't true, I'll fall.

How can he?

Is it out of pity?

The thought has the ground crumbling beneath my unsteady feet, and I gasp, "Why? Why would you say that to me now?"

"I flirted with you because my heart already knew what my mind couldn't comprehend. Because that's how much I fucking love you, Mila. It was inconceivable that one person could mean so much to me. I realized it the Thursday night before the attack. I was going to tell you that Friday."

Three years of guarding my heart make his words sound like a dream. One, I'll wake up from any moment.

My doubt has me saying, "What if it's out of pity?"

"Do you honestly think I can breathe in a world without air? Because that's what you are to me. The fucking air I breathe. Pity has nothing to do with my feelings for you."

My eyes stay locked on his as my doubt begins to fade, and hope blooms into a flower that's reaching for the sun.

"There will never be anyone else for me, Mila. It will only be you today, tomorrow, and every day after that. I want all your smiles. I don't want you fighting with anyone but me because I'm a selfish bastard, and I want those fierce eyes of yours only on me."

My sight blurs, and I blink the tears away, wanting to see Jase clearly as his words wrap around me, giving me warmth and security I haven't felt for a long while.

My voice is hoarse as I say, "You really love me?"

The same look of awe Jase had earlier on his face as he watched me orgasm settles on his features, and the expression makes him unbelievably attractive. It's fierce, lighting his eyes with flames. It's intense and demanding – and everything I ever wanted from him.

His hands slip into my hair, and he leans close until I can feel the words on my lips. "You are the most important person in my life. I can lose everything. But not you. God. Not you."

I don't know how it happened, but a God fell in love with a broken soul. He collected every piece and put me back together, using my only dream as glue.

I can't stop the tears of happiness as I press my mouth to his, and then I begin to rain kisses all over his gorgeous face as laughter bubbles up my throat.

I pull back, and I get drunk on the love shining from his eyes.

"Those eyes. God, your eyes give me life," I whisper.

JASE

I glance around at the broken doors, and gripping Mila's hand, I pull her to my room. "You should just move into my room, seeing as yours has been converted to a cave."

Mila's laughter bubbles like the finest champagne, and it etches a permanent smile on my face as I shut the door behind us.

She's my fountain of life.

Mila climbs on the bed while I go to my walk-in closet. This time my eyes are locked on her face as I unbutton my shirt while stepping out of my shoes.

"Ooooh, I like where this is going," she teases, lying on her right side and resting her head on her hand.

"Yeah?" I slowly pull the shirt off my shoulders and drop it on the floor. "Admit it."

Her eyes burn over my abs and chest before they find mine. "Admit what?"

I unfasten the belt and pull it free from the loops. Unbuttoning the pants, I pull the zip down, then say, "I'm better than Channing Tatum."

A burst of laughter explodes over her lips, and then she fucking shakes her head, her eyes alight with the spark I'm addicted to.

I push the pants down, and only standing in my boxers, her laughter fizzles away. Her lips part, and her tongue darts out, wetting her bottom lip before drawing it between her teeth.

The desire on her face has me hardening, and walking to the bed, I crawl onto it. Looking down at her, I drop my voice low. "Admit it."

She lies back on the bed and wraps her arms around my neck. "You're better than Channing."

309

I press a kiss to her mouth, then demand, "And Clark Kent."

A burst of air fans over my face as she laughs. "Now, you're pushing your luck."

I lie down on my side, and facing her, I pull her one hand from behind my neck and bring it to my chest. I press her palm to my skin and move it down to my abs.

"Crap," she breathes. "Yeah, you're definitely better than Clark Kent."

I chuckle, and pride fucking swells in my chest because Mila's so affected by me.

It's not the only thing that's swelling.

"I want to strip you naked so fucking badly," I admit. My mouth feathers a kiss over hers before I brush my lips down to her throat. Sucking on her skin, I let out a moan filled with need.

"Okay," she whispers, and it has my head snapping up.

My eyes dart over her face to make sure she's not uncomfortable, then I grin, "Oh yeah? You wanna get naked with me?"

Her hand on my abs drops to the band of my boxers as she nods, and that's all it takes for me to devour her mouth.

MILA

My fingers explore the hot as hell V that curves down from Jase's hips and disappears into his boxers.

His tongue sweeps through my mouth, lashing at mine with hard strokes. It makes my abdomen tighten, and my stomach explodes into a million stars, all burning for him.

Jase begins to pull at my shirt, and I help him get it over my head. He unsnaps my bra, and then he crawls over me, his hands dropping to my sweatpants. He grips the fabric and my panties and then slowly draws them down my legs.

His eyes drift over my body, and watching the desire grow on his face gives me the courage to climb to my knees.

"Lie down." Jase's eyes fly to mine, but he does as I ask.

Taking hold of his boxers, I pull them down, and only when I discard the fabric on the floor do I allow myself to look at him.

This man is so... stunning. Every inch of Jase is perfect.

I straddle his thighs, and leaning down, I press a kiss to his right nipple. My mouth explores every hard plane, and my tongue joins as I reach his hips, following the curve of them down to his cock.

Jase's muscles tighten, and he reaches for my hair, moving it to the side. "You're killing me."

I glance up at him before I bring my gaze down to his cock, and then I wrap my fingers around his length. I revel in the feel of muscle and skin.

"Fucking wrecking me," he groans.

I begin to stroke his length, and when his hands grab the covers, I tighten my hold around him. My eyes go back to his face, and the heated look etched on his features has me increasing my pace.

Having Jase at my mercy is a powerful feeling.

"Fuck, babe," he grinds out, and his hips begin to thrust into my hand. "Christ, harder."

I tighten my grip on him as hard as I can, and wanting him to orgasm so badly, I lower my head and suck him into my mouth.

"Fucking..." he gasps as his hips lift off the bed, every muscle in his body unyielding and tense.

Jase jerks against me, and then I taste him on the back of my tongue. Not knowing what else to do, I swallow as fast as I can. He slumps back against the bed, gasping for air.

I press a kiss to his abs and then stare down at him, feeling proud of my first hand and blow job combo.

A grin spreads over his face, then he asks, "You swallowed me?"

I nod, admitting, "I didn't know what else to do."

Jase darts up and pushes me onto my back, and then his tongue dives into my mouth, and he licks me as if he's trying to taste himself.

Holy shit.

I knew he was wild, but damn, I never knew just how hot-blooded.

He begins to move down, his mouth burning a path over my breasts and stomach as if he's starving, and I'm his only sustenance.

By the time his shoulders spread my legs, my body feels like a crashing wave tossed around by the tide that is Jase Reyes.

His mouth latches onto my clit, and the sensation is so intense, I buck off the bed, my mouth open in a silent moan.

Jase doesn't relent, his teeth and tongue demanding my body give him every drop of my release. The orgasm spasms through me, and I lose all control.

A breath manages to explode from me as rapture seizes me.

Jase laps at me as I come down from my release, and then he crawls up my body and crashes his mouth against mine.

And I get to taste the intoxicating mixture of us.

JASE

Naked, we crawl under the covers, and I pull Mila against my chest, admitting, "Totally blew my mind, babe."

"Thought I'd repay the favor and give you a little taste of what it feels like to be me," she sasses me.

"Yeah?" I love how brave she's becoming, not holding back what she thinks or feels. "You can repay the favor any time."

"Mmh... so greedy," she murmurs as she snuggles into me.

"You love my demanding ass," I remind her.

"Yeah, I do." She lifts her head, and her eyes glide over my face. "I love you, Jase. It's only been you."

"You know," I say as I wrap my one arm under my head, "I always thought you were picky, and that's why you didn't date."

"And in the meantime, it was all because of you," she chuckles.

"Since you were fifteen?" I still can't believe I never picked up on it. "You're damn good at hiding things."

"I was going to tell you, but you forgot to pick me up from school because you were with a girl." She thinks for a moment. "Angela."

I try to recall it but come up with nothing. "I'm sorry I forgot to pick you up," I say, and lifting my left hand to her hair, I pull my fingers through the silky strands. "I was clearly a dumbass at the age of nineteen."

Mila's gaze drops to my neck. "It's okay. You're with me now."

"Show me those eyes," I murmur low in my throat. Mila lifts her gaze back to mine, and I stare deep into her green irises. "There she is. My girl."

A grins tugs at her lips before it stretches into a smile. "My man."

"Kiss me," I demand.

Mila pushes up and presses a sweet kiss to my mouth.

When she pulls back, I growl, "Now kiss me like you mean it."

She lets out a chuckle, then crashes her lips to mine. Bringing her hands to my jaw, her tongue slips into my mouth, and time slips away.

Chapter 28

MILA

The weight of the attack doesn't feel so heavy as I attend my classes. The other students' stares aren't as bothersome, and I don't even hear the whispers.

I'm too busy replaying the past weekend in my mind, like a favorite movie. Every couple of minutes, goosebumps spread over my skin as I remember Jase's kisses and the feel of his hands on my body.

He loves me.

God, it feels like I'm high.

When the accounting lecture ends, Jade, Fallon, and I head out of the building.

"You've been smiling a lot," Jade comments, a mischievous grin on her face. "Anything you want to share?"

I shake my head, but knowing she won't stop asking, I say, "I just feel better today."

"I'm glad to hear that." Jade wraps her arm around my waist and gives me a squeeze.

"We should celebrate with junk food and facials," Fallon comments.

"Oooh, that sounds like a great idea," I agree.

And then I spot Jase and Jessica standing near the dorms, and my good mood evaporates.

He leans down to her, and my heart sinks. The sight of them rocks my entire world.

Jessica reaches for Jase's arm, but then he yanks away from her, and when he turns, I see the anger on his face. He takes a couple of steps away.

"Everyone thought we were a couple," Jessica yells for the whole campus to hear. "I thought if I could get Justin and Mila to date, she'd leave you alone."

Swinging back, Jase shouts, "Have I ever said we were a couple?" He closes in on her, and Jessica has enough sense to take a step back. "You fucking encouraged that fucker to pursue Mila. You're just as fucking guilty as he is!"

Jade grabs hold of my arm and drags me closer.

"I did it for us, Jase!" Our approach catches Jessica's eye and a scowl forms on her face. "If it weren't for her, none of this would've happened." She points a finger at me, and it makes my eyebrow pop up.

Jase glances at me, his eyes smoldering with rage, then he fixes a look of warning on Jessica, "Don't fucking go there."

Jessica's chin trembles, and she's dangerously close to tears. "But things were so good with us until Mila wormed her way between us."

Jase's expression darkens, and he looks downright scary as he growls, "Careful, Jessica."

A tear spills over her cheek, and she turns her eyes to me. "Are you happy now? See what you did?"

I feel Jade tense next to me.

I stare at Jessica, and instead of feeling shame from all the rumors, anger begins to bubble in my chest. "Enlighten me. What did I do?"

She takes a step closer to me, but Jase's hand darts up between us, and he pushes her back, and it has Jessica screaming at him, "Don't you see what she's doing? Since the so-called attack, you've been glued to her side. She's freaking playing you. Everyone on campus knows this. How can you be so blind?"

A week ago, her words would have reduced me to nothing, but after this weekend, I raise my chin and say, "Fuck you, Jessica. You're a vile person."

Her frantic gaze sweeps back to me. "Fuck you, bitch. How can you walk around pretending to be all traumatized just for a little attention from Jase? You're the laughing stock of Trinity."

Jase turns his back to Jessica, grumbling, "God help me." His eyes land on Jade. "I can't fucking hit a girl. Help me out."

Before I can grab hold of my cousin, she darts forward, and then a sickening punch connects with Jessica's face. She staggers backward, then falls on her butt. Jade follows Jessica to the ground and straddling her, she begins to deliver one blow after the other.

Finally, I manage to move forward, but then Jase wraps his arms around my waist, and he pulls me back to his chest. I glance over my shoulder at him. "We have to stop Jade!"

He shakes his head hard. "No."

Watching Jade hit Jessica has me covering my mouth with shock. I've only seen my cousin lose control like that once before, and it wasn't pretty.

Fallon finally pulls Jade from Jessica, and she struggles to keep hold of her as Jade keeps fighting against her grip. "I'm not done!" Jade screams.

I break free from Jase and rush to my cousin, and once I wrap my arms around her, she begins to still. Her breaths explode over her lips, and her entire body is wound tight.

I frame her face and lock eyes with her. "Calm down, Jade. You made your point."

She sucks in deep breaths and finally relaxes enough that I feel comfortable with letting go of her.

I turn to where Jessica is sobbing as she spits blood from her mouth.

Jase glares down at her, no pity anywhere on his furious features. "Someone clean up this fucking mess." His gaze snaps to Fallon. "And make sure she never sets foot here again."

Fallon nods, then Jase grabs hold of my hand and drags me after him.

All the adrenaline from the fight still has my heart hammering in my chest, and I only manage to catch my breath when Jase pulls me into his room and slams the door shut behind us.

His whole body is wound tense as he turns to stare at me, and it makes me swallow hard. Then he snaps, "Why didn't you tell me?"

Confused, I stare at him. "What?"

"About the fucking rumors, Mila!" Having his rage directed at me feels like I'm facing off with a grizzly bear.

But I stand my ground as I answer, "Because your mom told me it would happen and to just ignore them."

A look of exasperation crosses his features, and he shakes his head. "You should've come to me with this." He moves forward and framing my face with his hands, his eyes burn down on me. "From now on, you tell me the second you hear anyone talk about you."

I nod quickly, then ask, "Was that what the fight with Jessica was about?"

Jase draws in a deep breath, and he seems to calm down a little. "Yeah, Nate told me Jessica kept encouraging Justin to date you. According to Nate, she made Justin believe you were in love with him. And then I overheard her talking shit to her friends."

I bring my hands to his wrists and softly say, "It doesn't matter."

"Everything about you matters." And then his mouth is on mine, and his kiss is so wild all I can do is hang on to him.

Jase wraps an arm around my waist, and he pulls me into him as he tilts his head to get a better angle. His teeth and lips take turns working my mouth into a passionate frenzy.

The hypnotizing effect Jase has on me is powerful. He clouds my mind and demands every sense to focus only on him.

When he frees my mouth, I stand and gasp for air like a fish out of water. "Wow," I breathe. "If that's your way of punishing me for not coming to you with a problem, I'm going to start hiding everything from you."

A sexy smirk pulls at his lips. "Don't you fucking dare. Next time I'm spanking you."

I can't resist as a grin settles on my face, and I lower my voice, "Is that a promise?"

"Fuck, woman. You'll be the death of me." He begins to lower his head again, but then there's a knock at the door, and it has Jase shouting, "What?"

Fallon pushes the door open, and when she sees us standing so close to each other, a broad smile stretches over her face. "I'm here to steal Mila." She takes hold of my arm and pulls me away from Jase. "Come on. We have a date."

"What date?" Jase begins to frown darkly.

"A girl's night. Chill." Fallon lets out a chuckle as we walk to the living room. "Time for facials and relaxing. We haven't done this in a long while, and my skin is drying out."

Hana and Jade are already waiting, and I go sit next to my cousin. Taking her right hand in mine, I brush my finger over the redness on her knuckles. "We should put ice on it." I get up and rush to the fridge.

Pulling a pack of peas out, I go back to Jade, who grins at me as she says, "I'm not going to lie. I'm loving the attention."

I press the pack to the back of her hand, and resting my head on her shoulder, I croon, "My hero."

JASE

While Mila is spending some time with the girls, I call the campus' office to make sure Jessica is removed from Trinity.

After taking care of business, I go take a shower. Resting my hands on the tiles, I let the water pour over the back of my neck. And then my thoughts return to this weekend and the kiss we just shared. If Fallon hadn't interrupted us, I would've had Mila naked by now.

Since I've seen her naked, it's sent my desire for her into overdrive, and I've been walking around with fucking blue balls.

I bring up the image of Mila's mouth on my cock. Her silky black strands scattered over my skin. I grip my cock, and I begin to pump it, imagining I'm finally getting to sink balls deep into her tight pussy.

I tilt my head back, letting the water run over my face and down my body. Pleasure sizzles down my spine, and I thrust faster until the sound of my hand pumping my cock fills the bathroom. *Fuck.* I suck in a breath and hold it as the orgasm shudders through me.

Christ, if it's that intense just fantasizing about Mila, what's the real thing going to be like?

I better jerk off a lot, so I last longer than a minute when I finally have sex with her.

I quickly wash before I step out of the shower and get dressed. Feeling lighter, I have a grin on my face as I walk out of my room.

Feeling lighter. I let out a chuckle. *You almost blew a hole in the wall.*

I go to the kitchen and grab a water from the fridge. I lean against the counter and uncapping the bottle, I drink half of it with my eyes resting on Mila. She glances at me, and the mask in her hands is instantly forgotten in her hands as her lips part.

Setting the half-empty bottle down, I stalk over to where she's sitting, and framing her face, I press a hard kiss to her mouth. I let it linger before I move my lips to her ear, and I whisper, "I just had the best fucking orgasm in the shower while fantasizing about you. But I still wish you were there." I pull back and grin at her.

Mila stares at me with a mixture of shock and heat, then she drops the mask on the couch and darts up. She grabs hold of my shoulders, and lifting to her tiptoes, she proceeds to rock my world with a hungry kiss, not caring that our friends are watching.

I want her legs wrapped around my waist so I can carry her back to my room, but knowing she has to spend time with her friends, I let her control the kiss.

When Mila pulls back, she winks at me before taking her seat again. Her gaze drifts over her friends' shocked expressions, and it has Mila saying, "Pick up your jaws from the floor."

Hana looks at me, then to Mila. "I like where this is going."

"That makes two of us," Fallon says, looking so damn happy.

Jade seems to be thinking about something, then she asks, "So if I marry Hunter and Mila marries Jase, that will make Jase and Hunter cousins, right?"

"That's stretching it a bit," Fallon laughs.

I grin like a dumbass, and my eyes settle on Mila as I say, "I like the sound of that, though."

"Yeah, you and Hunter might as well be related," Hana comments.

I walk to the hallway, saying, "Not what I meant, Hana. I was referring to Mila marrying me."

"Don't drop a bomb like that and walk away," Jade yells, and it has me laughing as I walk into my room.

That should give them something to talk about while they do facials.

Chapter 29

MILA

I finally get time to paint my nails, and I opted for a soft pink.

Jase walks into the room and coming to sit on the bed, he looks at my fingers as I blow on them to speed up the drying process. Taking my left hand, he blows on the wet paint, and it makes me stare at him with a grin.

"How long does this shit take to dry?" He asks.

"It's quick-dry," I reply, and when he gives me a look stating it doesn't answer his question, I chuckle. "One to two minutes."

A wicked grin spreads over his face, and he pushes me back on the bed. "So, I have you totally powerless until then?"

I nod, a contented feeling filling every corner of me.

Keeping his body raised above mine by resting on his hands and knees, he just stares down at me. "God, you're beautiful."

"You're pretty, too," I tease him.

A disgruntled look settles on his face. "Pretty?"

"And hot."

He lifts an eyebrow.

Chuckling, I continue, "And sexy."

"Keep it coming," he demands.

"And strong." My gaze softens on him. "You're perfect."

Lowering his head, he kisses me softly, then says, "Only in your eyes, babe."

Then he glances at my hands. "Are they dry yet?"

I test them quickly, then nod.

"Good." He pulls me up. "Because my mom is here to see you."

"What?" I shriek. "You made her wait?" I rush out of the room, and when I burst into the living room, I ramble, "I'm so sorry, Mrs. Reyes. Did you wait long?"

She smiles at me as she rises from the couch. "Not at all."

I go to give her a hug, then sit down. "Would you like something to drink?" I shoot up again and go to the fridge. "We have coke, water, and... milk." Turning to her, I offer, "I can order something?"

She pats the couch with a smile on her face. "Nothing for me. Come sit."

I do as Mrs. Reyes asks, then I smile at her.

It's so important that she likes me. Now more than ever.

There's a pleased look on her face as she says, "You seem to be doing better."

I nod. "Yeah, every day it gets easier."

"I'm glad to hear that." She leans back into the couch and gets comfortable as if we're old friends visiting. "How are the nights?"

I turn my body to her, resting my shoulder against the cushion. "I only had one bad one. Other than that, I haven't had any nightmares."

"Want to tell me about it?"

I give her a grateful smile. "I was stuck in the dark, and there was… something evil clawing at me."

"Yeah, I had those too," Mrs. Reyes admits.

"But they went away?" I ask, hopeful.

She nods. "They do. How do your ribs feel?"

She's so freaking considerate it makes me feel a little emotional. "They're healing. The pain isn't as sharp anymore, and I'm getting used to it."

She places a hand over her heart, and patting her chest, she asks, "And how are things in here?"

A soft smile plays around my lips. "Good. Very good."

"You met with Mr. Green on Saturday?"

"Yeah," I nod. "He apologized."

Her eyes narrow on me, then she whispers, "It doesn't give closure, does it?"

I shake my head, admitting, "I was hoping it would, but honestly, his words meant nothing to me."

"But still," she reaches for my hand and squeezes it, "you look like you're doing so much better than when we last visited."

I hesitate for a moment, then bring my eyes to her blue ones. "It's because of Jase."

A smile jumps to her face. "Yeah?"

I can't stop the stupid grin from pulling at my lips. "You have an amazing son, Mrs. Reyes."

"I know."

I let out a chuckle because that answer is so Jase-like.

He might look like his father, but he has so much of his mom in him. The same sharp gaze that doesn't miss a thing.

She pats my hand, then offers, "And please, call me Jamie."

"Okay."

Jase walks into the living room, then says, "Aww, look at my mom bonding with her future daughter-in-law." He slumps down on the couch while I stare at him with wide eyes.

He did not just say that in front of his mom?

Jamie lets out a bark of laughter at the expression on my face. "Yeah, Jase has no filter."

"Right?" I gasp. "He just says whatever he's thinking."

"We were at a Christmas function for CRC when he was... oh, I think three years old."

Jase jumps up and replants himself on the couch beside his mother, wrapping an arm around her and covers her mouth. "Mila doesn't need to hear that story."

Jamie laughs and mumbles past his fingers, "He yanked his pants down in front of all the attendees and walked around, butt naked."

I begin to laugh, more because of their antics as Jase tries to stop Jamie from talking than the actual story.

Jamie cracks up, laughing to the point that she's struggling to get the words out. "Every couple of steps... he'd stop... and wiggle his butt... yelling... shake that ass."

I crack up at the sound of her laughter, and Jase giving up, sits back with a broad smile, just watching us. "You should've charged everyone for the show. My hot ass would've made you millions."

JASE

Seeing Mom and Mila laughing fills my chest with pride and warmth.

When they calm down, and Mom looks at me, I blurt the words out, "I love Mila. She's the one for me."

"I know," Mom whispers. She places a hand against my jaw. "I knew the instant I saw you at the hospital. I'm happy you found your one, my baby."

I don't give two shits that she still calls me her baby. I love hearing it because no matter how strong I have to be for everyone else, I know I'll always have someone to fall back on when the pressure becomes too much.

Mom turns her gaze to Mila, and it has her sputtering, "He made me work my butt off for it. I loved him first."

Mom chuckles. "Yeah, all the Reyes' men are like that." She glances between us, then asks, "So will it be okay with the two of you if I called Mia and arranged for us to spend Thanksgiving together. I feel we have a lot to be thankful for this year."

My eyes dart to Mila, and she answers, "I'd love that."

Mom gets up. "I should get going. I have to pick up Carla from school. We're redoing her winter wardrobe."

"Give her a hug from me," I say. I should call my little sister and hear how she's doing. We haven't spoken during the past two weeks, and it makes me feel guilty. "I'll call her later."

"Do that," Mom says. She presses a kiss to my cheek then hugs Mila. "Don't be strangers."

I walk her to the door, then she pauses. "Oh, your dad said you made a good call with the deal. He's proud of you."

A smile spreads over my face. I let Mom out and shut the door. When I turn back to Mila, she tilts her head. "What deal?"

Resting my forearms on her shoulders, I answer, "I've been training with my grandfather every week. On Saturday, he asked my opinion on a deal my father is working on."

A light frown forms on Mila's forehead. "So all those times I thought you were out with a girl, you were actually visiting your grandfather?"

I nod. "Yeah."

"Why did you let me think you were a player?" she asks.

"I didn't. You just assumed."

"Yeah," she widens her eyes. "Assumptions are the mother of all fuck ups."

It's seldom I hear her curse, and it makes me grin. "That's a turn on."

"What?"

I lean closer. "You saying fuck." Dropping my voice lower, I murmur, "Makes me think of thrusting my cock..." I close the distance more, "into your wet..." I nip at her lips, "pussy." And then I fucking kiss her until she's gasping and clinging to my shoulders.

Mila bites at my bottom lip, and pulling back, she gives me a seductive look. "Who knew that dirty mouth of yours would be my undoing?"

When she turns away from me, I slap her ass before gripping a hand full. "Enough to get you naked?"

"Who's getting naked?" Fallon asks as she walks into the living room.

Playfully, I scowl at my cousin. "How do you always manage to walk into the middle of a conversation and hear the worst possible sentence?"

"Not the worst," Mila mumbles under her breath.

Fallon shrugs. "So are the two of you a couple now?" She takes a bottle of water from the fridge and drinks some.

"Yeah," I grin, wrapping an arm around Mila's shoulders.

"Good. I'm happy for you," Fallon says before she goes back to her room.

"I need to get some studying done," Mila mutters. "Or I'm going to fail accounting."

"I'll tutor you," I offer.

"Let's go get some work done," Mila says, and when we walk into my room, she adds, "And no getting naked until I've studied enough to get an A."

Chapter 30

MILA

It's been three weeks since Jase told me he loves me, and I still find myself wondering if this is real or just a dream.

If it's a dream, I never want to wake up.

Hunter arranged for the doors in my room to be fixed, but Jase still refuses to let me sleep in my room. I look at the outfit on my bed Jase asked me to wear to the Halloween Ball. I slip on the white medium length, off shoulder pencil dress and instantly notice the slit comes up to my thigh.

Grinning because the outfit makes me feel sexy, I step into a pair of heels.

We have to dress up as all-time couples, and I have no idea who we're going as.

I check my hair that Jase asked me to wear up, then walk out of the room. When I reach the living room, my jaw drops open, seeing Jade and Hunter dressed as

Daenerys and Jon Snow from Game of Thrones. Jade looks stunning with a white wig on.

"You two look epic," I gasp. "Wow."

Then Fallon joins us, and she looks freaking powerful in the tight-fitting black dress that feathers out around her feet.

"Where's my Gomez," she calls.

Kao comes rushing into the room, and when his eyes fall on Fallon, he freezes and stares.

Fallon goes to hook her arms through his, then grins at me. "We're Morticia and Gomez from The Adams Family."

Damn, my friends went all out for the Halloween ball.

Hana and Noah paired up for the dance, and I grin, asking, "Sandy and Danny from Grease, right?"

"Yes, it was the easiest to pull off," Hana explains.

Fallon lets out a bark of laughter, staring at something behind me. I glance over my shoulder, and the moment I lay eyes on Jase, I clap my hands. "Oh, my God."

He's dressed in a black suit, wearing a pair of reading glasses. The white dress shirt hangs open, and he had the Superman symbol painted onto his chest.

Damn, those abs.

Walking to my very own Clark Kent, I frame his jaw and press a kiss to his lips, then go back to staring at the S on his chest.

Yeah, I'm about to start drooling.

Jase adjusts the glasses. "Hey, Lois. You look totally fuckable in that dress."

Since we became an official couple, Jase doesn't care who's around to hear. He just says exactly what he's thinking.

And I love him for it.

JASE

"My girl wanted Superman, so goddamn, I'll give her Superman," I say, and wrapping my arm around Mila's waist, I pull her closer.

Her hands come up, but then they don't know where to settle, and she just rears back. "I don't want the body paint on my dress."

I yank her right against me, then lower my head to hers. "It won't. Now fucking kiss me."

She keeps the kiss light, nibbling at my lips.

Then I brush my jaw along hers and whisper, "I have a surprise for you tonight."

She pulls back, and her eyes sparkle up at me. "Yeah?"

"Well, actually a couple." I bring my arm from behind my back and hold the box to her. "Starting with this."

Mila's eyes first dart to my face before they lower to the gift. She carefully takes it from me, and when she flips it open, her lips part.

"I chose emeralds because they're green like kryptonite." Lifting the emerald encrusted diamond necklace, I place it around her neck and clasp it. "You're my only weakness."

"Holy shit, who knew Jase could be romantic," Fallon whispers.

I had the necklace and teardrop earrings set made for Mila. I'm just glad BVLGARI was able to get it to me on time.

Mila's eyes are shining with unshed tears as she puts on the earrings, then she wraps her arms around my neck and looking deep into my eyes, she says, "And you're my only strength. Thank you so much for the beautiful gift. I'll treasure it."

"Always, babe." I press a quick kiss to her lips, then glance over her head at the others, and say, "Let's get this night over with."

Linking my fingers with Mila's, we leave the suite, and for the first time, I take the lead with Hunter and Jade following at the rear.

Yeah, I guess the dynamics of the group are still going to change a lot.

I keep my pace slow as we walk to where the function is being held in.

"Nice costumes, guys," Nate compliments us as we enter the hall.

Mila begins to pull her hand from mine, and it has me frowning. "Where are you going?"

"To sit." She gestures to our designated table at the front.

Shaking my head, I say, "I have to make my rounds first, and I'm not letting you leave my side."

"Oh," the words pop from her lips.

Every table I stop at, I make sure to greet students from families who do business with CRC Holdings.

I keep Nate for last, and when I reach him, I hold out my hand.

There's a weary look in his eyes as he shakes it.

341

"I assume your father told you about the deal we just closed?" I ask.

Nate nods. "Thank you for not letting what happened between you and my friends affect the business deal."

I keep hold of his eyes for a while, then say, "You're the only one who told me the truth. I'll always remember that."

A smile spreads over Nate's face. "I look forward to working with you, Jase."

"Likewise."

Done with the business part of the evening, I lead Mila to the dance floor and pull her against my chest. Placing my hands on her lower back, I nod at the band I organized for this dance.

The lyrics to *Superman* by *Rachel Platton* float into the air, and I tighten my hold on Mila as I begin to move.

My eyes are locked on her face, and I watch as the emotions play over her features as she listens to the words.

Bringing my hand up to the back of her head, I fold myself around her and press my face into her neck, sucking in a deep breath of her.

Mila moves her hands under my jacket and shirt and then holds on tight to my back as we sway to the music.

When the song ends, I pull back and press a kiss to her lips before I let go of her. "Stay right here." I walk to the stage set up in the corner and take the microphone from the singer while saying, "Thanks."

When my gaze glides over the tables, every pair of eyes are locked on me.

I clear my throat. "This is an official statement that Mila and I are a couple, so you can all stop wondering." I pause so my words can sink in, then I lock eyes with Mila. "She's my girl. Mine." I take a breath. "Don't fuck with her. I won't tolerate anyone talking about her. She's crazy as fuck for choosing me, but as long as she keeps choosing me, she'll be mine. And I fucking love her."

Dropping the microphone, I walk off the stage, and I don't slow until I can wrap my arms around Mila, and then I kiss her as if I might die if I don't get to taste her.

Because without her, I might as well die.

She's my entire universe.

MILA

One thing about my man? He freaking loves dropping bombs.

I smile against his mouth, my hands lost in his hair.

When he breaks the kiss, I hope he can see every emotion I feel for him. "My Superman, I love you."

He grins at me, then we make our way back to the table where our friends are sitting with happy smiles on their faces.

I sit down next to Jase, and my chest feels like it might burst from all the elation I feel. I've survived the darkest fairytale. I'm choosing not to focus on the attack but on what I gained from it. A new life with the man of my dreams.

"That was impressive," Hunter says. Then he scowls at Jase. "But you're making the rest of us look like losers in the romance department."

Jase lets out a bark of laughter. "Not my fault I'm that awesome."

I chuckle at his arrogance. God, this man knows no end.

We visit with our friends for a while, before Jase gets up, and taking my hand, he helps me to my feet.

"We're hitting the road. See you all Sunday."

My head snaps up to him. "Why only on Sunday?"

"One of the surprises."

I wave at our friends, and with my hand tightly gripped in Jase's, we leave. We don't even stop at the dorm but head straight for his car.

Jase stops to button his shirt, and I mourn the loss of the hot view of his chest and abs. He tucks the fabric into his pants and removes his jacket, throwing it onto the back seat.

Once I'm strapped in, and Jase is behind the steering wheel, he finally says, "I'm abducting you for the weekend."

"But I'll need clothes then," I say quickly, while we're still on campus grounds.

"I packed a bag for you," he explains as he steers the car out of the gates.

I rest my head back on the seat with my eyes on Jase.

After a while, he reaches for my hand and places it on his thigh.

And the moment feels perfect.

Chapter 31

JASE

The atmosphere is relaxed between us as I pull up to the lodge. Climbing out, I hand the keys to the valet, and grabbing our bags from the back seat, we walk inside.

I've arranged a ranch house for us, so we'll have privacy.

Mila glances around the rustic elegance while I get our key.

"Got the key. Let's go," I call to Mila. Once she's back at my side, we make our way to our own little slice of heaven. The house is all wood and already has a fire burning in the living room. I first go to set down our bags in the bedroom before exploring the rest of the house.

"This place is beautiful," Mila breathes as we step out onto the porch.

I sit down on one of the plush couches and pull Mila down onto my lap. Wrapping my arms around her waist, I smile softly, and not wanting her to think otherwise, I say,

"I just wanted to be alone with you. I have no ulterior motive by bringing you here."

A mischievous gleam darkens her eyes as she teases, "Well, damn, and here I had high hopes."

My eyebrow pops up. "Oh, yeah?"

Mila moves on my lap until she's straddling me, and then she wraps her arms around my neck. Her eyes turn serious, and for a moment, they drop to my chest before she brings them back up. "There's something I want to talk about."

I nod, focusing all my attention on her.

Her gaze darts away again, then she takes a deep breath. "That night." She exhales. "Just before you found me, I thought this was not how my first time was supposed to be." Her eyes lock on mine. "I wanted to give my virginity to you." The corner of her mouth lifts slightly. "And then you were there, saving me."

That fucking fucker. I seriously would have killed him if he had raped her.

I lock my jaw to keep quiet and to give Mila all the time she needs to talk. I wasn't aware she's a virgin, or I would've been more careful with her.

"Since then, I've had this constant fear that someone would take it from me." Frustration clouds her features. "I

347

hope I'm making sense." She takes a moment to collect her thoughts, then continues, "I want you to be my first and only, Jase."

When I don't respond quick enough, she pulls the cutest awkward face and mumbles, "Now's a good time to say something."

Pulling her closer to me, I press my forehead against her. "I'd be honored, Mila." I hug her tightly, and unable to keep the words in, I say, "Fuck, I'm so glad I got to you in time." I pull back and, framing her face, I press a hard kiss to her lips. "So fucking glad."

My gaze burns into hers. "Can I make love to you tonight?"

MILA

I nod, feeling much better after getting that off my chest.

Then anticipation starts to flutter through my body, setting it alight with a buzz of a million wings.

Jase taps my hips. "Get up."

Really? Right now?

My stomach tightens into a knot as I climb off his lap.

Jase takes my hand and leads me back inside. "I first have another surprise for you."

I let out the breath I was holding. I'm ready to have sex with him, but it doesn't mean I'm not nervous.

Jase leads me up to the bedroom and then digs a small box out of his bag. His eyes lock on mine, and he takes a couple of breaths.

And then he opens it, and my jaw hits the floor as I stare at the emerald ring.

Oh. My. God.

My eyes dart back to his.

"This is a promise ring," he begins to say. "It's a promise that I am yours, and you're mine. One day I'll replace it with an engagement ring, and then a wedding ring. But until then, this is my promise that I'm committed to you, Mila. There will only ever be you."

He removes the ring, and taking hold of my right hand, he slips it onto the ring finger.

I feel all emotional as I turn my eyes back up to his, and I admit, "I'm actually speechless right now."

He points to the bag he packed for me. "There's a bathing suit in there. Get dressed while I wash the body paint off."

"Wait." I grab hold of his arm and lift myself on my tiptoes. I kiss him softly, then say, "I always knew it would be mind-blowing to date you. I just never imagined how much. Thank you for returning my love. You made the only dream I ever had come true."

A sexy grin forms on his face. "Yeah, wait until I get you into that hot tub."

I let out a chuckle, and as Jase heads into the bathroom, I go pick up the bag. Zipping it open, I frown when I don't recognize any of the clothes. I pull out sweatpants and t-shirts, then my eyebrows shoot up. "Ahh... Jase?"

"Yeah?" he answers from the other room.

"Lingerie?"

I hear him chuckle, and he comes out of the bathroom, dressed in only the suit pants. My eyes drop to the Superman body paint on his chest. I'm so glad he hasn't washed it off yet. "Can I borrow your phone?"

Jase frowns, but he pulls the device out of his pocket and hands it to me. Bringing up the camera, I take a couple of photos of him. "I wanted a picture before you wash it off."

I drop his phone on the bed then point at the bag. "What's all this?"

A smirk tugs at his lips as he picks up a black sheer baby doll dress. "This is my gift to myself."

"Yeah, and here I thought you had no expectations," I tease him.

"But I sure as fuck was hoping," he chuckles as he goes to clean up.

I unpack the rest of the bag out of pure curiosity. Then I reach the bathing suit, and my mouth drops open again.

Holy shit, it's sheer black and seriously covers nothing.

Okay, then. So this is what Jase likes?

I slip out of my dress and underwear, then place the necklace and earrings carefully on the dresser before putting on the bathing suit. There are three slips of fabric, if you can even call it that, and they only cover my nipples and between my legs.

I glance around the room for a robe, and not seeing one, I peek at the bathroom before digging in Jase's bag for one of his shirts. Finding one, I grin as I pull it over my head.

Just then, Jase comes into the room, and he laughs when he sees me in his clothes. "Not what I had in mind, but I like it."

"Yeah, I just wanted to cover myself for now." I tug at the shirt.

Jase moves closer to me, and lifting his hands to my arms, he rubs up and down the length of them, as he explains. "I'm a visual person, but if you're uncomfortable with any of the clothes I got, then you really don't have to wear them."

I quickly shake my head. "I just need to get used to them."

"Want to climb in the tub while I get us something to drink?"

I nod and walk out on the balcony. With it being dark I can't see much of the view around us, but looking up, I smile when I see how clear the stars are.

A couple of minutes later, Jase comes back with two flutes of champagne. "I figured we had something to celebrate."

He holds a glass out for me to take.

"One second," I say, and grabbing hold of the shirt, I pull it over my head.

The smile Jase had on his face falls off at the speed of light, and a predatory look tightens his features. "Babe," he breathes, "I'm going to make you scream this weekend."

I take the champagne from him and gulp down a big sip before climbing into the water. It's warm and has an aromatic scent to it.

Jase places his own glass on the side of the tub, then strips out of his pants and boxers. My eyes drop to his cock that's definitely ready for action.

The sight of his muscled body sends a wave of goosebumps over my skin.

He steps into the water then glides over to me. Placing his hands on the side of the tub, he cages me in. The water laps at my breasts as his eyes drop down to them.

Biting his bottom lip, he shakes his head. "I'm one hell of a lucky man."

His compliment makes me smile.

Jase pushes an arm behind me and then pulling me to the middle of the tub, he skims a finger over my hard nipple.

I rest my hands on his biceps as we stare at each other, and I can feel his cock pressing against my abdomen. The feel of him is like electric shocks to my insides.

He pulls me tighter against his chest as his hand slips between my legs. "I love touching you. God, it's addictive."

A breath hitches in my throat when he slips a finger under the fabric and circles my opening. "I love being touched by you," I manage to get out in a low moan.

Jase moves back, and as he sits down, I straddle him, which gives him better access to my clit. His mouth claims mine in a dirty hot kiss that has my heart soaring to the stars in no time. His fingers work me toward an orgasm, and when I'm close, I let out a gasp.

Jase immediately stops and growls, "Eyes on me and let me hear you."

They snap back open.

"I want to hear what I'm doing to you, babe," he says as his finger dips inside me before circling my clit.

"I can't," I whisper breathlessly.

His eyes are sharp on my face, and he knows the second I'm close again, and he freaking stops again.

"Jase," I growl with warning.

It makes a hot as hell smirk spread over his face. "See, you can."

He begins to alternate between thrusting his finger inside me and pinching my clit. It has my hips bucking wildly against him. My gaze burns into his, and my breaths explode over my lips.

The orgasm hits hard from all the teasing, ripping the air from my lungs in a low moan. My body shudders uncontrollably, and I grind myself down on his hand.

"Shit," I gasp as the release relentlessly tears through me, and then noises I've never made before spill over my lips, and it sounds like something between a whimper and a moan. My hands move to behind Jase's neck, and I grab fistfuls of his hair as my body tightens, on the border of pain and pleasure.

"Jase," I pant, unable to take more, and only then does he free me from the sweet torture as his hand moves up to my breast and his mouth slams against mine.

I've never experienced anything this intense. My mind is missing in action, and my body melts against his.

There's only Jase and me.

Chapter 32

JASE

Mila's a wet dream come to life.

We've been making out for almost an hour when I reluctantly pull back from her. "Time to eat. You get out first so I can see that sexy ass of yours."

She's much more comfortable now and even gives me a seductive look as she gets up and turns around. Before she can move away from me, I grab hold of her hips and bite her left ass cheek.

"Fuck." I raise to my feet, and pressing my cock against her ass, I rub it shamelessly between her cheeks before I have to force myself to let go of her, or I'll end up fucking her right now.

"Go," I growl.

She lets out a chuckle, and when she gets out, she twirls in a fucking circle, and I get a full view of her hot as fuck body.

"Christ, babe, I'm going to fuck you raw if you don't cover yourself," I warn her.

Another chuckle bubbles over her lips as she walks into the room to grab a bathrobe. I climb out and take the one she offers me. I slip it on, then grab hold of her jaw and grumble, "I want to do dirty things to you." I bite her bottom lip and then suck it into my mouth before letting go. "But first, I need to get food in you. Then I can get my cock in that pussy of yours."

We leave the room and head down to the kitchen. I asked them to prepare a meal for us, and opening the fridge, I remove the food.

Mila takes a seat at the counter, then groans, "Oooh sushi. I haven't had that in a while."

I grab us each a bottle of water as well, then sit down next to her.

While eating, I keep feeling Mila glancing at me, and when my eyes snap up, she lets out a burst of laughter.

"What?" I ask, a smile tugging at my lips. I love seeing her so giddy.

"I'm just happy," she admits before taking another bite. She chews and swallows, then adds, "It feels surreal being with you."

Tilting my head, I stare at her and try to put myself in her shoes. If I had to love her like I do for three years while she wasn't interested in me… God, I'd lose my mind.

Getting up, I move closer and framing her face, I nudge it up. "I'm so fucking sorry I was such an asshole, and for not realizing sooner you were the one for me. I wish I could go back and smack my nineteen-year-old self upside the head for being such a dumbass." I kiss her tenderly, then add, "But I will spend the rest of my life making it up to you."

Mila shakes her head. "You already have."

I glance down at the plates. "You done eating?"

She nods and slips off the stool. I go lock the front door and turn off the lights before following Mila back to the room.

Taking her hand, I lead her back out on the balcony. "Let's just soak in the water for a while."

I want her as relaxed as possible before I make love to her.

When she drops the robe to the deck, I let out a groan. Fuck, I'm going to worship her tonight.

We sit across from each other, and Mila's hands drift over the bubbles from the jets I switched on. My gaze follows the fluttering movements, and then I murmur, "You have beautiful hands."

"I really like yours as well," she sasses me.

Winking at her, I say, "They love you as well."

Wanting to divert the conversation away from anything sexual, I mention, "How do you feel about spending Thanksgiving with our families?"

Mila shrugs. "I'm actually looking forward to it. Just us and our families will be nice. Will Carla be coming as well?"

"I never know with my little sister, but I'm sure my mom will drag her there if she has to."

"Oh," Mila gasps. "I almost forgot. Noah and his family are also coming over, with our fathers being twins and all."

I let out a burst of laughter. "Then we're in for a ton of fun. Carla and Noah have this hate thing going on between them."

"Yeah." Mila frowns lightly. "I picked up on that."

"Honestly, I think my sister has a crush on your cousin, but she's too stubborn to admit it."

Mila lifts an eyebrow at me. "I wonder who she takes after?"

I laugh then shake my head, "Yeah, it runs in the family."

Mila glances up at the stars, then asks, "Are you excited to start working this summer?"

I think about her question before I answer, "I'm both excited and nervous. So many people depend on me. I'm fucking scared of screwing up."

"You won't."

She says the words with so much conviction, it has me asking, "How do you know?"

"Because you thrive under pressure, Jase. Look at how you were with me. You took charge, and honestly, you made it so much easier for me to deal with the ordeal."

I think over what she said and realize she's right. I've doubted myself, but every time shit has gone down, I've managed to handle it.

My mouth lifts in a relieved smile, and my eyes rest with love on Mila. "You know me better than I know myself."

"Yeah, except for your choice of pajamas," she teases. "And speaking of, I'm going to get changed."

My eyes devour her body as she climbs out, and grabbing an outfit off the bed, she slips into the bathroom.

Getting out of the tub, I use one of the bathrobes to dry myself, then go to clear everything off the bed. Reaching in my bag, I remove the box of condoms and take one out. I pull the covers off, only leaving the sheet, and I slide under it.

The bathroom door opens, and I tuck the condom quickly under my pillow, then my eyes freeze on Mila.

She looks breathtaking in the sheer black lingerie. Sexy and all woman.

My eyes feast on her as she comes closer. She crawls onto the bed, then sits in a kneeling position at the edge.

And all I can fucking do is stare.

She loosened her hair, and the silky black strands fall straight down her back.

"How's it possible that you're from this world?" I murmur, caught in a trance.

My words seem to give her courage because she crawls closer until she reaches my hip.

She takes a deep breath then blurts out, "Okay, I'm really nervous right now, but don't take it the wrong way. It's just... I've been waiting for this moment a long time, and it means a hell of a lot to me."

Fuck, her words make my own nerves kick to life because I don't want to disappoint her.

I swallow the shit down because there's no way in hell I'm letting it ruin tonight.

I reach for her hand and link our fingers. "Want to talk about what's going to happen?"

She shakes her head, then her eyes widen slightly. "I'm on the pill. I thought you should know that."

A smile stretches over my face. "I'm still going to use a condom because I'll be fucking pissed off with myself if I get you pregnant." Feeling I need to explain my words, I continue, "I don't want to share you any time soon with a baby. I'm selfish like that."

She lets out a burst of laughter. "I'm totally fine with that. I want to graduate and work for a while before having a child."

"Come lie by me," I order. I first need to get her to relax again.

Mila snuggles against my side and resting her chin on my chest, she glances up at me.

I lift a hand to her hair and pull my fingers through the strands.

"Ryker's taking over from your dad, right?"

A frown appears on her forehead for a split-second, then she nods, "Yeah. Thank God because I suck with anything law related."

"So, what are you going to do with your MBA?"

"I'm not sure what I want to do. I'm just getting it, so I'll have something behind my name."

"You're not interested in hospice like your mom?" I ask, scooting down until I'm eye level with her.

"No. I'll cry myself to death if I had to watch people die," she admits. "I'm not too worried. I have four years to figure out what I want to do."

"Stephanie is retiring with my father, so you can always become my PA, and then we can have dirty office sex."

My comment makes her laugh. "No thanks, I don't want to work under you."

"Yeah?" I flip her onto her back and drop my voice low, "I'll get you addicted to being under me."

Mila brings her hands to my jaw and pulls me down until our mouths fuse together. I don't give in to my hunger to consume her and force myself to remain in the moment, so I don't lose control with her.

Once she's used to me, it will be a whole different story.

MILA

My heart is pounding in my chest with anticipation.

Jase slows the kiss, and his tongue massages mine sensually. His left hand finds my breast, and my back arches into his touch.

He kisses me until my lips tingle, then he pulls back. With his eyes on fire and his voice deep, he says, "I'm going to get myself off, so I last longer than a second once I'm inside you."

I nod, and I begin to move my hand down to his cock, but he shakes his head, and taking hold of my wrist, he pushes my arm down next to my head.

Then he lifts his chest off of me and keeps himself up by resting on his right forearm. His left hand skims down the side of my body, and then I feel his knuckles brush over my clit as he takes hold of his cock.

My eyes dart down, and seeing Jase touch himself makes a wave of heat rush through my body.

Damn, that's the hottest thing I've ever seen.

I draw my bottom lip between my teeth and watch with desire and fascination as he starts to rub his cock over my clit.

The feel of him between my legs is… just right. It's arousing and heady.

Not able to just lie still, my hands move down his chest and abs, and slipping over his waist, I drink in the feel of his toned back.

Lifting my head, I latch onto his neck, and tasting him, draws a moan from deep in my throat. I suck and lick at his skin, and when I hear his breaths rush over his lips, I pull back. His features are tense, and wanting to be part of his orgasm, I push my hand down between us, and he lets me take over. I wrap my hand tightly around the base of his cock and continue to rub him against me.

He brings his other arm up and, leaning on both, he stares down at me while thrusting against my hand. The friction makes my abdomen sizzle to life.

Knowing it's a turn on for him, I forget about my own inhibitions and groan, "Fuck, Jase. You feel so good."

His eyes darken, and it feels like I'm staring into flames. His muscles tense, and when his lips part and he begins to jerk against me, my own release tightens my abdomen before rippling through me.

"Christ," he grinds the word out between his clenched teeth.

I feel the warmth as he comes on my abdomen, and I love it.

When we both come down from our highs, Jase lowers himself against me, and my eyes widen. "Shouldn't I clean up first?"

He continues to rub his cock against me and shakes his head. "I fucking love feeling myself all over you."

"Mmmh…" I frame his jaw and begin to pull him toward me. "Give me that dirty mouth."

He grins right before our mouths collide. We devour each other's mouths until Jase is ready again. He reaches under one of the pillows and pulls a condom out. Ripping it open with his teeth, he leans on his side and rolls the condom on.

All the fluttering wings are back in an instant, creating a chaotic flight in my stomach.

He settles back between my legs, and his eyes lock onto mine. "Ready?"

My head bobs up and down super fast.

"Need to hear the words, babe," he grins.

"Yes, I'm ready. I've been ready for years."

His smile turns tender, and he presses a soft kiss to my mouth. "Thank you for fighting so fucking hard to protect what's mine."

My heart. It explodes into a kaleidoscope of vibrant color.

Jase begins to push inside me. Using short strokes, he keeps going deeper, and when I flinch from the sudden sharp pain, he freezes.

"I'm okay," I whisper. "Keep going."

He enters me another inch, and my body stiffens against the intrusion. Jase's eyes never leave my face, and I smile to put him at ease.

His body begins to tremble against mine as he continues to keep it slow. When he's finally all the way in, we both take a moment to breathe.

Jase lowers his head, and pressing his forehead to mine, he pulls out. His features are tight with concentration, and it has me saying, "You can go faster."

"No," he growls, his jaw clenched with restraint. "Not yet."

The first couple of thrusts, Jase keeps it slow before he begins to speed up. His lips part, and when a satisfying groan slips over his lips, I feel it in my bones.

I've been so fixated on his response that it only hits me now, Jase just took my virginity. A wide smile spreads over my face, and tears mist up my sight from an overwhelming sense of relief and love.

The corner of Jase's mouth curves up, and his eyes turn to molten lava as he whispers, "I love you so fucking much, Mila."

I brush my hands down his back and gripping hold of his ass, I open my legs wider and begin to lift my hips as he thrusts inside me.

"Fuck, babe, that's not helping," he groans. "I'm trying to last longer than a minute."

He pushes his hand down between us and starts to rub my clit feverishly. My head tilts back into the pillow, and then Jase latches onto my pulse, his lips and tongue lashing at my skin.

"Jase," I whimper, and I'm surprised when I feel my release start to build. "Harder," I groan, needing him to let go of his self-control.

Jase pulls his hand away, and it makes my eyes snap to his face. He plasters his whole body against mine, and with a rocking motion, his pelvis rubs against my clit. It makes fireworks explode behind my eyes.

"Oh, God." The words are ripped from me, and my lungs refuse to suck in another breath as my body tenses beneath his.

As I begin to shudder, Jase again increases his thrusts until he's driving into me, and air explodes over his lips.

He jerks against me, and his face tightens with that look of awe I love so much.

Our mouths crash against each other, and we drink each other's moans as we ride out our orgasms.

Chapter 33

JASE

God only knows how I managed to stay in control. That's easily the second hardest thing I've ever had to do.

After I discard the condom, I wet a facecloth with warm water and walk back to the bed. Sitting down next to Mila, I watch her eyes widen as I softly wipe between her legs and clean the mess I made on her stomach.

I go rinse the cloth out, then say, "Let's get back in the jacuzzi so you can relax. Hopefully, you won't be too sore tomorrow."

"Who knew you could be so attentive," she teases as she slides off the bed. Once we're in the jacuzzi, I pull her onto my lap.

She rests her head against my shoulder, and I feel her breaths fan over my neck. My eyes drift shut and smiling, I murmur, "That's my favorite feeling."

"What?" she whispers.

"Feeling your breath on my neck."

She presses a quick kiss to my pulse, then relaxes against me. "Don't let me drown if I fall asleep."

"I won't." I lean my head back and stare up at the night sky, holding the woman I love more than life itself in my arms.

When I nod off for a second, I decide it's time for bed. "Babe, are you awake?"

"Mhhh."

"Let's dry off and climb in bed." I help Mila stand and first step out of the tub, then reaching for her, I lift her out. Holding her to my chest, I walk us to the bathroom before setting her down on her feet. I hand her a towel then grab one for myself.

After we're dry, I throw the covers back over the bed and lie down so Mila can snuggle against my side.

"Night," she whispers as her head finds its spot over my heart.

"Night, babe."

We only wake up when the sun is high in the sky.

Mila stretches, then groans, "I need food."

"Room service, or do you want to go to the restaurant?" I grumble as I rub the sleep from my eyes.

"Let's go eat at the restaurant, and then we can walk the food off and explore the resort."

"Okay." I throw the covers back, and the last of the sleep clears from my head at the speed of light when my eyes get to feast on Mila's naked body. "How do you feel?"

"I don't know yet. I haven't moved," she chuckles.

"Get your sexy ass up then. I want to know what I can and can't do today."

She scoots off the bed and walks to the bathroom.

God, please let all the soaking and prep work from last night pay off.

I hear water running, and then Mila opens the door and grins at me. "Want to shower with me?"

"Hell yeah!" I'm up and out of the bed and rush into the bathroom. Wrapping an arm around Mila's waist, I yank her against my body. "And, what's the verdict?"

"I feel fine. We're good to go." She even gives me two thumbs up, and it earns her a slap on the ass.

"Are you sassing me?" I growl.

"If I say yes, will you spank me again?"

"Christ, Mila," I groan. Then I remember to get a condom. "Get in the shower. I'll be back in a second." I go grab one and roll it on before I head back to the bathroom.

It's her second time. Take it slow.

MILA

After we got some food in our stomachs, we walk in the direction of the lake.

Surrounded by the sounds of nature, we sit down under a tree. Jase pulls me between his legs, and I lean back against his chest. My thoughts wander to the past month, and I find myself reveling in how much everything has changed.

I soak in the feel of Jase's body behind mine and grin when I once again realize I can touch him any time I want to. The emotions are overwhelming as I whisper, "You're mine."

He turns his head toward my ear and says, "I better be."

I let out a chuckle, but it quickly turns to laughter as Jase moves his hand down my front and palms my vagina. "Who does your pussy belong to?"

When I take too long to answer, Jase jumps up, and before I know what's happening, he has me tossed over his shoulder.

"Put me down," I shriek, my laughter back full force. "I'm going to puke all over your back."

The palm of his hand connects with my ass, and it has me shrieking louder.

I realize he's walking toward the water, and I begin to squirm. "Don't you dare throw me in the lake."

"Who does your pussy belong to?" he asks again, his voice thick with laughter.

"You! God, it belongs to you. Put me down!"

Jase lets my body slide down the front of his, and the second my feet touch the grass, I slap him upside the head and dart away.

It's totally unfair that Jase is so much taller. He catches up to me in no time, and I let out a screech of laughter as his arms wrap around me. He takes us down to the ground, and I manage to squirm free.

"Christ, you're like an eel," Jase chuckles.

Crawling away from him, another shriek bursts from my lips as his hand connects with my butt.

Jase pushes me onto my back, and I struggle to gasp for air from all the laughing.

A shadow of a memory creeps around the edge of my mind, and my happiness dims a little.

"What?" Jase instantly pics up on my change of mood.

Staring up at Jase, I know he's so much stronger than me, but the thought doesn't scare me. He just gave me another thing back I thought I'd lost.

Lifting my hand to his jaw, I say, "I trust you."

"Yeah?" A look of confusion furrows his brow.

I consider my words, wanting to explain it to him properly. "Even though you can, I know you'll never hurt me."

He grins down at me. "Unless I'm spanking your ass."

I chuckle. "You're such a caveman."

Jase grips hold of me, and pulling me to my feet, he throws me over his shoulder again.

"Come on. I just ate," I complain even though there's a huge grin on my face. Then my eyes land on his perfect butt. "Nice ass."

"Enjoy the view, babe," he chuckles. Jase walks us back to the tree, and we get comfortable again.

We stare at the view around us, and after a long silence, I ask, "What are you thinking about?"

"You. Me. Our future."

I lean my head to the side so I can see his profile. "What about our future?"

"Whether you'll be okay with the long hours I'll have to work," he murmurs, keeping his eyes on something in the distance.

"Well," I sit up and turn around to face him, "I can always be your PA."

A grin instantly spreads over his face. "So, you like the idea of hot office sex?"

With a smile, I shake my head. "I'm not opposed to it, but I was thinking more along the lines that we'll get to spend time together, and I'll be able to help you carry the load."

Jase tilts his head, and his gaze lingers on me for a while. "You want to help me?"

I scoot a little closer, and taking hold of his hand, I pull it to my lap. I brush my fingertips over the veins stretching up his arm. "I know you'll be under a lot of pressure, and I just want to do what I can to make things easier for you."

Jase narrows his eyes, a serious expression settling on his face. "What if it fucks up our relationship?"

I shrug. "Your grandfather and Stephanie made it work. Also, your dad seemed fine working with his stepmother."

The worry in Jase's gaze begins to lessen. "Fuck, babe. You really want to work with me?"

I lean forward and press a kiss to his mouth. "Yeah." Pulling back, I lock my eyes on his. "That way, I can make sure no one hits on my man."

"Yeah?" he lets out a chuckle, "What will you do if one of the young secretaries try their luck?"

I move onto my knees and glare at Jase. "I'll throat punch you."

"Why me?" he asks incredulously.

"Because they should know right off the bat you're taken, and none of them stand a chance."

Jase's mouth lifts at the corners into a sexy grin. "It's hot seeing you all possessive. How do you feel about mirrors in the bedroom because I really want you watching me while I pound into your pussy."

Letting out a burst of laughter, I climb to my feet. "I guess we'll have to see if we can get mirrors delivered to our room."

Jase is up in a flash, and I have to quicken my pace to keep up with him as he rushes back to our ranch house.

JASE

"You seriously got a mirror?" Mila asks.

I position the free-standing mirror at the foot of the bed. Grinning, I turn to her. "Yeah, get your ass naked and on the bed."

I yank my shirt over my head and quickly step out of my jeans and boxers. When she takes too long for my liking, I move closer, and grabbing hold of her hips, I toss her onto the bed. Mila lets out a surprised shriek and then stares at me as I grip hold of her jeans, yanking them down her legs.

"Someone's in a hurry," she teases.

"To fuck you?" I growl as I turn Mila over, so she's on her hands and knees. "Always." I climb on the bed and spread her knees wider apart. When I see her reflection in the mirror grinning at me, I slap her pussy.

Mila's lips part, and she lets out a moan. Then she fucking wiggles her ass at me.

"Fuck, I love this kinky side of you." Gripping hold of my cock, I rub it over her opening and clit a couple of times. "You're so fucking wet for me."

Our eyes lock in the reflection, and then Mila says, "I want to feel you bare inside me."

God, this woman is my perfect match in every way.

Heat explodes behind my vision, and before I can gather my senses, my hips jerk forward, and my cock slams into her pussy.

Mila's hands fist the covers, and she lets out a gasp. Her body tenses for a moment, and then she orders, "Again."

"You like that, babe?" I ask as I pull out of her.

"Yes."

I place another light slap between her legs and her lashes lower over her eyes.

My pelvis drives forward and the sound of our skin connecting echoes in the room as I fill her.

I reach for the condom I tossed on the bed earlier, but Mila shakes her head. "Just once, I want to feel you come inside me."

Her words are my undoing, and it creates a wildfire inside me. One only she can extinguish.

Grabbing hold of Mila's hips, I sink into her and keeping the pace hard and fast, I watch as her cheeks flush and her breasts sway. The sight is erotic as fuck, and then her body shudders, and she lets out a cry, "Fuck me harder, Jase."

I let go of the last of my control. My fingers dig into her skin as I yank her ass back, meeting my fierce thrusts with loud slaps.

Mila's cry turns to whimpers as her body keeps trembling, and it only spurs me on to pound harder into her. Pleasure ripples over my body, and it feels as if my balls are tightening. Knowing I'm close, my eyes lock on Mila's face in the mirror's reflection, and I growl, "Look at me."

Mila's gaze locks on mine as I slam inside her, and then I gasp, "Christ."

My pelvis jerks against her ass as I come, and knowing that I'm filling her with my seed makes the moment a million times hotter.

I ride the last of my orgasm before I pull out. When Mila begins to move, I tighten my hold on her hips. "Hold still."

"Ahh... okay?"

I watch as my cum runs down the insides of her thighs and let out a satisfied groan. "Best fucking thing I've ever seen."

Chapter 34

MILA

One month later...

Jase's mouth latches onto my breast, and I stretch lazily out with a grin spreading over my face, murmuring, "Morning."

He lets go of my nipple with a pop. "Time to get your sexy ass up and dressed, or we'll be late."

I let out a groan and turn on my side, snuggling back into my pillow. "Just five more minutes."

Jase slaps my butt, and I feel him move off the bed. "Okay, but then you'll only have ten minutes to get ready."

"Ugh," I huff as I sit up. I rub the sleep from my eyes then glare at Jase, where he's busy pulling on suit pants. "It's all your fault."

A hot smirk tugs at his lips. "You didn't seem to mind last night when you were begging me to fuck you hard."

I scoot off the bed and go to stand in front of Jase. Grabbing hold of the bulge in his pants, I massage his cock as I drop my voice low, "Can you blame me? Having your huge cock slam into my pussy is my new favorite addiction."

The words have the desired effect as Jase draws his bottom lip between his teeth and lets out a growl.

I let go of him and dart into the walk-in closet. "Oooh, will you look at the time? We have to hurry."

"Don't start something you can't finish," Jase barks.

"You sucked my nipple first," I tease him as I pull out an outfit from my side of the closet. I gave in to Jase, and now we're sharing a room.

His arms wrap around me from behind, and he nibbles on my ear. "You're looking for a spanking?"

"Mhhh," I moan as I turn around in his embrace. "Until I orgasm?"

"Christ, woman." Jase pulls away and frowns at me. "I fucking created a monster."

Winking at him, I ask, "What was it you just said?" I pretend to think, then pushing past him, I continue, "Don't start something you can't finish? Remember that next time you suck on my nipple only to leave me hanging in bed."

My sass earns me a slap on the butt. I wiggle my hips then dart away before Jase can reach for me.

We get dressed quickly, and when we're brushing our teeth, and I catch Jase's gaze on my mouth, I slow my movements. He tilts his head and narrows his eyes at me. "You want me to walk around with a hard-on all day?"

I rinse my mouth then mumble, "I don't think my dad would approve."

While I check that I have everything in my purse, Jase presses a kiss to my neck. "For winter break, I'm booking us a cabin in the fucking mountains so I can tie you to the bed and make you scream right through Christmas and New Year."

"Oooh… sounds perfect."

JASE

I take a bite of turkey, then lean back in my chair. My eyes go to Mila, and watching her interact with our families, there's no sign of the trauma she endured two months ago.

Everything I thought I knew about her has changed. Mila was feisty before we became a couple. I knew that much. But she's continuously blowing my mind.

Her sass has increased tenfold, and she doesn't miss a chance to drive me wild.

Beneath my ever-constant desire for her lays a love I couldn't imagine existed. Her spirit is so vibrant, it demands to be seen, to be worshipped.

She's my goddess.

"I'm so in love with you." Only when Mila's head whips in my direction, do I realize I said the words out loud. My eyes dart around the table, and everyone has stopped eating, staring at me. Not caring two shits, I shrug, "It's not like it's news to any of you."

Everyone continues with their meal and the conversation I brought to a sudden halt, except for Mrs. West. Mila's mom takes a deep breath, then pushing her chair back, she excuses herself. "I'm going to check on the pie."

I wait a second, then rise to my feet, "I'll be back in a minute." I walk to the kitchen and find Mrs. West standing by the sink, a glass of water forgotten in her hand as she stares out of the window. Worried I might've upset her, I ask, "Is everything okay?"

She quickly glances over her shoulder, and a quivering smile wavers around her lips. Her eyes shine with tears, and it has me walking to her side. I place a hand on her shoulder, my worry growing.

Mrs. West sets the glass down, then turns to me. Her face softens with emotion, then she says, "Thank you, Jase. My only wish in life was for my children to find happiness. You've done so much for Mila." She sucks in a deep breath, then leans forward and hugs me. It eases the concern I had. "I'm so glad you're the one Mila gets to love all her life. I know I won't have to worry about her because she'll be safe in your hands."

I rub a hand over her back, murmuring, "I'm the lucky one."

Mrs. West pulls back and gives me a grateful smile. "I'll make sure to keep the biggest slice of pie for you."

"Oh yeah? From the cherry one?" My eyes dart to the counter where the pies are cooling off.

Mrs. West goes to cut one of the pies in half and sets it aside. "What you don't eat, you can take home."

"Careful, I can get used to this," I warn my future mother-in-law.

"I sure hope so," she grins. There are so many similarities between Mila and her mother.

I go to wrap my arm around her shoulders and pull her back in the direction of the dining room. "Will you teach Mila to make the gravy."

"No," she blurts out, then a teasing grin settles on her face, "That way, I have a way of bribing the two of you to visit often."

I nod slowly. "Oh, I see how it is. Now I know where Mila got her sass from."

MILA

After the meal, we're all suffering from having eaten too much. I'm lying on the couch with my head on Jase's thigh while the men watch a football game.

My eyes drift to Carla, Jase's little sister, and not having had a chance to catch up with her, I get up. I catch her eye and gesture with my head for her to follow me.

When we leave the living room and walk out into the garden, I smile at Carla, "How have you been? It feels like it's been ages since we've talked."

387

Carla glances around the landscaped lawn. "Oh, you know how senior year is. I've been studying, so I'll get better grades than Jase did."

The competitive streak is strong in the Reyes family. I let out a chuckle. "I'm sure you'll kick his butt."

I hear laughter and loud voices from the house, and both Carla and I glance toward the open sliding doors. Noah and his family just arrived.

"God, there goes my Thanksgiving," Carla mumbles under her breath.

My gaze darts back to her. "Because Noah's here?"

I picked up on a weird vibe between them during the welcome function at Trinity.

"Yeah." Her eyes find mine and a look of frustration crosses her beautiful features. "I swear he hates me ... ugh... just for freaking breathing."

"Did anything happen between the two of you?" I ask, worried my cousin did something terrible. I'll slap him so hard upside his head he'll be seeing stars for the rest of his life.

Carla shakes her head, then admits, "No, he just treats me like a six-year-old." She shrugs. "I shouldn't let him get to me."

There's a five year age gap between them, and Carla is Jase's little sister. I can't fault Noah for treating her like a kid.

"Hey," I hear Noah's voice and turn toward him.

"Hey, how's your Thanksgiving?" I ask as I give him a hug.

His gaze settles on Carla. "It was great until I heard we're babysitting."

Carla rolls her eyes, and walking away, she mutters, "Screw you too."

Crossing my arms over my chest, I scowl at my cousin. "Seriously? Was that necessary?"

Noah grins at me. "Yeah, totally worth it."

My lips part as the realization hits. "Do you have the hots for Carla?"

Noah pulls a disgruntled face. "Ewww. Come on. She's my friend's baby sister."

I let out a chuckle, and patting him on the shoulder, I say, "We both know Carla's no baby, Noah. But you keep telling yourself that."

I walk back to the house and go to greet the rest of the crowd. Not even an hour later, the place is bustling with life because all the families ended up at my parents' house.

I have a constant smile on my face as I watch my uncles and aunts joke with each other.

I glance at my own group of friends and ask, "You think that will be us in twenty years?"

Everyone looks at our parents just as Mr. Chargill slaps Mr. Cutler upside the head. Hunter and Hana's fathers are always fooling around.

Hunter lets out a bark of laughter. "Yeah, I'll be the one beating on Jase."

"My god-babies!" I hear Miss Sebastian, my godmother, screech. A wide smile spreads over my face, and jumping up, I run to hug her.

"You made it," I say as I hold her tightly. "I missed you." Pulling back, I let everyone hug her first. She's been gone for way too long, and it feels like the heart of our family has finally returned.

It takes a while for Miss Sebastian to do all her rounds, but then she comes to sit next to me. Taking hold of my hand, she says, "I'm sorry I wasn't here, my baby girl."

I lean into her, giving her a comforting hug. "I'm fine. Don't worry about it."

Pulling back, her gaze searches my face, then she asks, "So you and Jase are dating now?"

I nod happily.

Then Miss Sebastian looks at Jase, where he's talking to my brother on the other side of the room, and she yells, "Jase, I have a gift for you."

Hunter begins to laugh as Miss Sebastian pulls a box out of her bag. Remembering what she did with Jade by giving them a huge box of condoms in front of their parents, I grab the gift from her and run out of the room.

"Mila," Miss Sebastian shouts after me. "Just make sure he wraps it before he gets any."

I burst out in laughter and don't make it much further before I lean back against the wall in the hallway.

God, there's no stopping my godmother when she sets her mind on something, and it seems she's making it her goal in life to tease us.

Jase comes out of the living room, and when he sees me, a bark of laughter escapes his lips. "Give me that." He takes the gift from me and walks back to where Miss Sebastian is.

Opening the damn box in front of everyone, Jase shakes his head. "Tsk, it's a great gift, Mamma G, but they're way too small."

"They're extra-large, you little shit," Miss Sebastian laughs.

Jase shrugs. "Can't help it I'm blessed."

391

Miss Sebastian shakes her head at him as she mutters, "Or overcompensating."

"Oh yeah?" Jase lifts his eyebrows at her, and then Miss Sebastian screeches as he throws her over his shoulder.

"Ohhhhh. Myyyy. Gaaawwwd, "she keeps shrieking as Jase walks outside with her. "Jamie! Stop your son."

Everyone cracks up as Jase breaks out into a run, jumping in the pool with a squealing Miss Sebastian.

When her head breaks through the water, she yells, "I'm going to drown your bedazzled ass."

Deciding to join them, I kick off my shoes and run out of the house. I manage to spray them with water as I jump into the water.

I wipe the drops from my face and let out a spurt of laughter as Miss Sebastian tries to doggy paddle toward the shallow end.

JASE

Getting back to the suite, I fall down on the couch, totally spent after the fun day with our families.

"Movie night?" Fallon asks.

"Definitely," Hana groans. "I'm first putting on my pajamas."

"Ugh," I let out a groan as I get up so I can go change as well.

When we're all dressed in comfortable clothes, Fallon makes a huge bed on the plush carpet before asking, "What are we watching?"

"Not anything Superman or Channing Tatum related," I grumble as I lie down on a couch.

"Party pooper," Mila mutters. I pull her down on top of me, and we snuggle into a comfortable position.

"How about a Lord of the Rings marathon?" Hana asks.

Kao lies down on the bed Fallon made. "Sure, I'll be asleep in no time."

Fallon selects the first movie in the series, then goes to lie next to Kao.

I tighten my arms around Mila and only manage to watch ten minutes before my eyes begin to grow heavy. Movement catches my attention, and I watch as Kao positions a sleeping Fallon's head on his chest. Seeing the love he feels for her written all over his face, I wonder why he hasn't made his move yet.

When he thinks no one's watching, he lets down the constant guard he has up around her.

My gaze lowers to Mila's sleeping face, and a smile tugs at the corner of my mouth.

Yeah, Kao still needs to realize Fallon's the one for him. Hopefully, he won't take forever like I did.

Bringing a finger to Mila's face, I trace over her features. My heart expands to the point where it feels like it might burst with the love I feel for her.

And then?

It can fucking explode and fill the whole goddamn universe with love for her.

My love for Mila is fierce, continually growing, and … fucking forever.

The End.

Want to read where it all started?

Go 1 Click HEARTLESS.

And when you're done with the Enemies To Lovers Series,

follow it up with Trinity Academy.

All the sale links are listed in the back matter of the book.

If you are ever a victim of gender-based violence, please contact a helpline near you.

South Africa
Stop Gender Violence Helpline:
0800-150-150

USA
Rape, Abuse, and Incest National Network
(RAINN) – National Sexual Assault Hotline
Hotline: 1 (800) 656-4673

National Domestic Violence Hotline
Hotline: 1 (800) 799 – 7233

Love is Respect – National Teen Dating Abuse
Hotline
Hotline: 1 (866) 331 – 9474
Text: 22522

For any other country, please contact a helpline near you.

The Heirs

Reading order of future releases:

Coldhearted Heir
Novel #1
Hunter Chargill (*Mason and Kingsley's son*)
&
Jade Daniels (*Rhett & Evie's daughter*)

Arrogant Heir
Novel #2
Jase Reyes – (*Julian & Jamie's son*)
&
Mila West – (*Logan & Mia's Daughter*)

Defiant Heir
Novel #3
Kao Reed (*Marcus and Willow's son*)
&
Fallon Reyes (*Falcon & Layla's daughter*)

Loyal Heir
Novel #4
Forest Reyes (*Falcon & Layla's son*)
&
Aria Chargill (*Mason & Kingsley's daughter*)

Callous Heir
Novel #5
Noah West (*Jaxson & Leigh's son*)
&
Carla Reyes (*Julian & Jamie's daughter*)

Sinful Heir
Novel #6
Tristan Hayes (*Carter & Della's son*)
&
Hana Cutler (*Lake & Lee's daughter*)

Tempted Heir
Novel #7
Christopher Hayes (*Carter & Della's son*)
&
Dash West (*Jaxson & Leigh's daughter*)

Forbidden Heir
Novel #8
Ryker West (*Logan & Mia's son*)
&
Danny Hayes (*Carter & Della's daughter*)

Stand Alone High School Romance

Black Mountain Academy Series

Not My Hero
Colton Lawson
(Brady from Coldhearted Heir's Brother.)
&
Brie Weinstock
(daughter of Serena from Trinity Academy)

Trinity Academy

FALCON
Novel #1
Falcon Reyes & Layla Shepard

MASON
Novel #2
Mason Chargill & Kingsley Hunt

LAKE
Novel #3
Lake Cutler & Lee-ann Park

JULIAN
Novel #4
A Stand Alone Novel
Julian Reyes (*Falcon's Brother*)
&
Jamie Truman (*Della's Sister – Heartless, TETLS*)

THE EPILOGUE
A Trinity Academy Novella

Enemies To Lovers

Heartless
Novel #1
Carter Hayes & Della Truman

Reckless
Novel #2
Logan West & Mia Daniels

Careless
Novel #3
Jaxson West & Leigh Baxter

Ruthless
Novel #4
Marcus Reed & Willow Brooks

Shameless
Novel #5
Rhett Daniels & Evie Cole

False Perceptions
Novel #6
A Stand Alone Novel
Hayden Cole *(Evie's Dad)*

Connect with me

Newsletter

FaceBook

Amazon

GoodReads

BookBub

Instagram

Twitter

Website

About the author

Michelle Heard is a Wall Street Journal, and USA Today Bestselling Author who loves creating stories her readers can get lost in. She resides in South Africa with her son where she's always planning her next book to write, and trip to take.

Want to be up to date with what's happening in Michelle's world? Sign up to receive the latest news on her alpha hero releases → NEWSLETTER

If you enjoyed this book or any book, please consider leaving a review. It's appreciated by authors.

Acknowledgments

There aren't enough words to describe how much I loved writing Jase and Mila's story. Jase... he's everything. I borrowed a lot from Sheldon's personality, so you can all imagine how much we laugh from his constant playful antics.

To my alpha and beta readers, Sherrie, Sheena, Allyson. Kelly, Elaine, Sarah, and Leeann – Thank you for being the godparents of my paper-baby.

Candi Kane PR - Thank you for being patient with me and my bad habit of missing deadlines.

Sybil – Thank you for giving my paper-babies the perfect look.

To my readers, thank you for loving these characters as much as I do.

A special thank you to every blogger and reader who took the time to take part in the cover reveal and release day.

Love ya all tons ;)

Made in United States
Troutdale, OR
11/18/2024

24991741R00224